Glass HousEs

stories

Glass HousEs

george rabasa

:: COFFEE HOUSE PRESS :: MINNEAPOLIS

Grateful acknowledgment is made of the publications in which some of these stories first appeared: "The Amazing Frog Boy," in *StoryQuarterly;* "The Lion. The Eagle. The Wolf," in *Other Voices* and *Stiller's Pond* (New Rivers Press); "Houses by the Water," in *Side Show;* "San Miguel at Dusk," in *No Roses Review;* "Jimmy Pearl's Blue Oyster," in *26 Minnesota Writers* (Nodin Press).

Coffee House Press is supported in part by a grant provided by the Minnesota State Arts Board, through an appropriation by the Minnesota State Legislature, and by a grant from the National Endowment for the Arts, a federal agency. Additional support has been provided by the Lila Wallace-Reader's Digest Fund; The McKnight Foundation; Lannan Foundation; Jerome Foundation; Target Stores, Dayton's, and Mervyn's by the Dayton Hudson Foundation; General Mills Foundation; St. Paul Companies; Honeywell Foundation; Star Tribune/Cowles Media Company; The James R. Thorpe Foundation; Dain Bosworth Foundation; Schwegman, Lundberg, Woessner & Kluth, P.A.; Beverly J. and John A. Rollwagen Fund of The Minneapolis Foundation; and The Andrew W. Mellon Foundation.

Coffee House Press books are available to the trade through our primary distributor, Consortium Book Sales & Distribution, 1045 Westgate Drive, St. Paul, MN 55114. For personal orders, catalogs, or other information, write to: Coffee House Press, 27 North Fourth Street, Suite 400, Minneapolis, MN 55401.

Library of Congress CIP Data
Rabasa, George, 1941-
      Glass houses : short stories / by George Rabasa.
          p.   cm.
     ISBN 1-56689-051-9 (pbk.)
     I. Title.
     PS3568.A213G57   1996
     813'.54—DC20   96-17292
                                              CIP
10   9   8   7   6   5   4   3   2   1

ConTenTs

AuThor AcKnowledgmenTs

It is significant that this craft of words is itself nourished by words. For saying the right things at the right time, thank you, Alvin Greenberg and Janet Holmes, Pat Hayward, Joe Helgerson, A.M. Homes, Mike Honey and Isabel Victoria, Pepe Jessurun and Rina Epelstein, Deirdré Peterson, John Rabasa, Mary Rabasa, Shantanand Saraswati.

For your words as prods, lifelines, stimulants, jabs, hooks, and the occasional sinker, thank you, Jonis Agee.

And especially, my deepest appreciation to Juanita Garciagodoy, my wife, my first editor, my truest reader, for love and support beyond language, as well as for the two most important words in this book.

A la meva mare,
Paulina Ribas de Rabasa

Glass
HousEs

FloAtinG!

Tim says this is the biggest thing to help our marriage since his vasectomy four years ago. He did that for love, he says. And he's doing this for love too. I felt guilty about the vasectomy; I know how seriously he feels about his thing. But I don't feel even a twinge on this hot morning in July just because two very big guys in hard hats are getting a lot of money for digging a hole in our backyard.

By nine, their shirts are off. The one without the beer belly does make me feel guilty because I'm enjoying looking at him. His chest is hairless and sinewy muscles pulse along his back and arms and stomach as he lifts a pickax, lets it fall to the ground, and then pulls out the sod, scooping out great chunks of the loamy soil. I like that he concentrates. His whole mind is tuned into the motion of his body. He's got the routine down to three parts: lift, swing, pull. And with each step, a different group of muscles dances along his arms and shoulders and torso.

I call Tim at work. This is unusual because I seldom call him at the office; the last thing he needs is the little woman interrupting to ask him to pick up broccoli on the way home or what it means when the red light under the thermometer in the car goes on. Well, I may be female and not very tall, but I know what little red lights mean and I'm capable of getting my own vegetables if I feel like cooking.

Anyway, most of the time I'm too busy leaning into my PC as I watch it project the purchasing likelihood of millions of households across the country. It's called modeling: A family in Bethesda, Maryland, purchases a seven thousand dollar big-screen entertainment center. They have three kids, a large dog and two cats, a gerbil and a guppy. They own a four hundred thousand dollar house, one large Japanese car and one small American one, they subscribe to *Esquire, Bon Appétit, Time,* and *Rolling Stone.* They eat out three-and-a-half times a week, they have eight charge accounts, they favor Republicans for president and Democrats for sanitation department and school board, and they have been mugged twice within ten miles of their home. Quick, list all the other families across the country who, because of their similarities to the Bledsoes, are also apt to be purchasers of seven thousand dollar multimedia entertainment centers. Then I take these names and sell them for pennies apiece, and they do add up. I've gone into all this detail because it explains what I do at home every day, all day long. Occasionally I crave human contact. But I still don't call Tim unless I have a damned good reason.

"Tim, what in the hell are those guys doing in back of our house?"

"I don't know," he says. "I'm here. You're there. Look out the window and tell me."

"Funny. Very," I say. "They're digging up the backyard with pickaxes."

Tim laughs in that nice light way of his. In person he just smiles. But on the phone he chuckles sometimes for no reason at all, just to be pleasant and avoid silence. Silence can be deadly over the phone; how's the other person to know you are nodding thoughtfully or smiling beatifically or lifting your eyebrows quizzically? Tim is proud of his phone technique. His wide variety of sighs and hums, throat clearings, chuckles and grunts are a language all their own. More emphatic, more melodious, subtler than mere words. But they don't tell me what's going on in our backyard.

I hang up on him and stand just outside the kitchen door for a few moments watching the two guys dig mechanically into the ground, first one, then the other, a one-two punch that in the last hour or so has cleared a pit about twelve feet long and eight feet wide, and growing. For a while they're unaware of me. I listen quietly to the deep *chunck chunck* of the iron tool digging into the earth, their breaths and grunts percussive, syncopated, as regular as a metronome. The one with the interesting ripples notices me after a while but still doesn't look up. I'll call him "Biff." The other guy, the fat one, I'll call "Bohorquez." Biff and Boho, a team of world-class diggers.

There is a big difference between Biff's digging and Boho's. Biff's pick hits the ground with power and precision and with an almost sweet, musical *chunck*. Boho works harder and does less. His pick teeters in midair just above his shoulders, then wavers and waffles in a topsy-turvy arc. After a while Boho stops to rest, and Biff follows with one more swing, just to show him, I think, who's the head dog, and then leans on his pick. This time he looks at me and tilts his hard hat in a rakish kind of way. I find it hard to look into his hard-edged blue eyes. I find it hard to look at his brown nipples. I find it hard to look at his flat belly. I finally focus on his brass belt buckle with the Harley Davidson logo on it. I certainly find it hard to ask him why the hell he and his buddy, the tubby, are digging up my backyard. It just wouldn't do to admit ignorance. Instead, I offer them ice water out of the fridge anytime they want a drink. They say good morning, ma'am, and thank you, and no, they won't trouble me at all because they have iced pop in their truck parked out front. "Good," I say. "So long as you guys don't die on me."

I march across the house to the living room and look out the window. Sure enough, there is a van parked out front. The bottom half is blue, the top is red. It gives the impression of being half underwater. The sign along the upper half of the van reads *Big Splash, Inc. Swimming Pool Sales and Service.*

That night while Tim and I lie in bed, all sweaty and buff naked on top of the sheets, sometimes in our sleep kicking and punching at the hot summer air that hangs over us like some invisible blanket, I wake up to the sound of earthworms crawling through our backyard. I'm not sure digging holes in back of a house is a wise thing. And the pit is big by now, maybe sixty feet long and at least eight feet deep. I picture the meek little worms, accustomed to the dark, moist soil, suddenly upset so that they twist and crawl around first in the sun, then in the hot night. I'm not a hundred percent certain it's earthworms making the sounds that awaken me, but what else would go *slish, slish* in the middle of the night, so soft it's like a whisper, so close it feels wet and tickly all the way deep into my eardrum?

It's a wonder they don't rise up in anger against us. The horror of Biff and Boho tearing at their environment, changing the whole ecological balance with a few well-aimed swings of a pick, would be enough to set lesser creatures on a path of harassment, sabotage, symbolic acts of protest. I can see the night crawlers when I close my eyes, spreading out and blanketing everything in their path, rolling and slithering in lockstep like a horde of lubricious little fascists. It wouldn't take them long to figure out that Biff and Boho are merely tools in the employ of the real brains behind the devastation, namely my husband Tim Wailer, who sleeps now beside me. Without question, the hole was Tim's idea. In my honor, he assures me, but his plan nevertheless.

"That hole, out there," I mention several days later at dinner. "Does it have something to do with me?"

"With us, my darling," he corrects me between bites of corn nibblets, instant mashed potatoes, steamed squash. (Not great cuisine, but Tim has rediscovered the yellow foods of his childhood.) "I know you've missed the ocean ever since we moved to Minneapolis." He's right about that. There are lakes all over the Twin Cities, but they're for boats, not people.

"It was meant to be a surprise," he adds meekly.

"It was," I assure him.

"Well, sure," he stammers. "But it's too soon. You were supposed to be surprised once they finished, not while they were still in the middle of it."

"It's never too soon to be surprised."

"Are you pissed?" he wants to know. "I thought a pool was something we could both enjoy. Celebrate our short summer. Have friends over, escape the mosquitoes, take nude dips during hot sultry nights." Then he adds seductively, "You could sit on the edge, close your eyes, feel the breeze in your face, and dip your toes in the cool water. It would be like back home in California."

No, it wouldn't. Tonight I realize L.A. is an island. Not officially, but in actuality; living in L.A. is like being surrounded by water that cools it during the summer and keeps you thinking you're on vacation year round. Most people who live in L.A. do not realize what a liquid place it is. You need to look at it from the sky, your 747 approaching at dusk from the east, dropping gently out of the clouds, skimming the tops of the hills and canyon cliffs, and everywhere below there are swimming pools, maybe thousands of them, scattered on hotel rooftops, and motel parking lots, backyards and parks. Everywhere the cool lozenges freshen the hot sticky pavements and the dried out canyons and the charred neighborhoods. Even in the middle of a drought, with the Santa Anas breathing hot and scary from the desert and the sky a pearly haze of exhaust and smoke, the city is tempered by the pools, pure like jewels, and then, off the edge, the mottled blue of the Ocean, the big P, huge like the Universe.

Tim's pool is very compact and efficient. You can swim a mile in about thirty laps. It is heated, so when you go in, you're surprised. You expect a cold hit right at the level of your chest that will make you gasp and your eyeballs pop; instead, it feels like bathtub water that's been sitting too long. It has underwater lights that cast a ghostly glow at night and make the water look fluorescent, as if it had been touched by some nuclear reaction that turns everything turquoise.

Tim's surprise dragged on for about three weeks, what with digging out a hole in the backyard and running the plumbing and electrical wiring and then lining the excavation with a special quick-setting substance called Plasticrete. One day I look up from my PC and it's all done. The flagstone steps, the tubular aluminum ladder, the humming of the filter system. Biff and Boho are gone. The worms are gone. And tonight I can't wait for the Gogertys to be gone.

Midge and Arnold Gogerty are the first couple Tim invites to swim in our pool. He works with Arnold and has met Midge at company functions. It's like a test flight. I don't know the Gogertys because I have a deal with Tim: I don't go to his office picnics, Christmas dinners, and goodbye parties, and he doesn't come to mine. He says I don't have company parties because I don't work at a company. I say that makes me twice lucky.

I think the main reason he invites Midge and Arnold is that they don't have great bodies. Not that ours are fabulous, but Tim's love handles and my down-in-the-butt center of gravity aside, we look like sylphs next to the Gogertys. Tim and I disagree on this matter. I would not have invited the Gogertys precisely because they don't look good with their clothes off. I mean, why not invite Biff the Digger? When I mentioned it to Tim, he blew up. What are we going to talk about with him anyway? I don't see any lack of stimulating conversation topics. We could talk about swimming pools. About how to swing a pickax. About whether he realizes his pectorals quiver as if an electric current was shooting right through them. I would bring out a mirror to show him. He would learn something about himself.

What I learn about Midge and Arnie is that they hate taking their clothes off; they accepted the invitation because Arnold must've thought getting partially naked with the Head of Sales and his antisocial wife would be good for his career. He even delivers his wife's jiggly body for twice the points. Arnie wears a pair of baggy blue shorts and one of those tank tops cut huge around the shoulders and back just in case you've got so much muscle mass you might rip through an ordinary T-shirt. Midge wears a two-piece with a ruffled top connected to a skirted bottom by about a foot of black mosquito netting to hide her sweet plump belly.

They both emerge from changing in our guest bedroom hugging beach towels. They try to appear casual and loose about the whole thing, but as soon as they spot our aluminum-frame-and-plastic-webbing patio chairs, they scrunch down into them and don't move until hours later, when they realize the weight of their bodies has pushed down on the plastic strips so that their butts are starting to graze the hot flagstones.

The four of us sit in a semicircle on the terrace that leads to the pool. We hold bottles of beer and handfuls of salty popcorn. Even though we exchange occasional, random bits of conversation, our eyes gaze out at the water, as if we expect something to happen there, something that will reward the attention we're paying it. Under the light of such intense concentration, every detail becomes a rarefied event. We notice things. The wind makes ripples on the surface. A leaf from a nearby poplar falls to the water. The four of us watch how the leaf is pushed here and there by the breeze, sometimes coming close to the edge, only to turn back at the last minute. Tim picks up a long aluminum pole with a flat scoop made of metallic netting and fishes out the errant leaf. We take deep contented breaths and continue to watch the pristine water moving, undulating, shimmering under the sun.

When the Gogertys finally get up to leave, they are sunburnt and the plastic strips from the chairs have left stark white imprints on the backs of their thighs. It's time they headed home, they announce. We insist they stay a little longer. But the sky has turned a glaring, milky white, hiding the sun yet still managing to cast down a blanket of heavy moist heat, undisturbed by the slightest breeze. We let them go.

That night I decide the visit with the Gogertys had been a success. They admired the pool, they liked my pasta salad, they didn't talk much. Tim, on the other hand, felt the whole event was a disaster. "Nobody went into the fucking pool," he says.

"Well, you did."

"You should've gone in with me."

"I thought it best to stay with our guests," I remind him.

"And they didn't want to swim."

"What's a pool for, if people don't swim in it."

"To look at."

And to listen to, especially at night when the neighborhood goes quiet and it's cool enough outside to turn off the constant hum of the air-conditioning and sleep with the windows open. Then the pool sounds like a living, breathing thing with a motion and a rhythm all its own. It even startles me awake some nights. I can hear the water lapping against the sides. Even when the night is still and there isn't the slightest breeze to disturb the surface, the molecules vibrate all the time. Especially under the lights that Tim likes to leave on at night because of the way they reflect moving water onto the ceiling above the bed.

And then there's the situation with the heating system turning on and off. It makes a clicking sound when the water gets too cold. So as the night gets cooler, the pool starts to go *click . . . click . . . click.* Every ten or fifteen minutes, just when I'm drifting off to sleep. There it goes. *Click.* It's like someone's pacemaker or something. Too weird.

One night Tim wants to go swimming with the pool lights on. It's about midnight and he has taken off his purple terrycloth robe and gone in naked. I can tell this is important to Tim, to be able to swim nude in his own pool. I stand on the edge and watch him. The lights make his pallid skin look all spongy and iridescent, as if he were dead, and somehow his soul were seeping out his pores. He turns over on his back and the water cascades off his belly, his limp penis flopping just below the surface, the pubic hair swaying like a clump of seaweed. He beckons with his hand for me to come in with him. Even while not aware of it, he's drifting farther and farther from the side, pulled by a subtle, silent undertow. After a while he seems to be waving farewell. I return his wave and go back inside the house.

When he comes to bed, even after he takes a long soapy shower, there is a smell to him that reminds me of overcooked scrambled eggs, of hospital corridors, of the stuff inside large brown glass bottles. I curl up, my head pressed against the pillow, and cling to the edge of the bed. The smell rises from his hair, his skin, his breath. It is the smell of the pool with its mixture of germ-killing, pipe-clearing, algae-fighting chlorine solution and alum salts.

Soon the house is divided into two camps, the swimmer and the nonswimmer. Tim comes home in the evening and jumps into the pool. We have dinner and watch TV, and then, just before bedtime, he goes in again. The next morning he rises out of bed and swims before heading out to the office. I wonder if anybody else can smell the chlorine on him.

Tim tells me that splashing around in the pool is the most refreshing thing he has ever done. It energizes him in the morning, unstresses him after work, and relaxes him just before bedtime. One day he asks me if I think he's becoming a fanatic.

"What do you think?" I say.

"I don't think I'm being fanatical," he says. "But I feel you think I am."

"I didn't say you were."

"That's because you don't talk anymore."

"You can't hear well when the water's up above your ears," I say.

"I'd hear fine, if you were in the pool with me," he says.

During the day while I work on my PC, I don't think about the pool much. It has become something that sits out there in the backyard. But when Tim is home, then the pool seems pretty much to take over. He's either getting ready to go in or he's in or he's drying out after being in. When he comes out, his skin is all pink and pruny.

He wants to know why I don't ever get in the water. One time I tell him because the water is too warm. Another that the water is too cold. At first he keeps changing the adjustments on the thermostat in search of some ideal temperature. After a while he gives up asking.

"You know," he says to me one night while he dries himself after his evening swim, "there is something about water that feels very natural. The way it wraps itself around every body crevice and cavity. The way it holds you up. The way your body adapts to the temperature. It's a very comforting kind of thing. Our bodies are 97% water, we are created in water, our ancestral species lived in water. Sometime I'll spend the whole night in the pool."

When Tim says this, he does not look normal. Not that he's babbling or foaming at the mouth or looking wild-eyed. But I know Tim. Standing naked in front of the bedroom window, looking down at the pool all lit up and glowing in the night, he has a quiet kind of intensity, a brightening of his eyes. Does he dream of floating in amniotic fluid all over again? Does he fancy himself an amoeba? Does he want to dissolve?

Tim buys things to play with in the water. First there was a Float-a-Bar, basically a Styrofoam board with recessed circles to hold a glass, mixed nuts, an ashtray. Tim has his wine, his morning coffee, his after-work beer in the Float-a-Bar. This means he need no longer stand by the edge of the pool to have a drink but can splash about, never farther than a stroke or two from refreshment. He says whoever invented it should get the Nobel prize.

He buys a Float-a-Pillow, a kind of neck brace made of hollow red-and-yellow plastic that attaches to the back of his head when he floats belly up. He's easier to talk to this way because his ears aren't underwater. This device also allows him to take naps without drowning.

Then there's Float-a-Babe, an inflatable vinyl reproduction of a blonde woman in a pink bikini. The effect is quite realistic, the skin tanned to a soft cocoa hue, the hair golden, like Barbie's, the eyes are sparkly blue, the half-open red lips smile relentlessly. Tim is learning to be self-sufficient.

I tell him the doll is in bad taste.

"It's just a toy," he explains. And that says it all, as far as he's concerned. Like who am I to stand in the way of fun, for Christ's sake? Especially if all it involves is some inflatable vinyl thing. To prove the point, he plays with the doll. He pushes it underwater so that when I least expect it, Float-a-Babe comes leaping through the surface all wide-eyed and smiley, like she really is having a good time. I turn my attention back to the PC and marvel at the close interconnection between regular flossing by unmarried females and their propensity to join book clubs.

The next time I look out, Tim's legs are wrapped around Float-a-Babe's hips and his arm is around her shoulders, the two of them bobbing on the surface. "Don't worry," he calls out from the center of the pool. "We're just good friends."

One morning just before dawn, Tim wakes me up to show me a trick he dreamed up in the middle of the night. In the past several days, he has mastered swimming underwater the length of the pool and back, diving clean as a knife blade into the water, plus a bewildering array of butterfly strokes and frog kicks and somersault push-backs. But this is special, he tells me. He puts on his favorite red Speedo bathing suit and stands in front of our bedroom window. Below, the pool glows. He slides open the window and a blast of hot air comes into the bedroom.

"Are you going to do something dumb?" I ask him.

"Watch," he says with a big grin. "Introducing the human cannonball!" He lifts himself onto the ledge on the other side of the window. He takes a deep breath and leaps outward, his body curling into a compact sphere of flesh and bone and muscle that hurtles through the air and lands in the middle of the pool with a huge splash. It feels like a long time before his head pokes out above the surface, and he waves at me.

After his swim, Tim sits at the breakfast table across from me. He still looks as if he has just stepped out of the pool, his shirt matted against his shoulders, his hair slicked back. "Nothing like a swim first thing in the morning," he says. He has that cheerful kind of lilt in his voice that he uses to irritate me. Today I'm not going to argue with Tim about him spending so much time in the pool, taking too many showers, too many trips to piss in the middle of the night. A more constructive idea is bubbling up through the darker deeper layers of my consciousness.

"That's nice, darling." I can't believe it's me talking like that. I don't ever use the word *darling*, and yet here I am, smiling sweetly, watching the water droplets drip down from the tip of Tim's nose. "Here, dry your face." I hand him a paper napkin. "You're dripping into your Wheaties."

The following night while he sleeps beside me, I rise up on my elbow and study him. I take a small flashlight and run the pinpoint of light all over his skin, first along his side, then down the middle of his chest along his stomach, which rises and falls with his even breathing, and finally down to his groin. What am I looking for? Scales, moss, barnacles.

I lean down over him and press my face to his cheek, his neck, his hair. He has a cool, humid smell to him, like wet concrete. His skin feels moist, as if the whole of his body hasn't yet dried out, even though he's been in bed for hours. I run my hands along his arms, his legs, his feet. The hair on his shins is matted down, drops of water bead up along the tops of his feet, trickle in rivulets down to his ankles. I get a towel and pat his body dry, very gently, so as not to wake him. He takes a deep breath and rolls onto his side. The sheet under him is gathered up in a topographic mass of wrinkles that swirl down the length of the bed, forming ridges and canyons and a small river coursing down to the footboard.

Throughout the night I realize water is taking over our lives. And I edge closer and closer to my side of the bed. Tim keeps getting up in the night. He hardly wakes up; just shuffles down the hall in the dark like a sleepwalker, wanders into the bathroom, rarely bothering to turn the light on, stands naked in front of the toilet bowl, and just when I'm falling asleep, there's the stream echoing inside the tiled bathroom followed by the loud explosion of flushing water and the flow of the wash basin tap.

Around two A.M., we cross paths in the hallway. He mumbles something about where I'm going. "Go back to bed, Tim," I say. I stand in the hallway for a moment, listening as he falls back on the bed with a soft contented groan. I step outside and close the door without a sound.

The air feels soft and summery; the night is silent except for the crickets and the distant hum of traffic from the freeway, and the clicking of the pool's thermostat. I walk around the pool; it seems to lie beneath me like some dangerous trap, an alien swampy thing glowing in the dark. I circle it several times, feeling the heat that rises from the water like the breath of some dark primeval sinkhole.

My plan is clear. I walk to the end of the pool where the filtering systems and the heater and the thermostat click and whirr in a small compartment hollowed out of the flagstone patio. I lift a trap door and peek inside. There are two large iron faucets as big as the palm of my hand, with clear indentations for the fingers. One is red with a big *E* for empty; the other is green with an *F* for fill. I turn the red faucet several times until it stops. There's a small sound like a baby burping, and then the steady flow of water rushing down the drainage pipe beneath my feet. After a minute or two I think I can see the level of the water going down.

By the time I get back in bed, the air feels drier. I place my hand on the back of Tim's neck and the moisture seems to be gone. As I picture the pool emptying, it's as if some primal balance were being reestablished in my life. Tim smells sweeter. The bed sheets feel crisp and fresh again. There had just been too much water. It will be better this way. As I curl up in the bed close to Tim, I make a mental note to be sure to wake up early to tell him not to do the cannonball this morning.

SaN miguEl at dUsk

In 1959 Harlan Ebersohl appeared for twelve minutes on net-work television. He got a free trip to New York, three days with all expenses paid at The Pierre, and a limo. There was more. The insider's tour of the NBC studios. The private dressing room. Meeting Bennett Cerf. And finally the coast-to-coast, prime-time appearance on *What's My Line.*

Harlan came out in a turtleneck sweater and a black beret so that everyone would think he was an artist. He was not prepared for the lights, the cameras, the audience. "I stand tall," he started nervously. "With the likes of Picasso, Miró, Chagall."

The panel never guessed what he did. And the studio audi-ence liked him very much because he stumped the experts.

When Harlan returned to Minneapolis, he was surprised how many people recognized him and wanted to talk to him about being on TV and meeting Bennett Cerf.

Harlan enjoyed his brief moment in the limelight, but he was an intelligent man. He had mastered the art of facing day-to-day reality. He knew the value of dressing appropri-ately, even when he was not at his job. He was well read in current events, art criticism, and the basics of Western Thought. He could tell quality from glitz, truth from sham. And he didn't take for granted why he was who he was.

"Really, Harlan, why on earth would a man choose to spend the past thirty-five years standing here?" he sometimes asked himself.

"Because it pays $8.65 an hour."

"That's hardly a good reason."

"It also takes very, very little effort."

"Harlan, there's no future in it."

"It's a little late to bring that up. Anyway, I love art."

"The same pictures for weeks on end?"

"They change. I move around."

The temperature inside the exhibit rooms is kept at a constant 72°. The light is cool and diffused. The humidity is controlled, and a record of its ups and downs is mantained by a nib that draws a thin squiggle on miles of rolled graph paper. Perfect climate is one of the things that makes Harlan happy.

Last year he found a measure of happiness in a new kind of shoe. On the outside, they looked just like the black oxfords he always wore to work, but the Feather Lites were wonderful inside, actually built like a long-distance running shoe, for marathons and such, with a solid arch and heel support. Cushioning by hundreds of air bubbles eased the pressure on his knees, and tiny pores allowed his feet to breathe.

After two days, the inside of each shoe had molded itself to every contour and hollow of Harlan's feet, from the plump toes and protruding ball up the curved arch to the blunt heel with its peculiar overhang. In a short time, the shoes had become organically one with his feet. He was so impressed that he wrote a letter to the shoe company.

"As a man who lives off his feet," he wrote, "I thank you for bringing out your new Feather Lites, which in the course of my workday have become the biggest single contributor to my health and comfort."

He typed the letter on museum stationery and signed it formally Harlan L. Ebersohl, Security. In reply, he received a personal letter from the president of the Feather Lite Company and a coupon worth five dollars toward the purchase of his next pair.

"Now, think for a minute, Harlan," he asked. "What exactly is it that you do?"

"I take care of things."

"Half the time you look as if you've fallen asleep standing up."

"I watch people."

Mostly, it's quiet in the exhibit rooms. Visitors walk with slow, deliberate steps from picture to picture. They'll stand for a moment, take a deep breath, murmur to themselves, occasionally cough and clear their throats. Harlan seldom speaks, but sometimes the pager hooked to his belt beeps insistently when the front desk needs him.

Emergencies do occur. In September of '85, for instance, the sleepy calm was shattered in one explosive moment by an angry art student who set fire to Salvador Dalí's *Gala Eating Black Cherries*. The young woman had been stalking Dalí's pictures for about an hour, a sinister figure swaddled in layers of black, feverish eyes burning from a pale white face topped by a shock of carrot-orange hair.

Harlan remembers noticing her and thinking she was early for Halloween. The thought made him feel both smug and guilty. He was in the middle of a silent apology when she broke from the group and rushed to the canvas.

In one fluid motion she was splashing gasoline across Gala's open mouth and squeezing a lighter so that the flame shot out like a torch. Harlan lunged at the woman and wrested the lighter from her grip while another guard rushed to press his coat against Dalí's wife. Actual damage was minimal, barely a smudge; Harlan was rewarded with a letter of commendation from the Tate Gallery, the owners of the famous painting.

On weekday afternoons there is a stillness in the exhibit rooms that feels like the texture of dreams. The very air takes on a different weight, a dense viscosity that slows the normal flow of time. There are seldom more than two or three people in the room at one time, usually alone, unhurried, with hours to fill between flights or appointments. They have the detachment of true time killers. Their dullness is contagious.

"Hello, Harlan. Are you still there?"

"Yes, yes, I'm here."

"Truly there?"

"Can't you see me?"

The stance is familiar. Feet planted evenly on the floor. The soft, squarish body rendered more shapeless by the polyester uniform, shiny navy blue down to his black Feather Lites. His milky hands are loosely clasped, sometimes in front, sometimes in back. His head, supported at the neck by the wide starched shirt collar, seems too large for the medium frame.

Sometimes while standing so still, his breath flowing in a thin, shallow stream, Harlan likes to think of himself as one more exhibit. Placed squarely under a cone of light from one of the overhead track fixtures, he is one of those sculptures where details count, and every lifelike touch brings on the gasp of surprise, the little moan of delight. Notice how delicately the tiny hairs on his wrist catch the light. Remark on the perfect pink of his fleshy earlobes. Study the seemingly random placement of a thin shaving cut.

A middle-aged couple, possibly out-of-town visitors, stops

in front of Harlan. As the woman reaches out to brush her fingers against the smooth sheen of the guard's polyester coat, the husband pulls her hand back in time. He steers her by the elbow to the large Miró just to the right and behind Harlan.

"I get it. This is fun, right?"

"*Interesting* is a better word."

Harlan drifts to the left, taking soundless steps on his Vibram-soled Feather Lites, while all the time he keeps a discreet, watchful eye on the couple standing in front of *Man Walking a Dog*. The woman glances to her left, but Harlan now hovers just outside the periphery of her vision. She turns her head until she meets his calm gaze. He holds her eyes for a moment, then nods his head in recognition. She blushes and turns her attention back to the scrawny little dog with the curled tail in the Miró. She manages to steady her breath, ignoring her husband's questioning look.

A moment later, Harlan has moved into the adjoining exhibit area and taken his place in a dimly lit corner where he washes into the background like a shadow against the wall.

When the couple turns from the *Man Walking a Dog*, Harlan is no longer in the room. The man doesn't seem to notice, but the woman's eyes keep searching all about, even as she follows her husband to the next exhibit area. The woman steps up to the guard and examines him until she is satisfied that this is a different man, younger and thinner than the one in the previous room. After shuffling from painting to painting for several minutes, the couple wanders down a narrow hallway into another room.

The walls in this room are sparsely hung with a few large canvasses placed far from each other. In the middle of the floor stands a guard. It's Harlan again. "We've already been in this room," the woman says. "No, we haven't," her husband insists. "Yes, yes, I'm positive we've already seen this stuff," the woman repeats, this time looking toward Harlan for confirmation, then turning away from his stare.

"Do you enjoy going around bewildering people?"

"Life is bewildering."

"It's you, Harlan. Not life."

"You're splitting hairs."

One gray winter evening as he punched out of the museum, Harlan saw a recent issue of *Popular Science* lying on his supervisor's desk. Most people would not give the cover picture of the bug-eyed mechanical midget more than an amused glance. To Harlan it was both a mirror of his limitations and an intimation of his future.

"You can trust your life to Gary the Guard," the caption read. Manufactured in South Bend, Indiana, by Priceless Robotics, Inc., Gary the Guard was fully mobile in three directions with a total action arc of 280 degrees. It could scoot, slide, bob, and weave with surprising agility. A built-in radio receiver and delicate sound sensors enabled it to react to voice commands and unusual sounds. Heat and motion detectors relayed radio signals to police and fire stations as well as to the museum security office. Meanwhile, through its 360-degree bank of photoelectric cells, Gary the Guard would spot a potential intruder or hostile visitor and, while emitting a shriek not unlike a martial arts cry, roll across the floor to intercept the attacker with a sharp clipping block behind the knees.

Like Harlan, Gary the Guard had his gentle side. At the touch of a button, it would speak preprogrammed bits in a warm baritone, on the gift shop hours, daily specials at the restaurant, locations of rest rooms, and a short biographical note on the featured artists.

"I wouldn't worry about the thing, Harlan."

"It moves faster. Sees, hears, smells everything. Remembers stuff."

"But you've got insight, Harlan."

Spring came early. By the end of April, Harlan was able to switch to his summer weight uniform and walk the ten blocks from his apartment to the museum instead of riding the bus. The pleasant weather helped his state of mind. Museum attendance dropped as people spilled out into the streets and parks. The crowds would be back in August. Not for the art. For the air-conditioning.

"You're being negative again, Harlan."

In spring Harlan had the place to himself. Unfortunately, the walls were dedicated to lesser works—flower shows, forgotten curiosities from the permanent collection, the annual exhibition of community artists.

"Nobody here, Harlan. You might as well go on vacation."

"Things are hanging."

"If nobody is here, nobody knows for sure."

"What am I?"

"You're somebody, of course, Harlan."

"But if nobody knows I'm here, then I'm nobody too."

"You win. You're here. The art is here."

"On the other hand, if I turn all the lights off . . ."

"You could go on vacation."

On Monday, Harlan walked into the Annual Community Artists Invitational Show, a confrontation of some forty-odd selections that made the walls bristle. During the first week, he found himself restlessly pacing and turning, searching for the exact spot where he would stand comfortably, the precise nine-inch square of parquet that marked a harmonious place within the scheme of walls, floor, and ceiling, his own mental island of blue between the surrounding extremes of color and whiteness.

He moved about for hours, standing only a few minutes in

one place and then finding himself repelled by some hidden force. At the end of the day, he still had not found the best place to stand in any of the rooms.

As a result, his feet ached even with his Feather Lite shoes, his belly swelled up with gas, his chest burned from the thin air. Evening found him at home, letting out a soft groan as he lowered his pink body into a tub of nearly scalding water, feeling the soreness in his legs and back gradually ebb as he gazed at the wallpaper that bubbled all around him in a pattern of coral reefs, seashells, and fanciful marine flora.

After the first week, word came that security staff would rotate stations every twenty minutes instead of every forty in order to alleviate the boredom. Punctually, the blue figures that had been slumping like melting candles would shudder back to alertness and slink into the next room.

Harlan would resume his restless search for the best place to stand. He searched for it confidently. Just as his shoes eventually molded themselves to the shape of his feet or some intelligence in the fabric of his coat learned how to slope over his shoulder, he had long ago discovered that once he found his place in each room, the malaise lifted and he would stand erect and poised, breathing in the perfect humidity-controlled museum air.

Today he felt he was close. He paced from one end of Room IV to the other, attracted by turns to a tray of cheese and fruit, to a wounded mallard diving from the sky, to the staring eyes of an artist's grandchildren. Watch Harlan turn. Watch Harlan pace. Watch Harlan fidget.

When it finally happened, it was in a single moment of absolute surrender. He let out a long sigh, his shoulders straightened, his arms hung loosely at his sides. Warm tears welled in his eyes. He looked around for the spot's exact bearings. He noted a door, a column, a fire extinguisher.

From directly behind him, a steady glow warmed the very center of his spine through the blue coat and the starched white shirt. He remembered the picture now. A low stone wall bordering a plowed field. In the foreground, the edge of a dirt road. In the distance, the soaring gothic towers of a church, its pink stone façade burnished by the late afternoon light and the dust that hung in the air. The wall would have been no more than three feet high and was built of rough stones piled on top of each other. The waning light struck the rocks and cast a golden hue over their hard surfaces, allowing thin metallic flecks to shimmer here and there. From a dark crevice in the wall where the stones did not quite fit together, a thin green stem reached out and exploded in a brilliant red peony.

Harlan closed his eyes. A soft westward wind soughed through the dry brush. There was the sudden flutter of birds' wings. The constant undertone of crickets. The pungent smoke from wood-burning stoves hung in the air. *San Miguel at Dusk.*

The next day, Harlan looked up the name of the artist, Felicia Sutton, a longtime resident of New Hope and a retired high school art teacher. He wrote her number down on a scrap of paper and carried it with him for two days. On Wednesday, Harlan found himself again standing in this one perfect spot with *San Miguel at Dusk* behind him. He turned. The red of the peony blazed out of the rocks.

"Yes, that's my name," the woman explained on the phone. "But I'm not the Miss Sutton you want. The artist is my mother, and she spends winters in Mexico."

"That sounds like a nice thing to do," Harlan stammered.

"In San Miguel," the woman continued. "That's where she did the painting you mentioned."

"Maybe you can help," he said. "I was curious as to whether the picture is from real life down there, or if it's a scene she imagined."

"Are you really connected with the museum?" the woman asked.

"Well, yes, I'm in security. I just have a personal interest in how your mother's picture came about."

"I'll give you Mom's address so you can ask her yourself," she offered cheerfully.

The information was in Spanish and he had to make her spell everything out so that he could write the name of the street and the town and the state with his neat, rounded script.

"When are you going to write her, Harlan?"

"I don't know, tonight."

"Hell, why don't you just pack up and go visit Miss Sutton personally?"

"Well, sure. I just might do that."

The next morning, Harlan called in sick and went to the Greyhound station on First Avenue. "Ah, yes, you'd like to go down to sunny Mexico. Wish I could," the woman selling tickets said as she traced a direct route on a map following I-35 all the way down to Laredo, Texas. That was around 1,500 miles. For just $99 in a special promotional fare, he could ride to Laredo, then walk across the bridge into Mexico and take another bus 350 miles down to San Miguel, a black dot in the middle of the mountain range that traverses the whole western side of Mexico.

"When do you want to go?" The woman started to tap out the information on her computer. With a prickle at the back of his neck, Harlan sensed the crowd that was lining up behind him. He said he would think about it and come back later.

Outside the waiting room, a battery of buses was lined up precisely between bright yellow lines on the oily asphalt, engines idling in a deep rumble, their red and amber lights like jewels in the gloom. Harlan looked at the route map again. The thought of packing a suitcase and locking up his apartment and leaving the museum to arrange for a substitute made him queasy. He sat for a moment on a bench and watched the buses, first waiting impatiently in their berths, then one after another taking off with shudders and hisses and bursts of bluish exhaust. The sick feeling in his stomach did not get better until he left the station and walked to the Country Buffet Cafeteria for tamale pie.

The next day the exhibit rooms were unusually well attended. A fine, clinging mist had shrouded the city all day, driving people indoors. It was not until closing that Harlan found himself alone in Room IV. He stood before *San Miguel at Dusk* and waited for the faint twilight glow to warm his face. He stepped closer to see the very particles of dust that hung in the air, as if at the previous instant someone had just driven by, stirring up the loose dirt on the road.

"Go ahead, Harlan. But only for a second."

"I couldn't."

"Just be careful."

He reached out, and with hardly any pressure at all, laid the fingers of his right hand on the canvas, right at the spot where the glancing light from the sun fell on the rock wall. He closed his eyes, and felt his fingertips travel across the the thick swirls and nubs where the oil paint had been layered with a few blunt strokes of the palette knife. He was suddenly out of breath, his back wet with perspiration. He watched his hand cling to the painting with an intelligence and a will of its own.

When he withdrew it, a thick chip of ochre paint remained stuck to the tip of his finger. Hastily, he buried his hand deep in his pants pocket, turned away, and walked out of the room and down the hall with the brisk steps of someone eager to bring the working day to a close. The sliver of dried paint burned like an ember inside his pocket.

When he reached his apartment, Harlan bolted the door, drew the curtains shut, and placed the small paint chip inside a clean pickle jar. He kept it nearby all evening long. It was right beside him while he ate some Mrs. Paul's fish sticks. He watched the late news and *Letterman* and reruns of *Cheers,* and all the time the jar sat on the table beside his comfortable chair. He kept it close enough to rest his hand occasionally on the glass and imagine he could feel a certain energy seep out onto his fingers.

The next morning Harlan was anxious to take his post. Promptly at 9:50, he went straight into Room IV. He assumed the familiar vigilant stance, legs apart, hands clasped behind his back, his eyes facing the center of the room. *San Miguel at Dusk* waited behind him. He put his hand inside his pocket and restlessly fingered a Gem nail clipper.

This time he worked out in his mind the exact sequence of movements. He knew exactly where to go to get what he wanted. He wouldn't need more than three or four seconds. With his hand still inside his pocket, he drew out the thin nail file with the curved tip. Then he took a couple of deep breaths and turned to face the picture.

In a moment, he had scraped a thick chunk of dried oil paint right off one of the brilliant red petals of the peony. The fleck of color fell to his feet. He placed the nail clipper back inside his pocket, and turned again to face the center of the empty room.

He stood at his post for several minutes and waited for his breath to settle. Then, after looking about to make certain he was alone, he bent down to pick the small red chip off the floor. At 10:20, he moved from Room IV to Room III.

That night, Harlan stood by a window and held the pickle jar up to the moonlight between his large white hands. The red chip sat next to the ochre chip like a drop of blood.

"Why Harlan, you've become a criminal."

"No comment."

"No comment?"

"That's correct."

HousEs bY the wAter

"I need a new tie," Russ Bolger says to the younger man sitting beside him in the taxi. "I can't walk into a presentation to Westco, in the middle of Beverly Hills, with a tie that says I'm from Iowa."

"You're from Minneapolis, actually," his friend says. "And that's definitely a Minneapolis tie."

"Big difference. I used to be from L.A., I lived in L.A. for twenty years, I understand L.A. That's how I happen to know that if you are not from L.A., or maybe New York, or maybe, just maybe, Chicago, you're from nowhere. No, Minneapolis doesn't count."

"Gee, Russ. L.A. doesn't look all that cool," the younger man says, gazing out the window as the taxi speeds past the warehouses of La Brea.

"I'll let you know when we're there, asshole." He holds up his tie and stares at it in disbelief. "How the hell did I end up in paisleys? That's what happens when you leave the house at five fucking thirty."

"Want to trade?" The young man pulls his own tie out, a design of yellow wooden pencils on a black background.

"No, thank you. It's a fine tie for a copywriter. I happen to be the account guy." Russ leans forward, slides open the plastic partition that separates the front seat from the back. "We want to make a stop at Beverly Center. Think the stores will be open?"

"It's after ten, they'll be open."

"We'll still need to get to Wiltshire and Carrigan by ten thirty."

"You shop fast, I'll drive fast," the driver says through a cloud of cigarette smoke.

"Thank you," Russ pats him on the shoulder. "You're a real professional."

"It's quarter after," the younger man says nervously.

"In L.A. you can buy anything in under three minutes. Watch me."

The cab stops in front of the Beverly Center entrance on Melrose, and Russ Bolger jumps out to buy himself a tie. Mike Long leans back against the seat and takes deep breaths. He tells himself that if Russ is not back by 10:25, exactly, then he will have to tell the driver to go and he'll make the presentation by himself. The thought makes him want to throw up.

At 10:22 he knows he is not up to handling the whole thing on his own. He wishes he could be as cool under the heat as Russ Bolger. It's not just anybody who will take the time to shop five minutes before pitching the biggest account the agency has ever had.

At 10:24 Russ jumps back in the cab and tells the driver to hurry over to Westco on Wiltshire. "You're the creative guy," he says as he pulls out the new tie from inside its flat carton. "Is this art, or what?"

They get to Westco right on time, and while the receptionist announces their visit, Russ slips into the men's room to change ties. When he comes out he seems to stand straighter, his chest puffed out under the new tie, an explosion of ripe petunias all pumped up as if they've been fertilized with steroids. "Relax," he murmurs to the younger man. "This is my town."

By 11:07 they're back in the lobby waiting for a taxi. "I think we wowed them," says Russ. "Talk about smooth. They couldn't wait to get to the storyboards. We make a hell of a team, you and I."

"I don't know," the younger man ventures. "They didn't ask any questions."

"These guys are fast reads," Russ says. "They know what they saw. They got it from word one."

"They were quiet."

"Stop with the quiet business," Russ says. "We came, we showed, we conquered. I've been there a hundred times."

"A hundred times."

"A thousand times. These guys are fast on their feet. They're talking right now, even as we sit in their lobby waiting for a cab."

"So what do we do now?"

"Lunch."

"Or we head for the airport and try to get on an earlier flight."

"Lunch," Russ repeats. "We just pitched a fourteen million dollar piece of business. You don't turn tail. You do lunch. We'll rent a car and head for the beach. You've never been to the Rose Café in Venice. All the guys from Chiat Day eat lunch there. The first time I saw Jay Chiat he was at the Rose. He was having lunch."

"Just like that? Eating, like any of us mortals."

"I've seen Steven Spielberg at the Rose. And Joni Mitchell.

And Seiji Ozawa."

"OK, OK, I'm impressed. Really."

Russ Bolger rents a BMW 735i for $150 a day. "Ah, but it feels so good," he exclaims, hitting the steering wheel with the flat of his hand. He makes a slow wide turn onto Santa Monica. "I used to drive one of these when I lived here four years ago. A car like this is almost a necessity in L.A.; it's something you wear." Mike and Russ buzz down the windows and stick out their elbows, letting the sunshine strike their faces, the balmy air tousle their hair. For a few moments, they know themselves to be right at the center of a bigger universe than the one they came from, right here in the middle of the labored stream of hot chrome and sheet metal that crawls toward the ocean.

The traffic slows down to a stop. "I even love the traffic jams in California," Russ says. "Where else would you be stuck with a million dollars worth of Jaguars and Beemers and Rolls Royces, all within spitting distance? That's the only thing that doesn't change about L.A. Every time I come here, another building has been torn down and a new one put in its place. Construction doesn't last ten years. Everything is in constant flux. Don't you just love that word ? Flux. Flux you. Fluxed in L.A."

"Why did you leave?"

"My life was in flux, too. Then things got intense. She was trying to clean me out."

"Your ex-wife."

"Yeah." He points to a low pink building just ahead and adds, "There's Pacific Printing. I did eight million a year with them when I had my own agency. Used to deal directly with Shigeru Iwamoto, smartest little guy you'll ever meet. And that's where Bay Productions is, or was, looks like the building has been pushed down to the middle of the block. I swear they used to be here on the corner. They can't do that, can they? Just push a building down the street? I remember many a night until three A.M., editing commercials for the Chevy Dealers Association. Great bunch of guys until one of them saw me driving the Beemer and tried to pull the account. Three days later, I went to the head of the association's dealership in Van Nuys and bought a Corvette right off the floor for $55,000 cash. I had them take a picture of me paying for it. Then I made postcards of it and sent them to every dealer in the state. Dumbest car I ever drove, but I managed to keep the business. They loved me. And they loved the blonde that used to pitch their cars. So did I."

"You married her," Mike guesses.

"Lesson number one: Never come on to the talent."

"Sounds like you're not on good terms with her."

"You could put it that way."

"Do you have any kids?"

"Nope, no kids."

"That's good, I suppose."

"Yeah, makes for a cleaner break."

When Russ and Mike get to the Rose Café, they learn Steven Spielberg is not there. "No," the waitress says. "Can't say I know him. Is he supposed to be joining you?" She stands there and peers at them through these great cat's eyes glasses, arms crossed, one hip jutting out, all the time being a real waitress and playing a waitress.

"You don't know him? That's great." Russ laughs. "He's a very well-known guy, eats here all the time."

"Nope," she says. "He's not here yet. Would you guys like to order something or wait for the other fellow to show up?"

"We'll go ahead and order," Russ says.

"Good." She pulls a pad and pencil from her pocket. "The salmon is wonderful today."

"What does Spielberg order when he's here?" Mike tries to keep the joke going.

She sighs. "Well, today, he would have the salmon."

"I'll have the salmon then," Mike says.

"Will that be two?" She barely glances at Russ.

"Actually," he says, "I will have the warm spinach salad, with Bacos instead of bacon, dressing on the side."

"Hey, now that's interesting," the waitress says, putting her pencil down. "You ordered what Steven Spielberg always has. Spinach salad, Bacos, dressing on the side. How did you know that?"

"Now *you* are pulling my leg. You said you didn't know him."

"No," she insists. "I think maybe you do know Steven."

Russ lowers his voice. "He wouldn't appreciate my going around saying I know him. It's become a privacy thing with him, especially since the Oscar and all."

"So you have seen him."

"Now and then," he says, with a vague shrug.

"I know, you don't want to impose," she says. "But would you give him a message from me, from Melissa at the Rose?"

"I can try." Russ smiles generously.

"Tell him I've done a rewrite of the script I told him about."

"I'm sure he'll appreciate knowing that," Russ asserts. "You're never so rich and famous that you can't take an interest in the work of new talent."

"And it's as ready as it's ever going to be."

"He'll be pleased about that. Shows you've been working."

"You know, I really thought you were putting me on about

knowing him," she says, shaking her head. "How about a couple of glasses of the good chardonnay, on the house?" She puts her pencil and pad away and rushes off to the kitchen.

"What a bullshitter you are!" Mike marvels as soon as the waitress is gone.

"Big deal, I know what Spielberg has for lunch."

"Yes, but you implied all that other stuff. She thinks you're buddies."

"She's actually bullshitting me too, because maybe, just in case she can't get Spielberg to help her, she might get me, whoever I am."

Russ parks the car by one of the docks at the Palm Bay Marina. "This is where I used to keep my boat," he says, turning off the ignition. "That was my slip over there." He points to a spot in the middle of the crowded grid of boats, their spindly, fragile-looking masts doing a bobbing, bristling dance to the gentle motion of the water. On either side of the narrow inlet, high-rise buildings tower along the shore. "How would you like to have a condo up there, overlooking the water?"

Mike shrugs. "It looks like the view would be of a very crowded parking lot."

"A very expensive parking lot," Russ adds. "There's not a boat here for under a hundred thou."

"What kind did you have?"

"A forty-six Morgan." The two men walk along the pier until Russ sees a boat with a long, graceful prow. "That one, with the name *Vagabond* on the side, is just like it. I called mine *Free Spirit*. It was like a little house inside, the stateroom had a queen-size bed, a head with a hot shower, a wet bar, and all kinds of clever built-ins. Very efficient. The deck was pure teak."

"Where did you go with it?" Mike asks, dutifully now.

"San Diego, Catalina, Baja," he says. "But the best trips I took didn't go anywhere, just floated up and down right here on the slip while we partied. You had to be a eunuch not to get laid with a boat like that. Every weekend I'd meet different women, college girls, flight attendants, models. We'd start with drinks over there in the club, and then they'd want to peek inside. I had it really cozy, with fuzzy upholstery and satin sheets; it just made them want to cuddle." Russ takes a deep breath, then shakes his head as if to shake off the wave of sadness that comes over him. "Then everything hit me at once. Getting older, getting divorced, getting poor, getting out of California. One day I was doing great, and the next I wasn't. Just like that."

"You're doing all right in Minneapolis," the young man puts in brightly.

"But it's not this, is it." He makes a sweeping gesture with his hand that encompasses the neat rows of boats, the club terrace with its pink-and-green table umbrellas, the glass and steel high-rises, and finally, the distant horizon line beyond the mouth of the inlet. "I know this might sound arrogant." Russ takes a deep, sad breath, then leans forward until his face is just a few inches away from the younger man's. "Down deep, right where I know what is true and what isn't, I know I deserve all this. That it's my birthright."

The black BMW rolls slowly, almost silently, down a winding blacktop that parallels the Palisades on one side and the beach just north of Malibu on the other. The houses appear large and unwieldy, jammed onto small lots, too close to each other, each calling for its own individuality, designed to stand alone, not to be part of this chaotic ensemble that ranges from the Cape Cod weather-beaten to the urban glass and concrete to the uprooted Victorian, all with big windows facing the ocean, all with fences and heavy doors with security system stickers that announce that in the event of an attempted entry, alarms will sound, guards will arrive, guns might go off. Russ Bolger points out the houses of people he knows.

"Hal Ferguson, the producer of *Days in Our Time,* lives here. Marisha Stone, who sold her last screen play for $750,000, lives over there. Ned and Artemisa Valle owned that one before they got divorced. These used to be my friends."

"You still know them," Mike says.

"I suppose someone might remember me, but it would be like seeing a relative after he's done time in jail. They would be embarrassed, I would be embarrassed. Nothing's very permanent in L.A. Houses get swept up in flames or wash down mud slides, careers stall after one turkey, marriages end after a few months. I would be a reminder of all that."

Russ brings the car to a stop in front of a gray, three-story house, its wood façade done in imitation salt pitted, wind beaten planks, broken up by two narrow windows and a simple steel door mounted flush against the outer wall.

"This is where I used to live." Russ switches off the car engine.

"It looks like a fortress."

"It's meant to. I bought it from the head of the gaffers' union, who at the time was fearing for his life. Paid three eighty, it's worth over five hundred now."

"Pretty good return," Mike says with a nod.

"Would be, might be, may never be." Russ laughs uneasily. "My wife has everything tied up until there's a final settlement. I hate her, just absolutely, unequivocally hate her." He gets out of the car and starts up the walk toward the house.

"Come on," he calls out to the younger man. "It's an interesting place."

The two men walk around the house until they are on the beach and facing a large deck that extends away from the house and is supported by pilons buried in the sand. "See that room by itself above the second story? That was my studio. Great view. On nice afternoons, I'd leave the office, grab something cool to drink, and perch up there watching the sea gulls and working on stuff. One of the better perks of being your own boss." He pauses for a moment, frowning. "I can't stand the paint job. It's supposed to look natural, weathered, with a grainy texture. This is just paint."

"How are we doing for time?" the younger man breaks in. "We should head for the airport soon."

"We will. I just want you to get a feeling for the inside of the house," Russ says, knocking sharply on the back door.

"Does your wife still live here?"

Russ shrugs. "We'll find out soon enough. If no one answers, I know a way to get in."

"That might be a dumb thing to do," Mike says.

"Don't worry. We'll be in and out in minutes. I need to make one last visit to the place, get it out of my system." Russ knocks again, then walks to a narrow window on the side of the house. He tries to slide it up with both hands flat against the glass. When the pane doesn't give, he turns toward Mike, who is standing nervously several feet away. "You got a quarter?" he asks.

"Sure I do." He laughs. "Will it make me an accomplice on a breaking and entering charge?"

"Throw me the quarter," he insists. "I'll get in and open the door for you. That way you'll only be entering."

"Sounds like a technicality to me."

"Technicalities are how people get away with stuff." He

walks to Mike and takes a quarter from him. He inserts it under the window frame, pushes up against the glass, and the window gently slides open. "Besides, half of this house is still mine. That's my defense. I'm breaking into the half I own."

A moment later, Russ opens the front door and calls out to Mike, "Ready for the House and Garden Tour? The whole place is empty, not a piece of furniture or an appliance anywhere. She must've moved out right after I did."

There is a heavy, closed-in feeling throughout the house, with a smell like soiled linens. Even with the large windows and the bright sunlight outside, the house feels dank and gloomy. The walls, which at one time glowed with earthy hues of peach mousse and cocoa silk, as the paint can labels would have put it, now appear faded and dusty. "This is the dining room. We had this great Spanish table, and we entertained three, four times a week. Spago or Ma Maison would schlepp. We had all kinds of people over. We had Troy Donahue. Remember Troy Donahue?"

Mike shook his head. "A friend of Steven Spielberg's, maybe?"

"Teenage heartthrob in the fifties. Wore a red sweater in all his movies. In fact, he had a red sweater on the night he came over. I did his advertising for a while. Healthy snack things like fat-free potato chips, soy flakes, freeze-dried carrot sticks. It's the kind of stuff he eats and the guy looks fabulous."

"So how long are we going to hang around here?" the younger man asks. "It makes me nervous, I don't mind telling you."

"I want to take a few minutes to say good-bye to the place. Why don't you look around? The bedrooms are upstairs; check out the bathroom with the sauna and Jacuzzi, and the study up on the third level. I sound like a real estate agent."

Mike climbs the stairs to the second story, where three

closed doors face an open sitting area that, like the down-stairs, feels cold and gray. He wanders through the bare rooms and finally enters a bedroom where the afternoon sun glows through curtains that match the wallpaper's pink and yellow bunnies.

"Hey, Russ," he calls up to the third-floor study. "Did you say you didn't have children?"

There's no reply. Mike returns to the bright room with the thousands of fluffy bunnies leaping all around him. He guess-es it belonged to a girl. There are small holes in the wall where the child's pictures must have hung. The carpeting is blue, and he can see the four indentations where the small bed would have rested beside the window. There is a heavy line of scuff marks along the bottom edge of the door, flaking wood-work around the frame, and a key still in place. Then, a cou-ple of feet above the floor, he sees the small handprint in faded maroon, the tiny palm and fingers pressed tightly against the wallpaper, and then extending into four parallel streaks which end abruptly at the edge of the door. Mike walks out of the room, closing the door behind him. He can't wait to get out of the house.

"The kid who lived in the house," Mike begins later while they speed to the airport. "Is she with your ex?"

"I never had any kids."

"Yes, you said that," Mike nods. "But there was this child's room in the house, so I wondered."

"That was for my wife's kid." He seems to underline the difference.

"A little girl, right?"

"Yes, her name was Mandy. She was a brat," Russ says.

"She must've been what, about four?"

"I don't know how old she was. Why do you say she was four and not six or ten?"

Mike remembers the small handprint by the door. "Just a guess."

"Listen," Russ says, with a sudden edge to his voice. "I'm not sure how we got on this subject, but do you mind if we wrap it up?" He swerves the car to the right and stops on a side street on the way to the Prestige Rental car drop-off. "What else have you figured out?"

"I'm not figuring anything out," Mike says. "You're the one who's been telling the story of his life."

"There's nothing else to tell," Russ snaps, hitting the steering wheel with the flat of his hand. "There was a wife, and there was a kid. They used to gang up on me. But now they are out of my life, the wife, the kid, the house by the water. Simple."

"Fine. Can we go to the airport?"

"As soon as I'm sure you don't have any more questions."

Mike takes a deep breath. He thinks about the silent gray house, and other houses he had known, houses where he'd had no right to be. "No, it's a wrap."

Russ nods and turns to face the road. He takes the wheel tightly in both hands, shifts into first, and sends the car screaming to the airport, away from L.A.

A smAll mYstEry

Even before the new neighbors moved in next door, Eleanor Wright concluded that Walter F. Pribble was a criminal, of some sort. She deduced this from a thick brown envelope addressed to him but which had ended up in her mailbox by mistake. She separated it from her pile of catalogs and bills and held it for several moments, observing its heft, its smell of institutional must, its secrecy evidenced by the strapping tape that sealed all points of entry. The return address was from Parole and Probation Services, Department of Corrections, Hennepin County.

This notion about the Pribbles kept snaking in and out of Eleanor's awareness; sometimes it bridged one thought to another, at others it hovered in the background ready to spring into focus at any moment. "The house next door has been bought by Walter and Deanna Pribble," she announced to her husband Matt over breakfast. "I think he's an ex-convict." She showed him the envelope before she took it to the adjacent mailbox.

He noted the return address. "He could be a lawyer."

"Lawyers get work mail at work. This is personal to Walter Pribble."

"An interesting observation," Matt said between slurps of coffee.

"Way too interesting. I think we should have been warned. Somebody must've known an ex-con was moving into the neighborhood. These things don't happen by accident. Some thought goes into determining where these people live after they get out."

"Calm down, honey."

"I am calm." She took a sip from her coffee. "Just because I wish something had happened that didn't happen does not mean I'm losing my cool."

"You lost your cool years ago." He looked up at her and smiled for the first time that morning. "That's what's endearing about you."

"You're calling me something," she said. "I just don't know what it is."

The day the Pribbles moved in, Eleanor stayed home from her job as a claims analyst at Midwestern Family Insurance to tighten up the security of her home. Canaan Hills was changing and they would have to change with it. She intended to send a signal to the Pribbles that she was on to them, that whatever they thought they had left behind was like a smell following them all the way to their new home.

She had hoped her husband would stand with her, but Matt was in the middle of planning the marketing strategy for a new species of breakfast grain-nut-raisin clusters. He couldn't take the day off, even with a household of convicted criminals settling in next door. She suggested he at least buy a gun downtown during his lunch hour.

"Not a good idea." He pointed out that criminals simply raised the violence level to cope with increased resistance. There was a law of physics defining the phenomenon, but he couldn't remember how it went. In any case, it was not clear that Walter Pribble was dangerous; Matt didn't want Ellie shooting innocent people.

Even as the Pribbles were moving in, the Wrights were having deadbolts installed on both their front and back doors. Throughout the morning, Eleanor welcomed in quick succession the truck from Gunderson Alarm Systems, the Air-Tite Locksmiths van, and a black Jeep with MAD DOG license plates. It belonged to the owner and chief breeder of Killer Kennels, Inc., who brought with him a family album of bull terriers looking for a nice home to protect. Eleanor had no intention of actually buying a dog; it was all saber-rattling meant to put Walter Pribble on notice.

In anticipation of her neighbors' arrival, Eleanor had picked out the best observation spots in the house. From the bedroom window she had a clear view of the Pribbles' front lawn and of the path leading to the main entrance. From her kitchen window, which faced north above the sink, she could see right into the Pribbles' curtainless kitchen and into a combination pantry and breakfast nook beyond it. She made sure her lime-green blinds were lowered and angled so she could spy unobserved. Finally, the east window on her second-story guest room provided a view of their detached garage at the end of the wooded lot.

Eleanor was sitting by her bedroom window when she saw the Pribbles drive up to the garage, but by the time she had run to the guest room to look out, the couple had already parked and entered the house through the kitchen door.

She speed-dialed Matt's work number. "They've arrived," she said breathlessly. It was an enlightened aspect of their marriage that they could call each other in the middle of work and jump right into a conversation. "Guess what kind of car they drive."

"Mercedes Benz," he said. "Gangsters drive Benzes."

"We haven't established they are killers or dope dealers or anything major," she said. "Just that the man is a criminal."

"I give up," he said impatiently.

"Is this a bad time?" she asked, hearing the edge in his voice. "Are you with people?"

"No, no." He was quick to reassure her, because he felt there were times when work had to take a backseat to the easy flow that their relationship demanded. "He drives a BMW," he guessed again. "A large one."

"Nope," she said, stretching out the game. "Lawyers drive the Beemers. Not their clients."

"I give up, Ellie," he surrendered. "Tell me."

She took a deep breath, and then, one hand shielding her mouth, she spoke into the phone as if afraid the Pribbles might overhear. "Ca-di-llac," she said. "Can you believe it? The color is royal blue, with gold doodads and tinted windows."

"Tinted windows on a Cadillac. There goes the neighborhood."

She felt reassured by his laughter. He wouldn't think she was being stupid if he was laughing along with her. "Now, do you agree they're criminals?"

"Tacky ones, too."

"Telephone scammers."

"Gambling. Welfare fraud. Con artists."

"I'll go ask them," she offered.

No, she was kidding, Eleanor reassured Matt. It was not her style to ask the Pribbles face to face what exactly the Department of Corrections wanted with Walter; she knew how to figure things out on her own. In the same way she coaxed the patterns of numbers in her claims audits to reveal the truth through inference and deduction, she would watch her new neighbors, and they would open themselves up like fudged books, innocent on first look, but full of evasions and contradictions once she broke the code.

It wasn't until late in the afternoon that she got her first good look at the couple. She had been slouching on a cushy gold chair near her bedroom window where a gauzy curtain billowing in the breeze hid her from view. Near her was a small table with the phone. She had been watching two big Mayflower men lug in their furniture. The variety of stuff reminded her of the unlikely combinations you might see at a second-hand store—a Victorian dining room, dark and oily, with tufted chairs, a zebra-striped couch, a bedroom set done in faux marble veneer. And the BarcaLounger, upholstered in maroon Nauga-something, trailing a power cord for the vibrator attachment.

Then, when she least expected it, there were the Pribbles themselves, in the flesh, standing in the middle of the walkway that crossed their front lawn. She hardly dared breathe for fear the slightest movement would send them scurrying out of sight, like deer aware of a hunter.

She saw them stand on the sidewalk and look around as if checking out the neighborhood for the first time. Eleanor held the phone to her ear in case they should look up at the open window. After a moment, she punched Matt's number again.

"They're out there," she whispered. "I think they can see me, so I need to make believe I'm talking on the phone and not just staring out the window."

"I'm in the middle of a meeting, Ellie. I'll call you back."

"Oᴋ, talk to you later," she said. "Oh, I think he wears a toupé. Details at six!" She disconnected but kept the receiver pressed against her ear.

Walter looked to be about forty-five, a big pear-shaped man with love handles that rolled out above the waist of his gray pants and spilled into a black-and-gold Mystic Lake Casino T-shirt. Everything about him appeared tight and confining except for his glossy black hair, all slicked back and pompadoured up.

Mrs. Pribble was a small, compact woman. Her face was round with big nervous eyes. She wore a crisp denim skirt, a blue-and-pink checkered blouse, and white walking shoes. She appeared to be in charge of the move, while her husband looked on anxiously at the steady stream of stuff lurching up the narrow path into their new house. Eleanor didn't think she looked as if she belonged with Mr. Pribble at all. What would a sweet farmer's wife-type be doing with a big-city sleazeball?

Mrs. Pribble placed a hand on her husband's arm, as if to gently restrain him, and said something that made him shake his head impatiently. He started to go back inside the house when something, perhaps the flutter of a curtain from the upper-story window of the house next door, caused him to turn his head too suddenly for Ellie to retreat into the dark bedroom. With the phone next to her ear, she shut her eyes and attempted to appear involved in some imaginary conversation. Her heart was racing; an instant before, Walter Pribble's eyes had met hers with a questioning, annoyed look.

That evening over dinner, Matt did not want to talk about the Pribbles. He was preoccupied with the marketing project at work, and Ellie felt again that he was fading away from her. "How's the new cereal going?" she asked.

He looked up from the strands of pasta curled on his fork. "Soggy one day. Too crisp the next. I'll bring a box home tomorrow so you can taste the latest formula." In his rumpled white shirt and loosened tie and hair plastered back with perspiration, he showed all the signs of having weathered a battle.

"What's it called?" She cheerfully drew him out.

"Grain, Fruit 'n' Nut Clusters." Matt forced his mouth to articulate the words as if he were pronouncing something disgusting. "That's the stupid boring name so far, according to research."

"It's an OK name. You expect it to taste good."

"You expect it to taste like a dozen other cereals on the shelves."

"Does it?"

"Kind of." He took a deep sigh. "I wanted to call it Clusterola. A kind of granola, but in clusters. 'Get Clustermania this morning!' was the slogan." He looked pale.

Now she understood his dark mood of the past few days. Every time one of his ideas was not adopted, Matt's career path turned erratic, and he felt he was dying inside. "So what happened?"

"Consumers are idiots. They said the name didn't tell them anything about what was in the cereal. They said it reminded them of Clusterphobia. Something to eat while in an elevator."

"Sounds like you have to call it a Grain, Fruit 'n' Nut *something.*"

He breathed a long unhappy sigh and spat out, "We tried Bunches, Bon Bons, Crunchies, and Chunkies."

"How about Pribbles?" she said suddenly.

He looked at her and his face brightened. "What's a Pribble?"

"Anything you want it to be. Grain, Fruit 'n' Nut *Pribbles.* It just sounds cute."

He reached across the table and kissed her on the lips. "Ellie, you can have my job anytime you want it."

"Pribbles taste right," she sang. "A flake, a nut, and a fruit, in one tasty bite!"

By Sunday, three full days after the new neighbors had moved in, Eleanor decided that she and Matt should introduce themselves. "If we wait another day, we'll appear weird and unfriendly." She pressed her lips with determination. "I mean, they're the ones who are supposed to act in a suspicious manner, not us." She did not tell Matt that the longer she waited after she had been caught staring at Mr. Pribble, the more awkward and foolish she felt.

"Oᴋ," Matt said. He lifted his arms in a lazy groaning stretch. "Let's go." He folded up the *Trib*'s sports page and dropped it on the rest of the Sunday paper scattered around him.

"It's not that easy," said Ellie. "I think we should call them first. And I should take a welcoming gift. Homemade bread would be nice."

"I thought you didn't want to consort with criminals," he said.

"We will just make believe when we are with them that they are normal human beings, just like us."

Matt read the paper while Ellie conjured a fragrant golden loaf of whole wheat and rosemary from her one-step Japanese breadmaker.

Matt and Ellie sat on the Pribbles' zebra couch, setting down the loaf of bread between them like a baby. Ellie had tried to hand it to Walter when he opened the door, but he said to give it to his wife Deanna, as if the responsibility for handling food was more than he could take on. Then when Deanna came into the living room, she couldn't take the loaf because she was holding a tray with four mugs and a pot of coffee and a plate of sugar cookies. After she had served the coffee and they were all sitting down, the bread remained forgotten, lodged between Matt's and Ellie's thighs.

It was Matt, when he realized his leg was pressing against something warm and moist, who held up the loaf and reached out to hand it to Deanna.

"Well, what a sweet, old-fashioned gesture," she exclaimed. "One doesn't expect fine manners from people younger than oneself, does one?"

"Now, Deanna," Walter interrupted gently from the depths of his BarcaLounger. "Good manners come in all ages." He winked. Which Ellie thought was a message directed at her, because well-bred people don't spy out of windows. She sipped her coffee and nibbled on a cookie and counted the minutes until they might graciously leave the company of the Pribbles, never to feel obligated to socialize with them again.

"Don't mind him," Deanna said. "He winks like that all the time. It's almost a tick with him. I've told him that winking habit is going to get him in trouble some day."

"You never let me have any fun." Walter pursed his lips in a mock pout, but even as he was joking, Ellie was sure she saw in his eyes a look of such sadness it made her queasy. He leaned back in the BarcaLounger and turned on the vibrator.

"Just don't mind him," Deanna repeated with a toss of her head in his direction. "This is too nice a neighborhood for the likes of him to be running loose."

"This *is* a safe neighborhood, isn't it," Walter asked as he suddenly turned off his vibrating chair.

Ellie gave Matt a small nudge with her elbow. "I think it is," he said. "A very nice neighborhood."

"There are very few one-hundred-percent safe neighborhoods left in this country," he said, sounding to Ellie much too knowledgeable on the subject.

"Well, there haven't been any incidents, really, that I have known about," she said. "Not in Canaan Hills anyway."

"Do you folks have a security system?" he asked Eleanor

directly. "I've considered getting an alarm wired in. Or at least a good hungry pit bull."

After that afternoon Eleanor continued to watch the Pribbles, even if she and Matt no longer talked about them all the time. Criminals or not, Matt said, they just weren't very interesting people. Still, she was conscious of them when she was reading, working in the kitchen, taking care of the yard. In the spirit of self-protection, she would assure herself, it became second nature to keep a wary eye on next door. But after that first day when they moved in, the place was as quiet as if it were deserted. Even on weekends the Cadillac stayed in the garage. The curtains to the living room and upstairs bedrooms were always drawn.

In the evening she stood outside in the middle of her front lawn, close to the hedge that separated the two houses, and became perfectly still, shutting her eyes, concentrating on the sounds around her. There was the silken murmur of distant traffic, and the rustle of the wind on the branches of the young poplars lining the street, even the gurgling music of her washing machine far away in the basement. She wiped these sounds from her awareness and directed all her attention toward the house next door. She knew the Pribbles were home because she had seen them arrive an hour earlier, the trunk of the Cadillac full of grocery bags, as if they were settling in for a siege. But from the house next door there was nothing but a profound, cottony silence, no TVs chattering, phones ringing, machines humming. No voices.

Occasionally, she tried to bring the subject up again, because she had a new theory that Walter Pribble was actually a Mafia informer and had been settled in their midst under an assumed identity. It wasn't fair. The normal people of

Canaan Hills were being used as cover. That explained why the Pribbles didn't look like people called Pribble and why Walter wore a toupé styled like Elvis and particularly why they were both always home with no jobs to go to in the morning and no jobs to return from in the evening. Matt didn't seem to care; he was into his cereal these days.

For the next few days the Pribbles and the Wrights didn't cross paths. Eleanor didn't see either one of them until one night around midnight, when she went into the kitchen for ice water and saw through the half open blinds above the sink that the Pribbles' kitchen was all lit up. She took a glass from the cupboard and filled it from the tap. Opposite her, she could see Walter Pribble filling his own glass with water. At first she hardly recognized him because his precisely swirled head of glossy hair was gone, and in its place was a round bald pate with a neat circle of fringe along the sides. She had been right about the hairpiece, she thought to herself. She would be sure to tell Matt.

Walter Pribble, shirtless as well as hairless, stood for several seconds with the glass in his hand, then set it down on the sink and grabbed both sides of the counter with his hands as if suddenly dizzy. She could see him clearly, his broad shoulders with tufts of fuzzy black hair placed on each one like epaulets, the outward slopes on either side of his thick middle. When he stood up straight to drink, she could see the whole of his torso from the coarse graying hair that curled toward his throat to where it became softer and sparser down his midriff to his protruding lower belly. His skin appeared milky white and vulnerable under the fluorescent fixture above the sink.

He rinsed the glass, and then, as he was about to place it in the yellow dishrack, his eyes became fixed on the opposite kitchen's dark window. When he turned to walk away, Eleanor saw his back and then a step later, the soft milky ass. He stopped and turned to face her window again. The hands on his hips framed a large erect penis.

A warm rush flushed Ellie's face. Her heart beat a rapid flutter as she retreated into the darkness of the kitchen and then made her way back to the bedroom. She lay very quietly on the bed, concentrating on Matt's rhythmic breathing beside her. She tried to reassure herself that nothing in Walter Pribble's expression, not the raising of an eyebrow, not the pursing of his lips, indicated he had seen her.

"Where were you?" Matt asked in his thick, half asleep voice when he felt her climb back on the bed.

"I was thirsty." Then she added cautiously, "I think Mr. Pribble saw me from their kitchen."

"You've got to stop spying on the neighbors," he said.

"I wasn't. Maybe he was spying on us."

"Because he was already in his kitchen? It sounds normal to me."

"Well, it wasn't."

"Fine."

"Are you tired of talking with me?"

"I'm tired of your obsession with the neighbors."

"But you still like talking with me, right? I mean, eight years is not so long a time to be married that we've run out of conversation topics."

"Of course not," Matt said.

Eleanor lay awake the following night and looked at Matt asleep beside her. For the first time in eight years, she had a secret from him. She got out of bed, careful not to awaken him, slipped on her light cotton robe, and moved silent as a shadow into her dark kitchen. She took a glass out of the cupboard and walked to the sink. She stood in front of the window for several moments taking small sips of water. Then, as if she had sent a signal, the lights across the way came on suddenly, flooding the Pribbles' kitchen and break-fast area with a cheerful light.

Out of a corner of the kitchen appeared Walter Pribble, again bare chested, but this time he wore his hair, which made the rest of him look even more naked. He walked across the kitchen floor, standing tall, shoulders back, his chest puffed out, and his belly drawn in. Gradually, as Ellie's breath settled, she felt emboldened to lean across the sink and lift the slats of the blind.

At first he seemed to wander aimlessly, as if he'd gone to get something in the kitchen and had forgotten what. Then she realized he was deliberately showing himself off, turning first one way, then the other, strutting around so she could see his back and the tops of his buttocks. He walked to one of the cupboards on one side of the kitchen and reached for the top-most shelf by standing on his toes. When he did this she could see the lower part of his belly, puffy like bread dough. Then he disappeared for a moment and came back with a small step stool. He placed it against the cupboard and stood on the first rung. He now had his back toward her, the full expanse of his naked buttocks looking pathetically vulnera-ble. Then very slowly, as if he were revolving on a pedestal, he turned to face her kitchen window. He held in his hand the gnarled erect penis that rose stoutly from his groin and point-ed its unwinking eye in Eleanor's direction.

"I know Walter's crime," Ellie said to Matt over dinner a few nights later. "Why they had to leave wherever they came from." The thought of their lifetime sentence of shame and silence made her shiver with excitement. By knowing their secret, she felt she had assumed some responsibility over their lives.

Matt kept on eating. He had shut his eyes and was chewing with great concentration, as if he wanted to preserve the particular sensation of that particular pasta salad for the rest of his life. Beside him was the rough draft of the marketing plan he had been working on. He had been reading the plan a few minutes before, but true to another of their rules, he didn't work while they ate.

"He's not really dangerous."

"Who? The neighbor?" Matt lifted his eyes to look at her. "As long as he doesn't sue us for naming a cereal after him."

"You didn't tell me you were going ahead with Grain, Fruit 'n' Nut Pribbles," she said, not showing the edge of anger she felt.

"I'm the hero at work, thanks to you, Ellie."

"Well, you can't use it."

"Sorry. The toothpaste is out of the tube. Everybody loves Pribbles."

"The exposure will kill them."

"Ellie, nobody is going to associate my cereal with the Pribbles of Canaan Hills."

"They will."

"It's just a word. It doesn't mean them. It means whatever we want it to mean with a nice little tune and happy singers and twenty-five million in TV spots. Pribbles *means* little bunches of cereal."

He concentrated on spearing the slippery pasta with his fork to include in one single bite a small floret of broccoli, two fusilli, and a pine nut. He was going about this with great precision when Eleanor picked up her plate, put it in the dishwater, and went to sit on the back porch to watch the evening settle over the cool woods just beyond her yard.

After that night, she never again brought up the new neighbors with Matt. By standing in the dark and watching, Eleanor had allowed herself to be entrusted with Walter Pribble's small mystery. It gave her some satisfaction that she could talk with Matt and not give the secret away. She would occasionally cross paths with Walter or Deanna, exchange small, cheerful greetings, and nothing in her expression would give away that she knew what she knew.

What kept appearing in her thoughts at odd hours was not the sight of Walter's nakedness; it was the look on his face just before she turned away from the window. His head was tilted back, his eyes closed, his lips were pressed shut as if to prevent the scream that boiled up inside him from tearing out of his throat.

Then there were nights when she would lie back on the bed and wait for the time when she could sense Walter Pribble wanting her to just stand still in the dark for him. His thoughts would ring in her mind with such desperation, the unspoken words so ripe with pain and loneliness, that she would give in and rise from her bed. Carefully, so as not to wake Matt, she'd slip through the silent house and wait at the kitchen window. He was always there.

JimmY PeArl's Blue OysTer

On nice days I like sitting in the parlor. At my age all days are nice days if you happen to be alive, with good digestion. The days are especially nice if the joints are flexible and the pain that occasionally starts in the middle of my right buttock and runs down the leg like a red-hot wire all the way to the back of my knee is somehow subdued and buried deep in the muscle tissue rather than snaking its way through the flesh until it strikes raw bone and gristle. But I don't complain; it gets me a government check once a month. When someone says, "Have a nice day," I say, "Amen."

A particularly fine day in the parlor of the Grand Hotel Winfield, which is not exactly a hotel but close enough if you don't insist on a reception desk or room service or bellmen, would be a warm spring afternoon with the sun smack against the windows as it courses above the alley that runs between the Tuck-a-Way self-storage and the Labor Exchange across the street. The dust that hangs in the air swirls and glows in the light and makes a man feel downright peaceful.

Most of the other residents are too dim-witted or crisped out to care whether the sun shines or not and, since the TV was moved to the cafeteria two years ago, not likely to get the oomph to hike up their sweatpants or tie their ratty bathrobes around their clacking bones and jiggling adipose and amble down to the parlor. Except for Moira and Jimmy Pearl and me.

We call the others the Living Dead after the famous movie because you can see them come into the cafeteria at meal-times, their slippered-sneakered-duckshoed feet shuffling in unison like they were some kind of dance group. Not kicking like the Rockettes, though.

After dinner, they scurry right back into their rooms, afraid to be left out in the dark. I'll ask Jimmy what time it is, and he'll say, "Oh, about twenty till the night of the living dead." That means it's ten P.M. because about twenty minutes later management turns off the lights. The three of us will chuck-le as we huddle together around our special table in the cafe-teria. As many times as we've gone through the Living Dead routine, it still cracks us up. We just can't get our minds away from all that grumbling and moaning as deep and mournful as the hooting of a distant wind.

Talk about the consequences of a hard, fast life. Just the thought of Mildred Higging and Casey Stanfeld and Sollie Rosen tripping back in the sixties is enough to give you a side stitch. The long faces and the disheveled hair and the blank eyeballs tell the tale. I mean, did they really think that becoming one with the trees and the moon and the tiny little blades of grass wouldn't cost them, somehow?

"I don't know what's keeping him," Moira grumbles from the other end of the parlor.

Startled, I drop last week's copy of the *Wall Street Journal.* "Jesus, Moira, I didn't know you were here."

"Who did you think I was anyway, the wicked witch?"

"No, Moira. I knew it was you. That raspy cigarette wheeze of yours is fucking unmistakable."

"Are you through abusing me?"

"I was concentrating on something."

"On last week's stock prices?"

"I'm after perspective, not immediacy. I can spot the trends, see the flow and ebb of the market's tides better when there's a little time between my attention and the events themselves. It's called perspective."

"You said that already."

"I know I said *perspective* twice. For your benefit."

"You read the old *Journal*s because it's Jimmy's subscription, and he's been a week behind in his reading since the fourth grade."

Once again our conversation comes around to Jimmy Pearl. Of the three of us, he is by far the most interesting. And the best looking. And at seventy something, old enough to be our father. So when the three of us are together, we let Jimmy do all the talking. And when he's not around, then sooner or later Moira and I will end up talking about him, or about something he said, or about what he does when he's away.

"Where is he, anyway?" Moira asks, rhetorically I'm sure, since I don't keep track of Pearl as closely as she does, mainly because she is in love with him. I personally love the man too, in a brotherly way. But I don't get wrapped up in his comings and goings.

It's bad enough that Jimmy's bladder and mine are in sync. Have been for about ten years. Even on days when we don't see each other, I can always count on running into him in the men's room when we both wake up at all hours of the night damn near the bursting point, and we wander into the stalls to let out a few measly droplets because our bladders have all the elasticity of shoe leather and our prostates are as big as persimmons. I mean, we would like to piss out real gushers, but we end up simply marking our territory like dogs encountering hydrants.

When I first moved to the Winfield Hotel and saw this little guy who always wore a double-breasted white summer suit, I knew we would be friends. We got acquainted while leaning into the urinal waiting for the flow and then shaking our wrinkled puds for a long time, knowing there would always be one last dribble after we'd tucked them back in.

"You're too young for this kind of routine," he said sympathetically. "How many times do you do it?"

"Just at night? Or in a twenty-four hour period."

"Don't get technical on me," he said.

"Five, six times."

"Eight to ten for me." He nodded thoughtfully. "It's a pisser, isn't it?" He laughed at his own joke. "It's unnatural. The night was made for sleeping and boffing."

"I haven't done much of either in years."

He squeezed his eyes shut and gritted his teeth and parted his lips in a grimace. "This place doesn't lend itself to sex. The only babe around here is Moira Jones. Great personality, too. Find me in the cafeteria one of these days. I'll introduce you."

That's how I met Moira, although in all these years I've never harbored romantic hopes about her. She is a fine looking woman; she just thinks she's smarter than the rest of us. Falling in love requires a measure of stupidity, and women like Moira never let their mental guards down enough to get involved. That's what I told her when she was complaining about not having married. I said to her she was just too damn smart for her own good. She said she didn't think she was a genius or anything, but certainly a lot brighter than any man she ever met. Except for Jimmy Pearl.

I think she would've fallen for him years ago, but he was just not interested in catching her. When a man has topless dancers on his payroll, why would he waste his time on some crank?

"I don't think I've seen him since supper last night," she says.

"He must've taken one of his trips to Jersey," I venture, remembering that I haven't seen him in the men's room.

"He just came back from Jersey."

"Owning a topless bar is complicated. Butko the Bouncer was threatening to quit. He probably had to rush back and hire another big guy."

"It wasn't Butko who was leaving. It was that other guy, the bartender."

"Jimmy calls him Lloyd the Slice, on account that he puts a slice of lime on every drink he mixes whether the recipe calls for it or not."

"I know as much about The Blue Oyster as you do," Moira snaps.

"I was just making conversation. I know you knew about Slice's nickname."

"You were patronizing me."

"I like it when you sulk. It makes you look sultry and ani-mal-like. Why don't you come over and sit a little closer?" I slide to the side of the sagging brown couch.

"Thank you, no."

"You're a treacherous tease, Moira."

All the banter in the world wouldn't let us forget that Jimmy Pearl was not around. He had gone off before, for days at a time. But he'd say his good-byes before he left.

When he returned, he'd be full of stories about his little bar in Jersey, The Blue Oyster. That was why he wore a white linen suit; the owner of a club had to project class. That was also the reason he talked on the phone so much, settling arguments among the three topless dancers who were forever breaking the rules—pay for drinks or get some schmo to pay for them, don't date customers, don't dope on the premises, don't fight, and share your tips with Butko because he is your protector and nobody ever, ever tips the bouncer. The Blue

Oyster was a big headache, but he stayed with it because, he said, it was a little gold mine.

When I asked him why, if he had so much money, he lived in the Hotel Winfield, Jimmy just said he liked the people, that it was people that made a place home. He must've been talking about Moira and me.

"You should go to his room and see if he's all right," Moira suggests after a while. I thought she had fallen asleep; her head had toppled forward, and her chin grazed the top of her blue dress with the big paisley print. Under the bright sunlight her red hair gave off tiny reflections that looked like sparks.

"You go see. I think he's fine."

"I bet he's not," she insists. "Besides, I've never been to his room."

"That's not what I've heard," I sing softly.

"Jimmy tell you something?"

"Right from the horse's mouth."

"Well, that proves you're lying. Even if it were true, which it is not, Jimmy is too much of a gentleman to blab."

"You think so? All guys blab. Blabbing is the best thing about having sex. Blabbing is so good, so satisfying, that you can blab about women that don't exist and sex that never happened, and the blabbing makes it all true."

Moira shakes her head in disbelief. I know she thinks I'm a real adolescent, but I know I've put a bug in her head. She takes out a cigarette and taps the end of it against her thumbnail. "What did he tell you, anyway?" she asks in her low throaty voice.

"That you were a fine woman, that you bucked like a wild mare, and that you drooled a little when you came. That you were better than the girls at The Blue Oyster."

"Well, he was lying."

"Maybe so, Moira. But the babbling makes it true."

After that, Moira is quiet for a long time. I can tell she puts up with me because I'm Jimmy Pearl's friend. But if we don't talk, there doesn't seem much else to do except watch the afternoon sun rise up above the parlor windows, the dried raindrops on the glass making everything inside look dusty and threadbare. I switch on the lamp with the brown spots scorched into the shade so I can see the commodities quotes a little clearer.

"I think I'll put some money in coffee futures. Coffee is bound to go up, don't you think, Moira? Jimmy says that people drink less booze these days. That's why he put in a six-thousand dollar Italian espresso machine at The Blue Oyster. He'd better be right."

"Jimmy Pearl hasn't seen six thousand together in his life."

"He'll be the first to admit The Blue Oyster is not doing so well these days. On account of the neighborhood demographics changing."

"Demographics?" Moira looks at me and laughs. Her laughing turns into coughing, until she lights another cigarette. "Do you even know what a demographic is?"

"Sure, it's Jimmy's name for customer. His customers used to be young Italian professionals."

"Gangsters."

"Now they are mostly Dominican."

"Gangsters."

"No, Moira, The Blue Oyster is a neighborhood bar. A homey place, where Lloyd the Slice knows your name, and Bouncer Butko is a rough but friendly guy, and Louella, Kim, and Thalia are your basic nice girls from small towns trying to make it in the big city."

"You crack me up." This time she doesn't bother to laugh. "I don't even think there is such a thing as The Blue Oyster. I mean, how could an old coot like Jimmy Pearl keep running some bar a thousand miles away."

"Oh, there's a Blue Oyster. It's the pride of Jimmy's life."

"Believe what you want," she sniffs.

Somewhere around five it becomes obvious that neither Moira or I will go anywhere until we find out what's going on with Jimmy Pearl. She suggests again I go to his room, but something makes me shy away from that. We're jealous of each other's privacy here at the Hotel Winfield, and our little 120 square-foot room is about all the territory any of us calls his own. The unwritten rule is that when the door is open, people are welcome to come in for a drink or conversation or whatever. But I checked Jimmy's door an hour ago when I went to take a leak, and the door was closed. That's a Do Not Disturb sign at the Hotel Winfield.

"Are you hungry like I am?" I ask Moira.

"No."

"You should eat, anyway."

"I'm just going to sit here until Jimmy shows up. You go eat."

"I'll get you a sandwich."

"Fine. Anything but Velveeta."

Moira and I eat our grilled cheese sandwiches and don't talk much. All I can hear is her crunching potato chips and gurgling down the Diet Coke. It isn't my fault Jimmy hasn't shown up. But you'd never know it to look at Moira. The pissseier she gets about him not being around, the worse the vibes she sends my way.

I'd have given anything for Jimmy Pearl's nonstop bla-bathon about The Blue Oyster. How to run a P&L on every single bottle of liquor to make sure Lloyd isn't getting too generous with his pals. Why coasters are a good investment when your bar surface is solid maple burnished to a silken gloss by time and a million elbows. Liability insurance on Butko. Turning your rest rooms into money makers with a condom machine in each one—eighty cents profit on every pop.

"If you don't go check on him, I will," Moira says around six, just as the parlor is sinking into a dusky gloom.

"Let's give it another hour, and if he doesn't show, we'll both go knock on his door."

"Fine," she says, in a tone that reveals it's not at all fine with her. "And what are we going to do meanwhile? Jerk our heads around every time we hear footsteps?"

"No, I'm going to continue my perusal of the *Journal,* and you can smoke three cigarettes. Then we'll go."

Of course we end up doing what Moira said we would. I do try to concentrate on the NASDAQ listings alphabetically, keeping a mental note of the ups versus the downs, and Moira smokes and coughs, and after I catch her directing hostile glances at me, I start looking straight back at her. But staring at Moira is like staring at the Sphinx, all stone faced and blank eyed and bigger than life. She has smoked so many Camels in her life that she's become part of the scenery on the package.

"Okay, let's go," she says finally.

She's breathing hard by the time we get to room 326 at the end of the third-floor hallway. "You wouldn't be winded if you didn't smoke so much."

"It's not the smoking. I'm trying not to panic. You'd be worried too if you weren't so insensitive."

When we're in front of Jimmy Pearl's door, she raises her fist to rap on the door, but in the end she can't make herself knock.

I tap softly at first. When there's no answer, I knock again, louder. "Jimmy, " I say. "These are your best friends in the world come to party with you. Moira is naked and I've got an ounce of *sinsemilla.* "

Somehow I'm not surprised there's no answer. There seems to be an aura of heavy, forbidding silence around the door, like a soundless exhalation that goes on and on. It takes a big effort to reach for the doorknob and turn it slowly. "Are you there, Jimmy?"

I go in first, followed by Moira, her raspy breath on the back of my neck. The room is very neat. The skinny bed is pushed up against the corner, a teetering card table is on the other side, and in the middle of the room, practically taking over the whole space, is a frayed La-Z-Boy he must've picked up at the Salvation Army because you just don't see those big mothers with the plaid upholstery anymore.

You can't miss him. Sitting up on the bed, leaning against the wall, wearing his white suit and his iridescent blue tie knotted in a Windsor is Jimmy Pearl, his pale blue eyes wide open, his head tilted down, and his jaw drooping toward his collarbone as if he were utterly flabbergasted to see us in his room.

"I knew it," Moira whispers hoarsely. "We should've come to see him sooner."

"When sooner, Moira?" I snap, pretty tired now of the woman's eternal dissatisfaction with the ways of the world. "It's not like he died because you weren't around to amuse him."

"We should call 911."

"Sure, Moira, like there's a big hurry." Even as I'm turning to leave, I give the place a quick look. On the wall above the table are several framed photographs. Jimmy at twenty with slicked hair and pegged pants on the Boardwalk in Atlantic City with three toothy women saying cheese. Then there's a shot of Jimmy tending bar in front of a wall of liquor bottles and a beveled mirror etched with the big Seagrams 7 logo. And there's Jimmy with someone who looks like Bing Crosby.

On the table itself is a round metal tray with a bottle of Canadian Club, two squat on-the-rocks glasses, some cocktail napkins with a progressive picture of the Mona Lisa going from her simpering little smile to a full blown, hysterical laugh. Stacked on the side is a pile of matchbooks with the image of a large oyster partially open to reveal a gleaming pearl inside and the words *Jimmy's Blue Oyster Lounge, Paramus, NJ Tel. MA6-3113*. I don't think Moira is looking, because I know she wouldn't approve, but as I lead her out of the room, steering her by the elbow around the La-Z-Boy, I tuck a couple of the matchbooks and one Mona Lisa paper napkin into my pants pocket.

The voice on the other side of 911 takes my name and address as if I were the one having a life-and-death crisis instead of old Jimmy. I go along; it's the best way to deal with public institutions. He promises to send an ambulance but not immediately because the victim in question is dead. That is, if I'm certain he's dead. I say yes.

Then I drop my last eighty-five cents until the first of the month to call the number on the matchbook.

"*Aló, quién habla?*"

"Is this the Blue Oyster?"

"The what . . . ?"

"Jimmy. Pearl. Blue. Oyster." I try to speak clearly and slowly.

"*Ay qué carajo . . .*" The voice trails off just before hanging up.

When I get back to the parlor, Moira is sitting off to one side of the green couch in the darkest corner of the room. I sit down beside her, half expecting she'll move away from me. But she stays put, even though I'm sinking into a hole in the couch that throws me close to her, close enough so my shoulder presses against hers. She doesn't even move her arm. I stay there too. I can feel the rise and fall of her body with every breath, and I can smell the cigarette smoke on her clothes, and I can hear her trying to breathe very lightly so as not to sniffle. I stay there even though a couch spring is digging in and starting to worm that hot wire into my butt and all along the back of my leg.

"I called The Blue Oyster," I say. "Just picked up the phone and dialed the number on this matchbook." She takes it, and I let her have it because I figure I've still got the other one. It's nice to have a memento from your friends.

"What did they say?"

"They said they were sorry to hear the news. That they'll miss him on account of what a great guy he was, a terrific boss, and a real friend to everyone there. That I should let them know the name of the funeral home so they can send flowers."

"That's sweet of them," she says. "Who did you talk to, Lloyd the Slice?"

"Yeah. He said he was going to invent a drink and name it after Jimmy. The Pearly Gate."

"What else?"

"I could hear the dancers crying in the background."

"And Butko?"

"Oh, he's such a bear of a guy, but you know, he was too choked up to say anything."

"What else?" Moira puts her hand on my arm and clasps her fingers tightly around it. "Tell me more."

"I don't know what else to tell you, Moira," I say, feeling now that talking is taking too much of an effort. "Things just aren't going to be the same anymore. Everyone knows that."

GettiNg aWay

The man and woman stuck in the waiting room of the steamy Puerto Vallarta airport had spoken very little to each other in the past two days. Each seemed absorbed by small nuisances—the woman ran a comb through the tangles in her long blonde hair, the man stared at the blurry print on their tickets. At forty, their bodies were lean and somewhat angular, their arms and legs too long for the narrow leather straps of the steel-frame bench.

It was clear from the way the couple stretched out, feet resting on their luggage, eyes gazing warily toward the crowd pressed against the airline ticket counter, their tanned bodies, perhaps from habit, drawn toward each other even across the empty seat between them, that they were content to travel together and might be relieved to return to Minneapolis on this, the last day of their first vacation in years. Still, returning from vacation has a different feel from going on vacation. The returners appear like the dumbstruck survivors of some violent tropical upheaval, rumpled and sunburned, sand in their shoes and their hair, the plunder from their zealous shopping overflowing the large straw bags with *Viva Puerto Vallarta* embroidered in pink yarn.

Twice before, a booming female voice had echoed in both Spanish and English over the PA with the announcement of flight delays. The gate area grew crowded with the arrival of passengers booked on later departures. The woman leaned forward to hear the singsong refrain of a slight brown girl who clung to her side and offered up a tattered box of Chiclets. Pulling off her large sunglasses, the woman tried to guess the flavors from the pink, green, yellow, red cellophane wrappers. She chose green, hoping for spearmint.

The man watched her long hands take the pack out of the box, then open the large straw bag between her feet to search for change. In their eight years of marriage, he had continued to marvel at the grace of her fingers in motion. Her every gesture seemed deliberate and important in itself. The first time they ever shared a meal—a quick pizza in the middle of their working day—he had noticed the way she carefully separated the tendrils of cheese that clung to the slice, and then so very gently, almost lovingly, it had seemed to him, laid the fragrant, doughy triangle on his paper plate.

"She's darling, isn't she?" the woman said with a nod toward the girl, who had marched on to the next group of American tourists in the waiting room. "I just love her little legs sticking out from inside those pink shorts."

"You must feel better," he said.

"Are you feeling better?" she countered.

"It feels good to be on our way home."

"But you're not feeling so hot, are you."

"It's not physical," he said.

"I never said it was physical," she said.

"But it's like a hangover."

"Without the fun to show for it," she said. "Will they let us upgrade to first class?"

"I'll talk to them again." He pushed himself up from the sagging leather straps. "Common sense will win out yet."

Marcie and Paul Farrar had promised each other that during this week in February they would be open to new sensations, court unpredictability, risk adventure. Indeed, a full week of freedom from the numbing gray winter and the chafing stress of the office was too rare a thing to waste by insulating themselves in one of the big Puerto Vallarta resort hotels. Playa Cruces, a small fishing village forty miles up the coast, offered pristine white beaches and a secluded two-story hotel in the midst of the noisy, flowering jungle.

The first thing Marcie and Paul did after finding their room along the open hallway was race to the beach. They pulled off their shoes and let the hard, packed white sand press against the soles of their feet. They chased the surf that lapped onto the beach until one large wave soaked them up to their thighs. In the distance the sun was setting in a blaze of violet skies and the reflection of the clouds made random brush strokes that danced on the water. Several feet away, just before the point where the waves began to roll in, they could see a greenish band that floated and bobbed with the rise of each swell of the sea. At first it looked like a school of fish floating lazily, their iridescent backs open to the sky.

"No, it's not fish," Paul said after a while, squinting against the glare.

"It's flotsam and jetsam," Marcie said.

"It's garbage," Paul nodded. "I see muck. I see heads of lettuce. I see dead fish."

For a long silent moment, they stood at the edge of the ocean and stared at the dark mass that rose and fell with the rhythmic push of the waves. "I see turds!" Marcie cried out finally, rushing back from the water.

Paul caught up with her on the beach. "They're dumping sewage into the ocean."

"We're not in Kansas."

"Probably the big resorts in PV. At least you can count on it being middle-class, suburban American crap."

"Not funny. Not clever." Marcie marched down the beach toward their hotel, faintly visible now under the darkening sky. She held her arms away from her body, her hands open before her, as if the possibility of brushing against her own clothes, of coming into contact with her own wet skin, would further contaminate her. "And please don't touch me," she said, as Paul caught up with her and began to walk beside her. "You were in the water, too."

Paul waited in line until he stood once again in front of the airline counter, holding out two wrinkled slips of glossy paper for the clerk to see.

"Just tell me one thing," Paul challenged. "Are these upgrades valid with our coach fare?"

"That is not the cause of the problem." The clerk, unflappable under his thin mustache and brilliantined hair, looked back at him with a blank expression.

"You have passengers flying up front who have actually paid a lower fare than I have but who also have coupons."

"There are rules, procedures. I do not make these . . ."

"I'm appealing to your sense of logic," Paul interrupted him. "The point is that my wife and I, who have the same coupons, plus paid a much higher fare than some of these people, have to sit in the back of the plane."

"Yes, but others got here first."

"Do you see how unfair that is?" Paul held out the two upgrades, one in each hand, for the man to see. "We are better customers than they are. My wife and I are in a state of great stress this morning and we require some undisturbed rest in First Class."

The clerk breathed a long sigh, as if he believed the end of this conversation was finally at hand. "The good news is I have room for one of you up front."

By the time Paul got back to Marcie's side, he was content with himself and with his small victory.

"Who am I going to talk to?" Marcie asked when he handed her the boarding pass. "It's a four-hour flight."

"I thought you'd be happy. You like First Class, remember?"

She smiled, perhaps for the first time that day, he thought. "Thank you. What did you have to do to get this?"

"Nothing much," he said. "Just be an asshole for a few minutes."

"I'm touched." She puckered her lips and tilted back the brim of her big hat. He leaned toward her, but the kiss must have landed in midair, because he never felt it.

On their first night at the Hotel de la Playa, the Farrars sat on a terrace by the pool sipping margaritas that were smaller but more potent than the ones back home. The night was warm and fragrant with the scent of night-blooming flowers, and the sky was brighter than they had ever seen it. They felt sophisticated and self-assured and vaguely superior to the other guests, mostly large Mexican families that included babies as well as grandparents, and a French woman who scolded her two wiry little boys, and a German couple who sat glum and uncommunicative in front of twelve empty bottles of Dos Equis beer. They had a second round of drinks and only then noticed the Mexican couple who sat near them on the terrace and who smiled whenever Paul's or Marcie's eyes met theirs. Finally, they invited the Farrars to come over to their table for a drink.

"We are the Caminos," the man offered his hand to Paul. "I

am Carlos and this is Rosa. We are in room 218. We are neighbors. We have been here for nearly a week."

"You can know this from our tans," Rosa said, pulling down the shawl around her shoulders to reveal a plump brown arm.

"It is interesting," Camino went on. "You are the first Americans we have seen staying here."

"Yes, we like to strike out beyond the beaten path," Paul said.

"Which path is that?" Camino asked.

"It's no particular path, just an expression in English for the choices most people make. For example, Americans tend to go to Puerto Vallarta, but we came to Playa Cruces."

"Aha, you are nonconformists," he declared.

"Well, yes, I suppose we are." Marcie shook her blonde hair and laughed. "I never thought of ourselves that way. But we must be. Don't you think so, Paul?"

"Why is this path better than the beaten path?" Señor Camino wanted to know. The four of them sat on low stools around a tiny table, their knees occasionally touching. Camino leaned forward and looked again from Marcie to Paul and back to Marcie. He seemed to squint when in deep thought.

"Playa Cruces is the real Mexico," Marcie replied. "It's less artificial."

"Oh, I think Puerto Vallarta is much more fun," Rosa said. "The hotels there are more luxurious. But expensive!"

"The real Mexico can be dangerous," Camino said. "You are more protected in the artificial Mexico."

Paul sat up. "Anything I should be worrying about?" he asked lightly.

"Oh, not any single thing," Camino teased. "You should look out for sharks in the sea, and scorpions in your bed, and cows on the highway." He lifted his shot glass and held it up to the light from the bright paper lanterns that hung all around them; he drank the tequila in one swallow. "But you don't look like the kind of man who has anything to be afraid of." Camino smiled first at Paul, then at Marcie. "Or you, señora."

"Sure, there have been occasions," Paul said.

Camino nodded and took his wife's hand. "True fear is a permanent condition. Like being bald, or fat, sometimes the awareness leaves you, but it always comes back, and then you realize even if you were not aware of being afraid at a particular moment, every cell in your body and all the little juices in your brain were all the time, all on their own, very busy being afraid."

Paul's face had set into a broad, convivial smile, even as he uncomfortably watched the Mexican couple exchange glances. He turned to look at Marcie, wanting to make sure she had also caught what he thought was a very odd look between the two, but she was gazing above the Caminos' heads toward the ocean. She didn't look his way until she heard Camino offer to buy the next round.

"I think I've had enough," Paul said quickly. "But this has been great. Just the perfect capper to a long, long day."

Camino made a face of mock disappointment. "Please, it is my pleasure that you and Señora Farrar accept a drink as a sign of our friendship."

On their first night home, Paul awoke with a start to the sound of waves crashing against the walls of his bedroom twenty stories above the empty downtown streets. He lay back quite still, reluctant even to let the sound of his own breathing interfere with the murmur of the surf, which sounded so real he thought he was back in Playa Cruces. He slowly opened his eyes to the glow of the lights from the neighboring buildings, reassured that he was home. Never had the lights burning through the inner-city grid held such a promise of warmth and security, even if they more accurately represented his fellow worker bees of corporate life buzzing through the night.

With a sigh, he closed his eyes and felt the weight of his body settle back down on the bed, the tilt of his head just right on the cool pillow, aware of Marcie's deep, rhythmic breathing. He reached out for her and felt his fingers brush against her thigh. For a moment he sensed her breathing pause in the middle of a long exhalation. He thought for a moment he had awakened her, and he waited for her to turn to him, to say something, so he could tell her about hearing the ocean just outside their room. Her breath settled back into its long rhythmic flow. He realized his hand was no longer touching her; between breaths she had somehow edged away from him.

He turned on his side and tried to will himself back asleep. He was sure he heard the waves again, this time in perfect synchrony with the even flow of Marcie's breathing. That was it, he realized, the sound of the surf was the sound of Marcie's breath. As she breathed, so the ocean moved. Inhale with the receding stroke of the undertow pulling itself together, breathe out to the rhythm of the crashing surf against the rocks that jutted out from the beach. It occured to him that from that night forward, as long as Marcie breathed, he would not forget the beach, the tumbling ocean waves, the long nights in their room in Playa Cruces. He wondered if they would ever get away from their sadness.

In the morning, as Paul and Marcie stretched out by the pool, their faces tingling under the sun, their bodies aglow with the sheen of sweat and SPF 30 sun screen, a shadow was cast over them. They opened their eyes and first saw their own image twice reflected in the large lenses of a pair of mirrored sunglasses; then the towering, pear-shaped form of Señor Camino, in pineapples-on-yellow matching trunks and shirt snug against his round belly, loomed above them.

"Forgive me," he said. "Clearly, your beautiful bodies and the beautiful sun were made for each other. I am only in the way."

"No, of course not." Paul waved the thought away. "It's good to see you, Carlos."

"Is Rosa still asleep this morning?" Marcie found herself being too friendly, but she wondered if, even at this early stage of their relationship, it was possible to retreat gracefully. After all, some time during the previous evening, the agreement had been made to be friends, to call each other Carlos and Rosa and Pablo and Marcia. Marcie had thought it a terrific idea. She kept saying to them, *"Mucho gusto, me llamo Marcia. Mi esposo se llama Pablo."*

"No," Camino smiled, still standing in the way of the sun. "She is on the beach collecting shells. She likes the seashells. Do you like the seashells, too?"

"I love seashells," Marcie nodded briskly, finding herself being agreeable even as she realized it was absolutely essential that they not display the remotest sign of a shared interest; the last thing anyone wanted on vacation, she knew and knew Paul concurred, was to get adopted by couples who would want to pair up because they were bored with each other's company.

"My wife is a shells connoisseur," Camino beamed. "Maybe you should go to the beach with her and look for special seashells together."

"Oh, no," Marcie stammered. "Not this morning. I am feeling much too lazy to be of any use this morning."

"Rosa would like the company; she would not expect you to look for seashells as if such activity were work."

"Perhaps tomorrow," Marcie insisted. "There will still be many shells tomorrow, don't you think?"

"Of course, señora," Camino said, suddenly more formal. "I will tell Rosita you are tired but that maybe you can look at her treasures this afternoon during lunch."

"They are so weird," Marcie exclaimed as soon as Camino was gone. "Did you see? He didn't go to the beach, he went straight into the bar."

"I think you hurt his feelings," Paul said. "It wouldn't have been too hard to take a walk along the beach with his wife."

"He had been standing a long time over us before we realized he was there. I thought he was a damn cloud."

"There are cultural differences," Paul argued. "I think he was being polite, not wanting to be too abrupt."

"There's something too eager about them," she said. "They look as if they'd like to absorb us."

After that, Paul and Marcie made a game of hiding from the Caminos. Whenever one of them would spot Carlos or Rosa, they would sound the alarm, a secret signal they had invented that sounded like an electronic beep. Marcie would go *"beep beep beep,"* and press her tongue against the inside of her cheek to point at the Caminos appearing in their matching yellow pineapple print robes. Then Paul and Marcie would casually move to a different part of the beach, or back by the pool if they had seen them on the beach, or to the bar if they had spotted them in the restaurant. Inevitably the Caminos trailed close behind. They even followed the Farrars when they took a taxi to shop in the village. Once in the market, the Caminos would lag behind a few steps, and pause at the same stalls, Rosa touching the scarves Marcie had looked at, trying on the same hats.

One night, the Caminos had dinner at a table right beside Paul and Marcie, close enough so Carlos could lean back in his chair and ask how the day had gone, if Marcia had found any interesting shells, what Pablo had thought of the fish because he himself felt it was not too fresh, which was inexcusable, being right by the ocean.

The Farrars finished their meal quickly, paid their bill, and found a pair of deck chairs on the dark side of the terrace overlooking the ocean. They slouched down until their heads were below the edge of the backrest; they held their breath and crossed their fingers and prayed the Caminos would not find them. They almost laughed out loud when they were startled by Carlos's deep voice behind them.

"The moon is so full tonight," he said. "So bright you can see your way without any lights at all. We should take a walk on the beach tonight. I have brought a bottle of brandy and we can enjoy the night together."

This time Paul was ready. "Thank you, Carlos. But Marcie and I are very tired. Too much fun in the sun." He laughed nervously. "Maybe another night."

"Ah, but this is our last night," Camino said. Then he stood on the low parapet around the terrace, lifted both hands to the night, and let out a high-pitched cry. "Ay, ay, hai, hai!" he yelled in a hoarse, anguished voice. "HAI, HAI, AY, AY, AY!" he cried out louder, head tilted back, hands rolled into tight fists at his side.

He balanced himself along the edge of the wall as if it were a tightrope. Then, still clutching the bottle, he jumped off the parapet onto the beach below. *"Adiós, amigos!"* they heard his voice call out from the darkness.

"I didn't know you were leaving," Marcie said to Rosa, who stood by the edge of the terrace and followed with her eyes the vanishing figure of her husband.

"It was nice of you to be our friends," Rosa said. "Carlos has many worries, but being with you cheered him up."

"That's what vacations are for," Marcie said.

"These are not problems Carlos and I can get away from."

"Still, a trip like this helps see a situation more clearly," Paul said. "Then maybe you realize things are not so bad."

"You think so?" Rosa said. The three remained silent for a few moments, watching Carlos walk down the beach and disappear in the dark.

"Well, you have to believe things will work themselves out," Marcie said.

"Yes, that is very true," Rosa said, suddenly cheerful. "Here," she reached into her straw handbag and pulled out a handful of shells wrapped in green tissue. "You should take these home with you. I've chosen the most special ones for you."

"No, you found most of them," Marcie said.

"I live closer to the sea. I can come here anytime." She laughed. "Anytime I have problems." Then she said good night and jumped off the low parapet onto the beach. "I will go find Carlos."

A week after returning to Minneapolis, the Farrars' two suitcases, a rigid metallic gray Samsonite with wheels and Marcie's yellow-and-brown flowered satchel, along with the big straw bags, remained unpacked in the entry hall to their condominium.

"I'm curious," Paul said on Friday night, after they had returned from dinner downtown. "Do you suppose we'll unpack anytime soon?"

"I can't deal with it right now, honestly."

"It's just a couple of bags."

"I mean the trip. Unpacking means coming to terms with the trip, deciding whether it was a good trip or not."

"I don't get it," Paul said.

"There is stuff you bring back, which maybe felt right when you got it, but once you get home, it turns into something else."

"It's mostly dirty clothes, Marcie," he said lightly. "I don't think they'll turn into anything else."

"You think. Those dirty clothes are permeated with last week."

"Cal Davis at work asked me if it had been a good trip," Paul said.

"What did you tell him?"

"That it had been a great trip. Just what we both needed."

"I said the same thing to Mom."

"So, what do you think?" Paul asked.

"I'll tell you after we've unpacked."

About an hour after they had gone to bed and turned the lights off, Paul whispered, "Are you awake?" When she muttered she was, he asked, "Have you been thinking about them much, Carlos and Rosa?"

"I've been too busy," she said. "When I do remember them, I tell myself I don't have time and just push their faces away."

"I think about how she sounded that last night," Paul said. "You just knew there was something heavy going on between them."

"Give it a rest, Paul. We're back in Minneapolis."

"You're not really home until you unpack."

"It's midnight, Paul."

"Let me do it," he said, jumping out of bed. "I'll just dump everything in the washer, get the sand and the salt and the sweat out of everything. By tomorrow morning, everything will be clean and smelling of Tide."

She could hear him in the dark hallway, dropping the heavy gray bag on its side with a loud thump, then marching into the laundry room, setting the dials with a series of sharp clicks to start the machine. He returned to the hallway and unzipped the satchel. "What do you want me to do with the seashells?" he asked, holding up the green package.

"You can do anything you want with them."

"She gave them to you," Paul said.

"Throw them away. They smell like seaweed," Marcie said, her voice muffled by the pillow she held over her head. "No, that's mean. Put them back in my bag."

The next morning, the next to the last day of their vacation off the beaten path, Paul and Marcie resolved to achieve a perfect, unblemished twenty-four hours. The sun would shine on them out of a clear, cloudless sky. Their skins would be baked, oiled, and burnished to such rich cocoa tones that their old, worn identities would melt away. They would not see the Caminos. They would be complete unto themselves, not replying to questions, greetings, or invitations.

"We'll just say *no hablo español,*" he said.

"Or *no hablo inglés.*"

"*No hablo,* period."

Down on the shore, the quiet was disturbed by a group of teenage boys and girls in skimpy fluorescent bathing suits, their bodies blackened by a lifetime out in the sun. One of the boys held a radio up on his shoulders as they danced to the brassy strains of a mambo. When they passed in front of the hotel's terrace, they waved at Paul and Marcie, and then gradually their music faded as they continued down the beach. After that there was only the breaking surf, the cries of the seagulls, the soft breeze stirring the palm fronds above.

Some time in the afternoon, the Farrars had guacamole with fried tortilla chips, and quesadillas dripping with melt-ed white cheese, and Bohemia beers so cold ice crystals clung to the necks of the bottles. The guacamole was fresh and made with large chunks of avocado, the green chiles sliced into daunting little circles gave it just the right amount of bite, and the fragrance of the hot corn tortillas was enough to make them nearly weep with gratitude that, here in the middle of Las Cruces bay, they could avail themselves of such perfection for just a few dollars.

Even when the sun was blocked by occasional clouds toward the middle of the afternoon and the air took on a sudden, unexpected chill, the Farrars' sense of well-being was not diminished.

A sudden gust made Marcie reach for her robe. She sat up on the recliner and hugged her knees close to her chest. Faintly, through the stirring wind, there was a woman's scream from the upper story of the hotel building. Marcie looked toward Paul to see if he had heard it too, but he remained stretched out prone on the recliner, his head pillowed in his arms.

The sharp bang of a door slamming made her look up as one of the young housekeepers dropped a bundle of white sheets and towels and ran down the open hallway, sliding on the shiny red tile floor, nearly stumbling down the staircase that led to the lobby. By the time Marcie looked again toward Paul, he was gazing in the direction of the building. A few minutes later they watched one of the managers from the front desk, a plump young man called Gómez with catlike whiskers, follow the maid up the stairs to the room. She stepped aside and waited several feet away from the door as he took her key and let himself in. A moment later he bolted out of the room, leaving the door open, and marched down the stairs, trailed by the maid, who had paused to pick up the bundle of linen she had dropped.

"Can you see the room he came from?" Paul asked.

"It wasn't ours," she said. "Ours is a couple of doors down."

"Was it the Caminos' room?" he asked.

"Maybe. I thought they had checked out already."

The air had grown chilly, and Paul and Marcie reached for their matching white beach robes. Clumsily gathering their sunglasses, sunscreen, sun hats, they padded their way across the lawn that led from the pool terrace to the rooms. As they walked down the hall, they could see that the door to room 218 was ajar. It was very quiet inside the room. Marcie stopped for a moment and was about to look in when Paul took her by the arm and pulled her back. After that, they stayed inside their own room even while they heard several men arguing loudly in Spanish just outside, followed later by the whine of a siren. Then, after a minute, there was the sound of running foot-steps and a gurney with one wobbly, squeaky wheel screeching down the hall into the room and back out. And then, a few minutes later, it rolled down the hallway for a second trip.

From that afternoon until the Farrars left Playa Cruces the next day, the sun never really came out again in full force. The food wasn't as good, the beer was tepid, the garden wilted under a hazy stillness. It wasn't until they reached the airport and sat on the leather-slung chairs of the lounge that Marcie wanted to know what exactly had happened to the Mexican couple.

"I don't know what happened," Paul said. "It could be anything. Sunburn. Food poisoning. Lovers' quarrel."

"We could have asked at the desk. Why didn't we ask?"

Paul shrugged. "Ugly things happen in hotel rooms all the time."

"Yes, but we knew these people." She insisted, "We knew their names."

"We don't know for sure if that was still their room. They could've checked out. We don't know that, Marcie."

"Their names were Carlos and Rosa," Marcie seemed to force herself to say. "Rosa said they had problems."

"That's all there is. We don't know anything else."

FaMily liNEs

This lunch has been two weeks in the making.

First, a woman called asking to speak to *Mrs.* Brunner, and Jill, my daughter, told her she didn't live here anymore but could be reached in Toulouse, France, where she had gone after our divorce to learn to be a pastry chef. A couple of hours later, a Mr. Grant asked for me and it turned out he was the husband of the woman who had called before. He said he wanted to invite my daughter and me to lunch so the four of us could meet and discuss something important "regarding your daughter's situation" is the way he put it. He suggested neutral territory, The Willows Restaurant.

There's nothing neutral about The Willows on an academic salary. From the moment we get here, I resolve to pay attention to every detail of this lunch, to what we eat, to what we say, and especially to what the Grants say, and what I think about what they say, and how my daughter takes it all in.

I glance around the restaurant, which is starting to fill up with men and women in the rigid blue suits, the unwrinkled shirts, the swirling ties of corporate drudges. Jill complains about the nice pleated skirt I suggested she wear because it is suddenly too tight around her waist. She says she is sulking because she knows she is not going to like the Grants and would rather not have to be part of this particular lunch. She pinches pieces of brown crust from a roll and chews thoughtfully. "Did you tell them how to recognize us?" she asks.

"I think they'll know once they see us."

"We're kind of uncool, right?" She takes a long look around the place. "From St. Paul rather than Minneapolis."

"No, honey, we look fine."

"I'm so nervous I could throw up."

"It's a great place for it."

"You're nervous too," she accuses.

"How can you tell?"

"You're doing your nervous laugh. The one that goes *heh-heh-heh* real quick, like you're clearing your throat."

When the Grants arrive, they look anything but nervous. I stand to shake their hands and try to focus on everything about them at once. They seem to be in their thirties; their skin is rosy and unwrinkled; their hair sits like poofy clouds on top of their heads; their clothes smell of a dizzying mixture of dry-cleaning fluid and cologne.

Martha (she says right away, "Please call me Martha") leans across the table toward Jill and looks into her eyes. "I'm so glad to finally meet you, Jill," she says in a conspiratorial whisper. "I've heard a lot about you, and you sound like a wonderful young woman."

"We're very close to your friend Jane Hunt's parents," Craig is quick to explain, although we both already know this from our earlier phone conversations. "When word got around about your status, we were naturally interested."

"Bad news travels fast," Jill says with a weak smile.

"Oh, but it doesn't have to be all bad." Martha tilts her head plaintively. "You have no idea. We've been trying for years. Every which way there is to try. Nothing's worked."

"The food is just great here," Craig says earnestly. He points out an item in the menu. "Aha, here they are, Shrimp à la Scampi."

I find my place on the page and notice they go for $16.95. I want to be able to tell Jill that this means it's okay to order anything up to that price. But before I can catch her eye, she says she will have the lobster. A deal at $24.95.

"Craig recommends the shrimp, honey."

"But I've never had lobster."

"Yes, you have." I force a smile. "Three years ago, Cape Cod."

Martha interrupts cheerfully, "I will have lobster, too. It makes this more of a celebration."

"So, tell me, Craig," I start in. "What do you do with yourself during the week, when you're not trying to buy a baby?" Even as I say the words, I'm already forcing a small laugh to show I'm making a joke, a little icebreaker, as it were. But the only laughter at the table is my own, the nervous one that Jill identified earlier.

"I'm in direct marketing," he says blandly. "I sell people's names and addresses. Long, long lists of names." He smiles because he thinks I don't understand what he does.

But I do. And I can't help calculating that even if he only earns a penny a name, he makes a lot of money. On the other hand, my wealth is the kind you find at the old DNA bank; a solid ectomorphic physique, a full head of hair, PhD-level brain cells. "I sell history," is the way I put it.

"I sell condos," Martha puts in cheerfully. "Although once Jill's baby is born and becomes our baby," she adds, "I expect to be a full-time mom."

The waiter, who has been eyeing us morosely since Jill and I arrived, comes over to take our order. He brightens a little after appraising the Grants and learning he's sold two lobsters and a bottle of chardonnay. Jill orders Diet Pepsi. It's all she has ever drunk since the age of two. I think she should switch to milk now.

"Now, about the daddy," Craig begins. "What can you tell us about him?"

"He told you," Jill says. "He's a history professor at Trent."

"That's your dad," Craig says patiently. "I meant the father of the baby."

Jill shrugs off the question. "I really don't want this getting around. He doesn't know yet."

"Is he in college?" Martha asks hopefully.

"No." Jill frowns. "He's in the shipping warehouse at Ward's."

"Do you know his parents?" Craig wants to know.

"I don't see how his parents have anything to do with this," Jill says.

"For what it's worth," I intervene, "I've known the boy for a couple of years. He's apparently bright, apparently healthy."

"Apparently Caucasian?" Craig looks at me for an answer, then at Jill.

Martha makes a helpless shrug. "I wish we didn't have to ask this kind of stuff. I told Craig to take it easy."

"What's Caucasian?" Jill finally speaks. "Is it only white? Or anything except black? How about the in-betweens, like Italians and Japanese and Spanish?"

"I know the Spanish are considered Hispanics," Martha says. "That's obvious, I guess."

"Well, they look just like Italians and Greeks. Does that mean Italians and Greeks are Hispanics too?"

"Not exactly," Craig snaps.

"So, if they're not Hispanic, they must be Caucasian. Right?"

"You could say that." Craig looks like he's trying to find another way to phrase his question, but Jill pushes on.

"You'd have to lump the Turks in with the Greeks and the Italians. And then you might as well throw in the Iranians because they look just like them, and so do the Afghanis, who look kind of Jewish, so you might as well bunch them in with Palestinians and Jordanians and Iraqis—in fact, all the Arabs can go into one bag except for the Egyptians, who tend to be mostly brown, which means they belong with the Inuit."

Under the weight of my stare, she pauses to take a long sip from her Diet Pepsi. "You can answer Craig's question, honey," I suggest.

"I was just getting to it," she says seriously. "I'm sure I'll have an apparently white baby, if that's what you're asking."

"It is, dear," Craig says. "Thank you."

Jill nods and finishes the last of her drink with a slurp.

Even as we trade low appreciative murmurs about the food, I'm considering the awkward, vaguely illegal kind of deal we're here to make. In truth, I'm less concerned about the murky ethics of the situation than about the simple practical realities of paying good money for the dubious benefits of raising a kid. I can't imagine what the bureaucracies of the world would do with free commerce in babies. We would need many more lawyers, for one thing. There would have to be minimum quality standards such as height and weight, coloring, life expectancy according to genetic background. The investment in the child would really pay off if it lived long enough to take care of its adoptive parents when they reached old age.

There should be warranties—three years or sixty pounds, whichever comes first. Service contracts might cover the gamut from orthodontics to psychotherapy. Consideration should be given to who actually sells the child: the mother as sole owner, a partnership involving both parents, or a privately held corporation that includes the extended families on both sides. Possibly the natural parents are only the agents of the sale, and the actual funds would be held in trust and paid directly to the kid upon reaching age eighteen, but only if it maintains a B average or better, does not take up any serious vices, and manages to stay out of jail. Otherwise, in compensation for the heartache of raising a difficult, unappreciative child, the whole of the purchase price, held in trust, goes back to the adoptive parents. With interest.

"And how is the lobster, ladies?" Craig asks, looking up from his food for a moment.

"Good." Jill nods vigorously as she tries to dig out a piece from under a mound of goopy white sauce. Not her favorite kind of food, actually.

"The scampi are great." I hold up one pink shrimp impaled on my fork and watch helplessly as Jill turns very pale.

"Oh, damn, I thought I was over this," she says. "I need to be excused." She pushes her chair back and heads toward the back of the restaurant, weaving her way around the tables, only to stop suddenly in the middle of the restaurant.

"Poor child," Martha says. "I'd better go help her find the ladies' room."

"I don't suppose any of this is easy on her," Craig says. He takes a deep breath and leans toward me as if he's about to make an intimate revelation. I try to meet his earnest gaze but become distracted by his silk tie with its design of geometry-gone-haywire falling limply from behind his jacket and hanging just above his plate. I start to warn him, but he suddenly sits back, as if changing his mind about what he was about to say. He then stabs a shrimp with his fork and leans again toward me with new resolve. This time the tie is not so close to the shrimp.

"You know," he says, "this baby thing has become an issue for Martha and me. More for Martha, actually," he corrects himself. "And we're damn near at the end of our ropes first with the fertility tests that proved inconclusive, then artificial insemination that didn't take, and for the last three years adoption applications that get us some address in Honduras, the name of a doctor in Sri Lanka, or a spot at the bottom of a waiting list for some all-American baby guaranteed to look like it came from us. Can you imagine? They match hair, eyes, complexion. Only thing is you pay through the nose and then wait for some girl who looks like your wife to meet a guy who looks like you, then they agree to have sex, and finally, on one precious occasion, lose the condom. The whole thing can take years."

I nod impatiently. "And here's a teenager that ends up pregnant first time around like there's nothing to it. No justice in the world, right?"

"I suppose that's what I'm saying," Craig admits. Then leaning forward, he adds in hushed, conspiratorial tones, "We want to do the right thing by your girl, you can be sure of that." This time the edge of his tie does skim the surface of the oil, but I see it too late to warn him.

"Good," I say with brisk enthusiasm. "She wants a hundred thousand dollars for the kid."

"Get serious," he blurts out while still leaning toward me across the table. Then he forces a deep breath, sits upright, and reaches for the glass of wine before him. I see his hand shake just a little.

"Just kidding," I smile at him. "Really, I just thought I'd say something to get us into the subject at hand."

"I didn't mean to get angry. But there are people out there," he says, vaguely indicating the outer reaches of the restaurant with a tilt of his head. "People who would try to profit from our predicament."

"I personally think Jill should have an abortion and put the whole problem behind her."

Craig purses his lips. "Is that what she wants to do?"

"She keeps putting off going to Planned Parenthood. She has a tendency to procrastinate until she's out of options."

"We will make it worthwhile for her to take the baby to term," Craig emphasizes. "Anything she needs, medical bills, tutoring, special foods, a little money for college."

"Just for argument's sake," I venture in, "how much do you suppose the baby would be worth?"

"You can't put a price on a human life," he shrugs.

"But you can put a price on the humiliation of attending classes big as a blimp, sitting out the prom, the lack of suitable roles in the class play."

Craig looks at me curiously. "Spell out what you're getting at, exactly."

"Exactly? Nothing." I shake my head. "I just wish there were a way to carry on the rest of this really very pleasant lunch."

Craig's face brightens with an idea. "I could have my attorney talk to your attorney."

"To Jill's attorney," I'm quick to correct.

By the time Jill and Martha get back, Craig and I have gone back to our eating of lunch and sipping of wine, but silent now, as if a difficult subject had been finally dealt with, leaving no energy for even the most perfunctory kind of small talk.

"Ah, the ladies are back," Craig says, acting cheerful again. "We were just talking, Jill, about how Martha and I want to be of help to you these next few months."

Jill glances at me suspiciously. "I'm sorry I got sick," she explains. "But for a moment the shrimp on your plates looked like a bunch of little embryos swimming around in olive oil." She looks down at the cold lobster under the thickening white sauce, prods it with her fork and, after a moment, folds her napkin and lays it on the table. "Could we just go home?" she asks me.

"There are still some things we should talk about, aren't there?" Martha wants to know.

"Of course, soon," I promise.

Craig gets up to shake my hand. "We'll stay in touch."

She has been asleep for hours since arriving home, while I sit in front of the TV just down the hall from her bedroom. I keep the volume very low, feeling like a guard posted outside the quarters of someone under threat. It's up to me to keep the Grants at bay, to filter out calls from what's-his-name at Montgomery Ward, to seal our windows and doors against the shrill politics of reproduction.

There are other threats too subtle to have a name or a face. In a Pepto Bismol commercial, the chalky pink syrup dissolves from an imaginary tummy onto my daughter's real womb and her resolute shrimp of a fetus, now also coated in the ubiquitous oozes of the nineties—pink gook as photochemical soup from the holes in the ozone, from the road paved with the living ashes of our dead garbage, and from those new diseases with their sticky little viruses.

Children are not safe anymore, not with those roaming bands of kidnapping pornographers, crack packs, the NRA, all Republicans, Saddam, Joe Camel, Melrose Place. (Oh, such a long list.) Even the neighbor's sweet Labrador, barking in their yard under cover of night, becomes the leader of a pack of hang-tongued fugitives from the pound, loping through the streets out to capture a human baby and hold it for ransom against the killer needles of the Humane Society. In time, they raise the kid as one of their own, at home in the inner city alleys, teaching him to scavenge in dumpsters, to snap at old men, to maul cats. (Things would turn out OK in the end: *Dog Boy Rescued! Rejoins Family, Barks Way Through Harvard, Marries Vet.*)

A leaden silence startles me awake and I realize the TV has been turned off. Across the dark room I can make out Jill, a large soft mound sitting on the couch with her legs folded beneath a shapeless black dress. Through the stillness, disturbed only by her shallow breathing, I sense the tiny, curled worm that glows like an ember, suspended in a deep red universe of buoyant tissue and mysterious fluids, biding its time, waiting to ripen.

"I keep wanting to throw up," she says. "Even when there's nothing inside me, I just keep on heaving."

"Part of you would like to be rid of it," I venture.

"It's the part of me that doesn't want to be rid of it that worries me."

"You can't worry about what you want or don't want. It just happens."

"I don't have to sell them the baby, right?"

"Do you want me to tell you what to do?"

"No, I guess not."

"So, for now, don't do anything."

"I feel like little Miss Rent-a-Womb."

One evening, a few weeks after our lunch with the Grants, Martha calls and says she would like to come over for a short visit. She appears with a heavy canvas shoulder bag from which she pulls out a box of assorted herbal teas, to get Jill off caffeine, she explains.

"I've been getting ready for this for a long time, you know," she assures Jill. "I know everything there is to know about car seat safety, and what plastics are good, and when's the right age to introduce a child to television and ice cream and guns. That's right, guns. Kids'll find them, so it's up to the parents to put guns in the right context. I intend to tell my child— our child, Jill—that guns are not toys, but tools that can help you solve certain kinds of problems. Then if he still wants to carry one, it's a decision he can take responsibility for."

"At what age do you think that should take place, Martha?" I ask, hoping Jill won't laugh.

"Age five is what I've read. By then a kid has some sense of other creatures' mortality, if not yet people's."

"What if he's a girl?" Jill asks blankly.

"Four and a half," Martha states. "Girls mature faster than boys. I've been studying this stuff for years."

Later, sitting around the kitchen table with our mugs of Red Zinger, Martha wants to know everything about our family, how many relatives have worn glasses, had diabetes, suffered heart attacks at an early age. She wants to know about baldness and farsightedness and obesity. Jill brings over a couple of dusty family albums started by her mother.

"This is wonderful," Martha exclaims, opening the first book. We pour over the milky Kodachromes and the yellowed black-and-whites of forgotten children frowning in the sun, old men and women sitting stiffly with looks of longing that reach far beyond the camera, grim bridegrooms rubbed the wrong way by their high starched collars. Martha demands information. She wants names, dates, places, events, which she ceremoniously repeats after me: Uncle Harry at Carlsbad, Jill's fifth birthday, Pauline who looked like Ingrid Bergman, Melissa's graduation from med school, Ambrose and Theodora on their wedding day. I find myself going on with numbing regularity, punctuated only by Martha's occasional interjections of delight or amusement.

"You know," she says finally, as she pushes the last of the photo albums away and reaches into her canvas bag, "I've brought some pictures of my own." She pulls out a black three-ring notebook. "Craig doesn't understand," she explains. "This is my baby book." She starts to hand it to Jill, then pulls it back until we promise not to laugh.

The book is filled with hundreds of pictures of babies, black and white and brown and yellow babies, naked baby bottoms and wriggly baby toes, nursing babies and tumbling babies and crawling babies, all clipped from magazine ads and labels for baby food and diapers and lotions.

"I've been collecting them for years," she smiles. "Ever since it was clear Craig and I wouldn't be able to make a baby of our own."

During the next few months, life for Jill is held at bay. College applications, new clothes for her senior year, the stock boy at Ward's, all are on hold. Mostly, she spends her time complaining of the heat and the humidity and the boredom. The high point of the month is her visit to the clinic. Here her progress meets with enthusiasm, her struggles against excessive weight gain are rewarded, the development of the fetus is applauded. Here we're told Jill will have a boy, something that makes Craig happy. Occasionally, I catch myself thinking about a grandson out there who may never know me. But I dismiss the sharp moment of sadness that comes unexpectedly; I only play a small supporting role in this thing.

One day, a Sunday, as I sit with the paper and the last of the lukewarm coffee, Jill wants to know if she will look normal after she's delivered.

"Sure you will."

"What makes you so sure?"

"Your mom went back to her usual weight."

"But there are these changes, right? Like the breasts hang different, and the stretch marks."

"You won't have any marks, honey." I try to sound convincing. "I used to rub lotion on your mother so she wouldn't get marks. That was my first contact with you." The memory is vivid, of my hands gliding along the creamy surface of my wife's young skin, of feeling the soft curve of a back, the small bump of a foot, the occasional traveling protuberances that swelled and recoiled along the drum-tight belly.

"Would you put some lotion on me, Dad?"

"Sure," I say as I go back to my reading.

"I mean now."

I put the paper away and look up at her. She is wearing the wrinkled pink flannel gown with the small white flowers. Her preference for staying around the house has made maternity clothes unnecessary. When she goes out, she wears one of my shirts and a pair of jeans with an expanding waist. During the past month she has been cutting away at her hair until it's now down to a short blunt length. Her face is coated with a pale, chalky makeup punctuated by bright red lipstick and blue eye shadow. "I don't want anybody to recognize me," she explained one time when I commented on her appearence.

"Come on, Dad," she pleads. "You don't want to be known as a procrastinator, right?" She hands me a bottle of lotion and stretches out on the couch. "First warm the lotion in your hands," she says, unbuttoning the middle of her gown.

"I've done this before, remember?" Still, I'm not prepared for the sight of the big, hard globe that rises from just below her enlarged breasts, peaks at the navel, and abruptly slopes down to her groin. The paleness of her skin, a stark eggshell-white marked by an occasional pink blush and a filigree of faint blue veins, is a foreign, forbidden sight.

I sit on the edge of the couch, holding a dollop of lotion in my hand. Jill has closed her eyes, and her breathing, usually shallow under the new weight on her chest, relaxes as she lies on her side. I exhale warm air on the lotion, then cup it with my left hand before spreading it on her belly with a smooth circular motion, thinning it out, rubbing it gently into her skin. My hand glides along effortlessly, the fingers skating on her skin, spinning whorls that seem to echo the patterns on my own fingertips.

At the first sensation of movement, I stop spreading the lotion and wait, keeping very still, hardly daring to breathe. The small lump that presses against the palm of my hand stirs once more. I imagine a tiny foot, or a hand with its five nubby fingers clenched into fighting readiness, or possibly the head butting impatiently at the walls of its cell. Speculating that some level of communication might be already possible, I draw small spirals on the milky film, circling with my index finger the restless bump that expands and contracts under the skin, thinking the slow punches and kicks are emphatic answers to the secret, wordless code of my touch. Mysteries wait to be revealed: is there thought before breath, lust before sight, pain before hunger?

The insistent beeping of the phone jars me from my thoughts. "It's Martha Grant." I hand Jill the phone and retreat to the Sunday paper and the last of the cold coffee on the kitchen table. From here, I can see Jill sitting up now on the couch, the large globe of her belly still visible between the edges of the unbuttoned robe. She speaks too softly for me to hear, but I see her nod emphatically, then take the phone and place it on her navel, hold it motionless, then very slowly move it a couple of inches at a time across the stretched skin, suddenly pausing and holding still for a moment, then moving it on a couple of inches until it has travelled the whole expanse of her belly.

"She wanted to hear the baby," Jill says later. "I told her the clinic let me hear the heartbeat, and she wanted to hear it too; I don't think she heard anything over the phone. She said she did."

A few days before Jill is due, Martha calls to say she knows it's going to happen any moment because she herself has been feeling something like contractions and, while there is no explanation for her having those sensations, she wants to know if Jill is feeling anything yet. "It's the weirdest thing," she says. "But I'm not making them up; it feels like a belt is being tightened around my insides. Even if it is all in my mind, it's still kind of remarkable, don't you think? I just know I'm meant to have this baby."

"She's been really weird," Jills tells me later. "She started getting morning sickness the day we met for lunch, and it stopped when mine stopped. She says she has gained weight, and her breasts are all swollen, and now she's getting ready to deliver. I might as well stay home and let her do the trick."

One evening, several days after Jill was supposed to start labor, Craig Grant calls because Martha is adamant that Jill will be feeling things any moment. Martha unfortunately can't come to the phone because while sitting on the couch watching TV, a sudden, viselike pain seized her lower back and gripped her insides.

I place my hand over the mouthpiece. "Craig says Martha wants to know what you're feeling exactly."

Jill closes her eyes, as if trying to become more attuned to the sensations inside her. "Nothing," she says, placing both hands on her belly. "Tell them nothing's happening."

"She's sure you must be feeling something."

"I'm always feeling things," she snaps. "I'm just not feeling contractions."

"Well, Craig claims that Martha is," I insist. "They want to know what's holding you up."

"Tell them if they don't fucking quit bugging me, I'll keep

the baby myself." She slams shut the door to her bedroom.

"Hello, Craig," I speak reassuringly. "Jill wants you both to know she is paying close attention to her body and all, but that she's not feeling a thing yet. She did say it might be better if you didn't call her; she's feeling a little pressured. You know what they say about a watched pot never boiling."

In the course of the next two days, Jill concentrates on sending her body messages that it's time for something to happen. She takes long walks, striding out into the street with even, ducklike steps; she eats enchiladas for the stimulating properties of the hot peppers and the cilantro; she consults the *I Ching,* which corroborates the obvious (Pi: Holding Together).

Martha Grant is having pains exactly twenty minutes apart. Something seems to be working, I catch myself joking. "I swear," she yells at me over the phone. "Something has to happen, and soon, because this stuff is not in my head. This is real suffering, you know."

"Martha," I try to calm her. "Maybe you should see a doctor. I don't know, a psychiatrist with gynecological experience."

I don't tell Jill about the call but she guesses anyway that there is turmoil in the Grant household. "Do you think Martha is too crazy to get my baby?" Jill asks cautiously.

"She has been under strain."

"She's not the one who's becoming a mom."

"Sure, she is."

"That's up to me still."

After another day passes, Jill is not in labor; Martha, however, does check into the hospital because nobody can figure out what is happening to her. Craig calls to say they have ruled out pregnancy, of course, but that they're checking into her gallbladder, liver, pancreas, colon, kidneys, appendix. It could be anything. "Please don't tell Jill I called," he asks me. "But let me know what we can do to help."

One evening, Jill has Craig get her front row tickets to hear a band she likes. She stands close to the speakers and lets the deep bass rumblings bounce on her body, sending tremors up and down her belly. For a moment, she believes that she and the musicians are in effect working together to break through the still amniotic pool with the clash of cymbals and hollow boom of the tom-toms, searing guitar riffs, and pervasive thud of two-chord bass. In the end, she comes out with only a ringing in her ears.

The next afternoon, I drive her to the hospital for one last examination to determine if they should induce labor. The nurses are brisk and unsympathetic. They tell her, "It's time, sweetie." They have seen all this before, and they hint darkly of drugs and procedures that will take over when the natural processes are stymied. Medical science, they assure us, can deal with this situation.

"I don't know why they call it a situation. Don't babies come out when they're ready?" she pleads while we wait for the elevator. When the doors finally open, Jill marches right in. I follow her, even though I realize it's going up instead of down.

"Shoot," Jill says. "It's going up. Maybe I should just stay in this elevator and go up and down and up and down until I start."

The elevator is full of green-and-white medical people. In the middle of this very hot July day, they have a wan, punchy look, as if only in the privacy of the elevator do they allow themselves to visibly fold. When the door opens on the sixth floor, about four stories above the maternity section, we are swept out by some people who scramble from the rear of the box to exit.

"We'll get it on the way back." I stab the down button.

"I have to pee, again," Jill says, heading from the elevator vestibule down a shiny green hallway. She hurries to catch up with a tiny, white-haired woman taking small steps with an aluminum walker. The woman nods and points Jill to the end of the hall.

When the elevator comes again, Jill is not back, so I wave at the group of medical types to go on without me. I venture a few steps down the hallway and notice a sign that welcomes us to the Women's Geriatric Unit. That explains the silence of the place. Missing are the mad dashes of medical people rushing down hallways with carts of steel and black rubber hardware. I sense that nothing is rushed here, that when a tired old heart stops beating or a leathery set of lungs pauses in midbreath, nobody panics much.

Thinking I'll find the restrooms down the hall, I go until I face a set of double doors to the Recreation Lounge. The room that opens up before me is large, with tall vertical windows that allow the sun to come streaming into an indoor garden of blooming planters and potted palms and ficuses and hanging baskets of flowers.

Suddenly, I become aware of soft, guttural voices coming from a corner of the room. A group of old women buzzes with excitement, and a few stragglers make their way to join them.

At the center of the tight circle is Jill, chatting away with a frail woman with wispy white hair and soft, cloudy eyes. The woman reaches out tentatively, and Jill takes the palm of her hand and lays it on the side of her belly. The old woman smiles excitedly, nodding to the others near her.

As word spreads around the geriatric floor, a line of women forms, their thin, angular bodies dressed in white hospital gowns, flannel robes, and faded cotton dresses. Each woman comes to Jill and touches her; from some, it's a caress, while others poke with their fingers or feel her breasts. She puts her arms around the shoulders of two women, tilting her head to listen to one, then the other. A blind woman reaches up to Jill's face with her fingertips. Tears well in Jill's eyes.

The women's voices mingle into a formless murmur that rises from their midst and courses toward the center of the group like the rush of flowing water. The hum seems to stir a deep, silent pool within Jill that pushes its way down, breaking like a thunderclap through the thin membrane. It bursts in a warm pink flood that at first comes in a gush and then thins out to a rivulet that streams down her legs, turning her jeans a deep blue. It puddles around her feet on the shiny linoleum floor.

As soon as I realize what is happening, I weave my way through the crowd of women. One of them rolls a wheelchair toward me. I position it next to Jill, and a woman with wildly flowing white hair helps her sit on it.

"Wait, Daddy," Jill says anxiously.

"We've got to move, honey."

"No!" she shouts, making me stop the chair by a set of phones. "I want to tell Martha it's time. Make her understand that she's not buying the baby. That she'd better get here and do some pushing."

The liOn, the eAgle, the woLf

At night, something comes between Claire and me. It's not Claire and it's not me. It is a third thing. It's not a thing you can see. I have never seen it. I have felt it. It always feels different. Claire has dreamt it. The dream of this thing is Claire's only awareness of it. She thinks that's all it is. This rift. A dream.

We've been married six years. In that time, some habits have become important to us. In summer we rise early and have coffee together. We share a cantaloupe and sit on the sunporch, enjoying the cool of the morning, the sunlight that streams in through the tender new leaves of the poplar. The melon is almost too ripe, a musky fragrance fills the still air as Claire splits it in half.

"This is it," I declare as I spoon out a morsel of its coral flesh. "The melon's apogee."

"Today was definitely its day." She agrees with me on many such things. "The peak of its melonness."

We know a thing or two, Claire and I, about melons and other matters. When we go to Lunds, people watch us go through the ritual of searching for the right melon. Claire searches through the bin and lifts the most promising one in her small hands. She feels its heft, turns it every which way, caresses its texture, her fingers running lightly along the rind, stopping at a slight ridge here, an unexpected bump there, a telltale softening at the poles. Then she'll hand it to me to smell.

It can take a few minutes to find a good melon, and all the time someone has been watching, following our selection process. People often ask us just what it is we look for to find the one perfect cantaloupe in the store. You read the melon, Claire says. The remnant of a stem at its navel means it was picked too soon. A premature melon is not good. There are other things. There is intuition.

They say thank you very much and push on before we can tell them everything. As they go, they'll reach into the melon bin and grab the one closest at hand. That's one way to buy melons. But not the best. Nobody is lucky every time.

By eight-thirty we've had our breakfast—fruit, coffee from Chiapas that I grind myself in a dandy little mill made by the famous German armaments manufacturer, and sometimes cinnamon toast. We've listened to some Albinoni and skimmed the *Trib*. We've put on our blue suits with the white shirts and a silk flourish of a tie. We look very much alike, Claire and I, dark blue and radiant on our way to work. She takes the Honda and I the Volvo. In the matter of automobiles, as in melons, we choose carefully.

"Wait." She stops me as I'm backing down the driveway. "I had a strange dream last night."

I know I'm going to be late. "What was it?"

"All I remember is being lost in a ghettoish sort of place. And being watched by people hidden behind broken windows, in doorways, inside parked cars with tinted glass."

"Interesting."

"It was frightening, actually."

Well, there's not much I can say in response to a dream except that it is interesting, sometimes. "Anything else happen?"

"No."

"See you tonight." Our lips brush in a quick kiss. I back into the street and head west. Claire follows and then turns east.

That evening we meet after work and have dinner at Café Brenda, a good, comfortable place. The trout for me, vegetarian croquettes for Claire. The service is good. The wine is good. The dessert we share is good. But we don't say much. A day's labor leaves us both edgy, our voices hoarse from endless meetings.

After dinner, Claire takes the Volvo and I the Honda, and we race each other home. That part is fun. I go about forty-five, run every stop sign and one red light. I win. Claire takes a shortcut but still comes in about a minute later. Winner gets to take the Volvo to work the next day.

It feels good to throw off my clothes and lie on the bed letting the breeze from the fan travel up and down my body. Claire sits on a chair. She shakes her hair loose and begins to brush it. I fall asleep long before she's through brushing. We're always closer in the mornings.

Around two, I wake up thinking it's light out already. Nights have become turbulent times for me. I get up two or three times to piss, sit up and read, check the clock, turn the light back off. Claire beside me sleeps like a stone. Her face in repose seems devoid of life and wit.

I kiss her dry, warm forehead and marvel at the unfamiliar touch of her skin. Do we become someone else when we sleep? Wide awake now, I lie on my back and stare up at the black starless void of the ceiling. I take a deep breath and marvel at how cold and thin the air feels. Beyond the ceiling, in all the vast region that stretches above my house, I am the only living, thinking, breathing thing. I float. Ah, how I float! Effortlessly rising from the bed, I'm lifted skyward, soaring up into the night, hurling into the chill heart of the universe, through the silent beats and rhythms of a language so abstract it is beyond song and meaning. Still, I know that somehow, to a rare few, this vacuum would make sense, its silence pregnant with revelation, every turn and every gust of dry wind a mathematical certainty. Ah, order! I know that even this arbitrary plunge from the comfort of bed and wife is steered by a sense of balance and purpose. There is nothing random about it—not in the sway and pitch of my body as it hurls into space, not in the unseen symmetry of the void or in the heady ether that I breathe. But even as I leap and soar and fall through space, I feel I must eventually regain control. Surely an adjustment here and there to the tilt of my body, a correction to the angle of my arms will allow me to manipulate the fates. Although I must admit that all the time a voice in my head says no, all is flight, there is no place to fall, that I must truly let go. Unfortunately, I'm just not the sort of person who pays attention to little voices.

I wake up a few minutes before the alarm goes off at six. Then, lying heavily on the rumpled bed, I open my eyes to the sight of so many good, familiar things. Ah, the lamp, the door, the window, the chair, the clock, the book, the plant, the shoe, the woman. I cry out with joy.

"What is the matter?" Claire wakes up suddenly.

"Nothing, I'm fine." After a moment, I add, "Relieved, actually. For a while I couldn't tell where I was."

"Yes," she agrees sleepily. "Like waking up in a Holiday Inn room that is just like every other hotel room, and yet not knowing where anything is."

It wasn't like that at all.

"When we first moved into this house," she continues, "I

expected the bathroom to be on the right side, like in our first apartment."

"Actually," I begin with something of an effort, "it was different from waking up in a hotel room. I was lost."

Claire is quiet, feeling, I'm sure, somewhat rebuffed. Yet I needed to set the record straight. Waking up in a hotel is not in the same league as returning from a trip to the center of the universe.

"Was it a dream?" She tries earnestly to understand.

"No. Not a dream."

"I had a dream," she says.

I feign interest. "What about?"

"I was watching a bird. It was flying around in circles, wide soaring turns, not going anywhere, just flying."

"What else?"

"Nothing else."

This morning we wear gray. Our shirts are pale blue, our ties liquid swirls of azure and silver. We eat kiwis, spooning the tender green pulp right out of the skins, we drink Earl Grey; we nibble on toast. Today we both want to be quick and lean and hungry out there. It's a Big Day for both of us. I don't particularly like Big Days. The effort of dealing with a new face, of trying to accomplish Something Meaningful, of arguing one's case before a group are all disturbing breaks from the comfortable monotony of my average business day. Claire loves a Big Day now and then. Her week is not complete without at least one confrontation, a test of wills and intellect that fires her up like a handful of diet pills. But then she is climbing up the ladder, whereas I'm already pretty well ensconced on one of the upper rungs.

After work we meet at the health club. We are silent, determined. We move among the high-tech riddles of weights, sprockets, cams, from one contrivance to the next, pushing ourselves at every turn, facing up to our frailties, from thigh flab and stomach bulge, to humiliating muscle failure after a mere dozen repetitions. I feel drained. Claire looks radiant. A surge of blood floods every vein and capillary and brings a glow to her skin. I like the way she looks afterward, clean wet hair hanging limply down the sides of her face, cosmetics washed off so her eyes look out clearly, her lips plain, like a child's. Lips that cannot lie. Eyes as clear as hers can only look upon what is good.

Sometimes, when Claire thinks I'm asleep, she leans over and looks at me. I wonder what she thinks, but since she believes I'm asleep, I don't ask. I simply lie on my back and imagine Claire's face imprinted on the back of my eyelids.

The eyes that stare at me on this particular night are not Claire's. She is asleep on her stomach, her face turned away from me, her breathing long and rhythmic. There's no shaking this observer that from the far corner of the bedroom watches every move I make, every tremor, every breath. Nothing is lost on this unseen seer. I blink my eyes. I stretch out my hand. I reach for the clock beside me. Everything is observed, no detail is so insignificant it goes unnoticed. I swallow, blink, reach, wriggle, breathe, shudder, scratch, sleep.

The next morning Claire and I go to the New French Café for breakfast. We each have a croissant that is in itself, even before tasting, impossibly beautiful. Its golden crust is folded over just right; breaking it apart to smear butter and jam on it seems unnecessarily violent.

"I'm just going to admire mine," she says, gazing down at the pastry.

I nod my head and continue devouring my now-demolished croissant. It's very good. I glance up and see that Claire has surrendered and is peeling off each buttery flake one at a time, placing them on her tongue like sacred wafers.

"Eat slowly," she admonishes.

I nod. I lick the jam off my fingers and feel like a barbarian.

"Did you have trouble sleeping last night?" she asks.

"I was awake for quite a while. But not particularly restless. Just awake."

"Do you have a Big Day today?"

"Medium."

"Me, too." Then she adds tentatively, as if searching for the right words, "I dreamt you were awake all night long. That you just sat up on the bed and stared at me, and I couldn't move or talk or ignore the fact that you were watching me with this suspicious look on your face."

I don't know how to tell her that she has her lookers and lookees, her subjects and objects, all mixed up. "Are you sure it was me in the dream?"

"Definitely."

Throughout the day at work, I'm aware of who is looking at whom and who knows he or she is being looked at and who doesn't know they are looking at someone who knows they are being looked at or does not know at first, and then turns, suddenly aware of being looked at. We sit around a long rectangular table for a Big Meeting on budgets. There are a dozen of us in our blue and gray suits with one guy in brown at the end of the table. Most of us take a moment to look at the brown suit. It's not a hostile or censuring stare. Being the only brown suit in the room, it draws attention from the blue and gray suits. I don't suppose Brown Suit knew about this meeting beforehand. I mean, you don't ordinarily appear in a brown suit when everyone else, including the powers-that-be, is in blue. If you do, you're going to get looked at. Until the novelty wears off.

In the afternoon, Claire calls me about weekend plans with friends, about a ping deep inside the Honda, about picking up wine on the way home, about donating money to the Orchestra, and about seeing a therapist.

There. The truth is out. Something has gone awry.

"I didn't realize anything was wrong," I venture.

"I didn't say anything was wrong," she's quick to defend.

"Then why the shrink?"

"I just feel I could be happier. And if I'm not absolutely, perfectly content, considering I've got everything, you know, the good job, the house, money, good friends, clothes, health and all, then something must be missing."

I notice she doesn't mention me, the good husband.

"Your mother says you need a baby."

"Like hell."

Claire decides to have dinner with a friend. Just like that. No other explanation. I bring home Chinese and settle in for *What's Up, Doc?* on TV. Even though it's not all that great a movie, it has one of my favorite sequences. It was done over and over in the silent movie days and still works for me tonight. Two men unload a pane of plate glass from a van and try to cross a busy street. To make things more interesting, there is a car chase going on. The guys with the glass pane seesaw from side to side, trying to stay clear of the caroming cars. It's all hopeless. It's wonderful.

I eat my way through the six little cartons of Combo #7, the Imperial Delight, and at last crack open the fortune cookie. The message it has for me tonight is "The unexamined life is not worth living." Sounds like Confucius, all right.

I expect Claire to be home from her friend's before the movie ends. I've seen my favorite part; it's all downhill from here. At ten till eleven, I call her friend. There's no answer. At eleven I go to bed, I tell myself I'm not worried or angry or hurt, and I fall asleep right away. I wake up after about an hour and feel the other side of the bed for Claire. I don't fnd her. I go back to sleep.

I wake up again some time later. This time I sense I'm not alone in the bed. But I'm unhappy about Claire staying out so late without calling, so I resist the impulse to reach out for her. Instead I lie flat on my back, quite still, just as on other nights when I've found myself thinking too much about unpleasant things. I am not, however, an insomniac. When I'm awake I don't particularly wish I were asleep or feel I should make some effort to pass out. Asleep is fine. Dreaming is fine. REM is fine. And awake is fine.

But tonight with every one of Claire's deep breaths, a pungent smell hangs in the room's still air. It drives me to curl up and cling to the far side of the bed, my face buried in the pillow. There's no escape. Gentle Claire exhales a storm of improbable smells. The cauldrons of hell. The carnage of war. Hitler's flatulence.

Even after I think I've drifted off to sleep, the smells rise like plumes hovering faintly at the edges of my consciousness. Am I being too sensitive?

The next morning I see Claire's side of the bed hasn't been slept on. I pad around the empty house. The Honda is gone from the garage. Coffee hasn't been made. There's no note by the phone. As I look for Claire, I realize I'm also searching for some remnant of the night's terrible smells. I point my nose all around the bedroom, inside the closet, down the stairs, in the guest bathroom with the bad plumbing, the disposal, the fridge, the garbage under the sink, in all the ghettos and mouse corners of our more or less modernized neo-Victorian home.

In my search, I open one of Claire's dresser drawers. I bury my face in a bouquet of lace and silk and inhale her scent. Clearly, what happened in the night was a bad dream. Claire is good and clean and sweet. Her smells are lavender, spice, mint, myrrh, sandalwood, chocolate.

I have coffee alone. I stare at the phone. I leave for work in the Volvo. As I drive past her friend's house, I notice the Honda is nowhere in sight. When I get to the office, I dial Claire's number at work.

"I'm not coming home for a while," she says, jumping right into the sticky part of the conversation. "I'll stay with Ellen for a few days. I've made an appointment with a therapist. I'll stop by the house later for some of my stuff."

"Can we talk about this over lunch?"

I suffer through the rest of the morning—a tightness in my chest, a shortness of breath, a ringing in my ears. Marital strife is tearing hell with my blood pressure.

We meet at Sobas. A tall waiter with an interesting haircut shows us to a small table with three place settings. "Three for lunch today?"

"No, two of us."

The waiter takes our order for blue cornmeal pancakes and Thai fettuccini. Very global. He leaves the third place setting even after I motion for him to remove it. I can sense the third blind presence rising between Claire and me, making our conversation awkward and self-conscious.

She begins, "About last night . . ."

"No explanations necessary," I say magnanimously. "I did worry about you, but now that I see you're all right, well, then everything is fine."

"It got late. I fell asleep on Ellen's couch."

"I understand."

"I had an awful dream," she continues hesitantly. "You found me repulsive. And then I woke up and knew that it wasn't just a dream. That you actually hate me." It's a subject that demands discussion, but we both need to get back to work.

In the evening when I get home, I see Claire has been there and taken most of her clothes. There is a new sense of emptiness everywhere. The bathroom is no longer cluttered with tubes and brushes and plastic bottles, gone are her combs and blow dryer, her diaphragm and contraceptive creams (the significance of this is not lost on me, though I give it no more than a moment's anguished thought), hair curlers, dental floss, toothbrushes, vitamins C, B complex, calcium, and iron. All gone. As are more than half the clothes in the closet we share and several books from the headboard bookcase. I feel numb.

I dial Ellen's number. "This is so stupid," I say when Claire finally gets on the line. "You took enough clothes for a year."

"Are you angry?"

"No. Of course not," I assert.

"I'm doing what I have to do," she says. "You don't have to get angry about it."

"I'm not," I repeat, slamming the phone down.

To tell the truth, I can't remember the last time I felt true, explosive, righteous anger. I never get angry at the office; it would be unprofessional. I don't get angry at slow waiters or dumb drivers, the weather or the time of day. I don't get angry at the Volvo or the Honda or at bicycles with flats or the toaster that burns my toast. I don't even get angry at Saddam or Newt.

But I am terribly angry at Claire. In fact, while I eat my dinner of Fish Florentine by Stouffer's Lean Cuisine and open a bottle of an OK chardonnay, I feel certain that if I live to be 108, I will still be angry at her with the same unflagging outrage I feel tonight.

I revel in my anger. I find myself retreating to an earlier, simpler time when emotions were allowed to spill out unbridled. To a childhood filled with primitive hate and elementary justice. Hating Claire seems ennobling. A clean break from the conventions that inhibit passion and rage and ecstasy. I feel I've been stuck in a world of emotional cripples. A place where lust, greed, vanity, and ambition are all right. But where love, hate, anger, curiosity, awe, and joy are not.

By ten, I've drunk over half the bottle of wine. I force the cork back in and run out of the house to the Volvo. I back up with a squeal onto the street, gun the engine down the familiar neighborhood streets to the house where my wife is sleeping. There are no lights in the windows, not a sound in the street. From the sidewalk, I call out, "Claire! I know you're in there. Come out and fight like a woman."

There's no response. I tip the bottle to my mouth and drink the wine in big gulps. "Claire! You coward, you deserter, you traitor."

A couple of windows from houses across the street light up. I step up onto the porch and try the door. It's locked. I ring the bell, wait for a moment, and then knock loudly with the flat of my hand.

"Come on out, Claire, or I swear I'm coming in for you."

I feel wonderful. Threats and accusations emerge from my chest with all the power and drama of grand opera. As my shouts echo through the sleeping neighborhood, I have visions in stark primary hues, of me kicking down the door, marching into the house, and confronting Claire. With both hands I clasp the door handle and strain to shake it open.

I feel suddenly faint as wave upon wave of anger and nausea wash over me, dragging out an eerie flotsam of ancient, ancestral memories. I am early man. I am the ocean's first burst of life. I am lion. I am eagle. I am wolf. I pace the whole length of the porch, stopping every time I pass the door to give it a kick or pound it with my fist.

I stop and find myself standing silently in front of the door. I take a couple of steps back. Calmly I unzip my fly, take out my penis, and unleash a long, gleaming stream of urine at the closed door. The piss arches smoothly from my center, from the very depths of my being, across the width of the porch, landing smack in the middle of the door and trickling down in yellow rivulets. Swinging from side to side, I draw circles and figure eights and the letter G along the floors and walls.

My bladder empty at last, I zip up and retreat to the sidewalk in front of the house. Lights go on in the upper story, then downstairs. Finally the door opens and Claire stands in the frame, the light behind her outlining her like a halo. She's a wondrous vision in a flowing nightgown that shimmers with lace and silk, her lustrous brown hair loose to her shoulders, her small feet bare. She squints, trying to make me out as I scurry in the dark from tree to bush to fence, as stealthy as a cat.

"Please go home," she calls out softly. "We can talk about all this tomorrow."

"First thing in the morning!" I say from behind a tree.

"Yes. But go home now. One of the neighbors saw you and is calling the police."

She stands before the lighted entrance for a moment, as if to make sure I'm really going, then steps back inside the house, shutting the door firmly. I hear the bolt turn and lock with a forbidding click. But even after the lights in the house have gone off, the image of her, glowing and pure, remains.

I stay behind the tree until morning. Some time in the course of the night, my anger finally leaves me. It seeps through my pores like some poison that has been sweated out. I feel elated, purged, cleansed. I nearly drown in sweet waves of tenderness.

LandScaPe of zEros

They couldn't help feeling a little nostalgic. Just last year Carl Skildum and his wife, the beautiful Lavonne, could still look out the east window of their farmhouse kitchen and see nothing for miles but green acres of nascent soybeans. They belonged to Burley Burleson's farm across the road.

On the other hand, when the Burlesons looked out of their west kitchen window, they were faced with the rolling black wasteland that had become Carl and Lavonne's place in the eight years since they inherited the farm from Lavonne's dad.

Not that Carl and Lavonne ever showed any talent for farming. Carl had been raised in the city and had made a good living selling advertising specialties—matchbooks, ballpoint pens, calendars, calculators, all imprinted with a logo and one-line sales message. Mowing a lawn was as close as he ever got to the sweet smell of ripe soil. Lavonne, as her father would have said, was born lazy. It came with being beautiful, everyone figured, but you can't be lazy and a farmer, too.

Still, as soon as they were given the deed to the farm, Carl and Lavonne jumped at the the opportunity to sell their house in St. Paul and move to the country, just twenty miles or so beyond the northernmost suburb.

"We'll live simply and frugally," Carl envisioned.

"We'll raise chickens and eat the eggs," Lavonne said.

"I'll still take care of my accounts, but we'll live rent-free."

"I'll bake bread. Put in a garden. Can fruit."

"I'll put an office in the basement and a warehouse in the barn."

"I'll get back into sewing."

"We'll live simply."

"And frugally."

That was before Carl and Lavonne got lucky. And before the day last year when the Burlesons finally surrendered to the same brand of good fortune that struck Carl and Lavonne.

It started out to be an ordinary spring morning for the two families.

"Rains came just in time this year," Carl said, gazing across the road. "Burley's got a nice crop going."

"It smells so fresh in the spring." Lavonne opened the window and took a deep breath as a crisp, clean breeze blew into the kitchen. "It's different in the summer. Then our place is all we smell."

"It's not so bad," Carl shrugged. "We could be raising pigs. Pigs smell worse than old tires."

"Chickens too, once you get up close."

"And cow manure."

"Sure, tires are not so bad, except in the summer when it gets hot and I have dreams about all that rubber melting and flowing and seeping into the house."

"Don't kick the tires, honey."

"I'm not. Believe me, I'm not."

"They're the best thing that ever happened to us."

"Of course they are. I just wish I could forget them for a while."

"Count your blessings. You don't have to look at them outside your kitchen window like the Burlesons."

"Do you suppose they hate us?" Lavonne asked after a moment. "Their boys look at me funny."

"You can tell what people think about you by the way their kids and their dogs act toward you."

They sipped their coffee thoughtfully for a moment, then the quiet was broken by the insistent ringing of the phone.

"Are we open for business yet?" Lavonne asked.

"Let it go, honey," Carl said. "They'll call back."

"Right. Let them call after nine. If we answer the phone now, they'll expect us to be available at any odd hour, night or day."

"Enough is enough."

"I can just hear the trucks pulling in, bringing more tires in the middle of the night. On Sundays. At the crack of dawn."

"We've got to control the flow."

"Right."

"The problem with the Burlesons is that they feel superior to us," Lavonne reflected. "I know they do."

"Their children sure love to come and play among the tires."

"Their dog, too."

"I heard Burley tell the kids it was dangerous for them out here."

"It's just a tire dump. They enjoy playing king of the mountain among the tires. Makes me feel that someday we should have kids of our own."

"Not too many families have hundred-foot mountains for their kids to climb around in."

"It would be educational."

"There's the phone again, honey."

"We open at nine. It's not nine yet."

Lavonne handed him a mug with fresh coffee and cradled the other one between her hands, breathing in the sweet fragrance of the sixteen dollar-a-pound Blue Mountain. "I bet we're the only people north of 694 drinking Jamaican coffee this morning." She pulled at the collar of her silk robe and held it closer to her cheek.

Lavonne occasionally needed to remind herself that as long as she didn't take their luck for granted, it would stay with them. Now, when she dared look outside the window toward the back of her house, she knew their good luck was temporary, with a certain, though as yet unspecified, end date. The black rolling acres of tired rubber would someday reach a point of overflowing, a time when the black mounds would begin to slide, and tires would roll off their land and onto the road. She was reluctant to answer the phone because she realized that while another shipment carried with it thousands of dollars in cash, it also brought their good fortune closer to an end.

Carl never worried about their luck running out, though he was aware that the land would only hold so many tires, that sometime after the middle of next year, there wouldn't be a way to squeeze in another Super Ply All Weather Steel Belted Radial. But he was a man of faith. He knew he had nothing to do with the first shipment of waste tires six and a half years ago, when a friend who worked in a salvage yard had put him in touch with New Age Waste Management at the time they were searching for a dump site. That was the work of the fates, and the fates, he was convinced, would work for him again.

Lavonne was worried about the future because she could not see her way clear beyond next week. Carl, on the other hand, had caught a glimpse of the future. "What do you do with four hundred thousand old tires?" he would ask himself.

The answer came to him one day between the pages of an old issue of *Science Illustrated.* It was an article about a technology developed in Akron, Ohio, that could shred old tires and then twist the strands of rubber into compact logs. Carl realized the tires could keep right on rolling in, and then, when the farm was full to bursting, he would bring heat and light to the Amazon, to the Gobi, to the Kalahari. Desert peoples and jungle peoples and arctic peoples would all be able to cook and take hot showers and snuggle on winter nights thanks to Carl. In his quieter moments, when Lavonne was roaring to the mall in her Corvette, he would settle back and lift the blinds of his bedroom window and gaze with awe at the thousands of tires piled out back. It warmed his heart to help people by taking on some of their waste. It was a Christian thing, in fact, if you stopped to think that modern man's biggest sin was wastefulness and that accumulation of waste was a just price for the endless, ceaseless throwing away of things. Blessed be the garbagemen, he silently congratulated himself, for they will store the sins of the world.

At 9:02 the phone rang again.

"They've got six tons," Lavonne said, putting her hand over the phone.

"Bring on the money." Carl smiled and toasted her with his mug.

"The dispatcher says the driver is out front, but there's some guy in the middle of the road, blocking the way into our drive."

Carl peered out the window through a narrow part in the curtains. "It's Burley Burleson."

"You'd better go see what he's up to," Lavonne said.

Outside, a semi with an open black trailer idled with a deep throaty rumble, its stack sending up plumes of oily exhaust. In the cab, the blonde driver was expressionless behind mirror sunglasses. He tapped his fingers on the wheel, occasionally stepping on the gas pedal and making the engine roar purposefully. When Carl bounded out of his house, the guy greeted him with two blasts of his horn.

Lined up across the road, the Burleson family stood shoulder to shoulder facing the truck's chrome grille. Burley was in the middle with his wife Marcella on his right and Scamper on his left and the two boys, Harold and Spencer, on either side. Marcella looked embarrassed to be part of the whole thing. Scamper sat on the warm pavement and scratched. The two boys looked determined; Harold, the ten-year-old, held a baseball bat; Spencer carried a plastic AK-47.

"Good morning, neighbor," Carl called from his front yard. "Anything I can do to help?"

Without taking his eyes off the truck driver, Burleson called out, "You can help. But you're not likely to."

"I don't know," Carl spoke softly, crossing the yard to the edge of the blacktop. "I'd like to do the neighborly thing."

"Well, you can send this guy off without dumping any more of his stink in our neighborhood."

"I couldn't do that, Burley," Carl raised his hands. "We've got a business deal, this driver and I. He brings old tires and I find a place for them in my farm."

"*Dump* is a better word."

"Dump, farm, whatever. It's my business. I've got a license to store waste tires on my property."

"Licenses can be revoked."

"Not without cause, damn it, Burley."

"You've filled over ten acres with old tires. Look around you, man. There's no room for more."

Carl stood erect, ready to hold his ground. He stared into Burleson's pale blue eyes. He shifted his glance to Marcella, her plump good-natured looks hardly up to the confrontation she had chosen to share with her husband. She looked sad, Carl thought. And determined. He wondered if Lavonne would be as supportive. But then, his situation was purely business. The Burlesons, on the other hand, were protecting their world.

"Look behind you, man." Burley grabbed his kid's baseball bat and used it as a pointer. "This was a beautiful place when Lavonne's dad had it."

"It was about to be taken over by the bank." Carl could feel the pale blue eyes of the four Burlesons bear down on him. He turned around for a moment and faced a landscape that had once been perfectly ordinary. The bright yellow farmhouse with the white wood trim was neat and carefully painted. But instead of the tender green fields of the new crop beyond the back porch and the vegetable patch and the red barn, a desert of black tires swept away from the road and sloped to a peak in the middle of the clearing. From a distance, the hill was a rugged, buoyant thing, sculpted into random indentations by the snowplow Carl used to contain the acres of old rubber that kept sliding slowly, inexorably, barely inches at a time, into the rest of the property and beyond. On coming closer, the black mounds became a sea of holes, a desert of donuts, a landscape of zeros.

"Can't we talk this over, Burley?" he asked.

"We'll talk as long as you like. But I'm not moving until this truck backs off."

"I'm not asking you to move. Just to reason with me."

"You can't talk around the fact that you've built a garbage dump across the road from us."

"It's not garbage, Burley. Just a bunch of old tires that may someday be brought back into the service of humanity. I'm talking recycling, Burley. The industry of the millennium."

"And cash for lazy folks willing to turn their home into a dump."

"True, Burley. But in the spirit of service."

"Bushwah!" he barked back. "Pardon my French."

"We're not going to get anywhere if you insist on a hostile attitude." Carl glanced up at the cab of the semi, and through the windshield he could see the young driver lean back against the door, his feet stuck out the opposite window. He seemed to be napping.

Carl looked toward his house and the wasteland beyond and felt isolated and shamed by the Burlesons straddling the whole width of the road, the quiet Mrs. Burleson with head erect, eyes narrowed to a defiant squint, the Burleson kids with their chests puffed out, trusting martyrs in this, their parents' own *jihad,* the whole family ready to be flattened by the truck.

He had moved to the middle of the road and was now facing Burleson with the semi at his back. He heard the door slam and the driver stepped to his side. He was about twenty-five. He wore a faded Metallica T-shirt and jeans rolled at the ankle just above his steel-tipped safety boots.

"You guys intend to work this out anytime soon?" he asked. "I need to piss."

"Go into my house," Burley offered. "The bathroom is right off the hall from the front door. Lavonne will give you a cup of coffee."

"If you go to his house, I'll assume you've taken sides," Burleson pointed out. "Right now, I consider you neutral."

The kid pulled out a comb from his back pocket and ran it through his hair. The possibility of having to make decisions had not occurred to him. With a long sigh, he replaced his comb in his pocket. He glanced at the tires piled on the truck trailer and said, "I guess I'll take you up on the cup of coffee, sir." He added apologetically to Burleson, "I'm going to have a problem with my dispatcher if I don't deliver my load."

"I'll go back to the house with you," Carl offered. "If these nuts choose to hang around on the road, that's their business."

"Well, they've got principles, sir."

"They've got principles? And what do I have? Un-principles?" They paused in front of the house. "It'd be nice to know whose side you're on."

"I'm on your side, sir." The young man paused for a moment. "There isn't any other side. I need to dump the tires, you need the tires dumped. I haven't figured out if that makes me a bad guy or not because somebody has to make room for stuff nobody else wants, and if you want to turn your house into a dump, that should be pretty much your business. But your house is across the road from his house. He can see your house, he can smell your house, he can't get away from your house. I don't know. I just don't know. I mean, the world needs a place to deposit its crap. But does he have to sit there and take it? The crap, I mean? I kind of wish you hadn't asked."

"Forget it. Go on in and take your leak."

A little later, Lavonne and Carl and the driver sat around the kitchen table drinking more coffee and eating muffins.

"You're famished," Lavonne said to the driver. "You must've driven all night."

"Pretty near an all-nighter, ma'am."

"Well, have another muffin," she offered. "There's one blueberry left, two poppyseed, and an oat bran that we should save for Carl because it's good for his cholesterol."

"Thank you, ma'am," the driver said, reaching for the oat bran muffin. He pulled it apart to make two halves and then spread a thick layer of butter on each. Through his mirror sunglasses he watched as the butter melted and soaked into the grainy texture of the bread. "I love this stuff," he said. "You know what bread is? Just an excuse to eat melted butter."

Lavonne and Carl watched the driver eat. He clearly worked hard at his tough trucker's look with the sunglasses he never seemed to remove and the greasy jeans and the thin white T-shirt with the pack of Marlboros rolled into the sleeve. He had good manners and he could carry on an intelligent conversation. It occured to Carl that this was the first guest they'd had since moving to the farm. Their friendships in the city had faded after they moved; forty miles for a visit was just too far to drive. The people of the community seemed to conduct their social life in the parish hall after church. And once Carl started dumping tires on his property, the neighbors grew increasingly hostile as the mountain of old rubber rose higher.

"Well, that was nice," the young man sighed and pushed his plate. "But I've got a load to deliver."

"Looks like they're prepared for a long stay." Carl parted the curtain and looked out the window. "Take a look," he said to Lavonne.

The Burlesons had brought out a couch, a coffee table, and a portable TV and set them all on a braided rug in front of the truck. "They're just sitting there," she marveled. "All four of them, and the dog, watching TV."

The driver joined Carl and Lavonne at the window. "It may be time to call my dispatcher."

"Wait a while. They're just trying to appear determined," Carl said.

"I'm supposed to call in if I have any problems."

"It's only ten—too early to say you've got a problem. They'll get bored in a while and you'll be back on schedule."

"I don't know about that, " Lavonne said. "Marcella is passing around a plate of cookies."

"I'd better get on the horn."

"No, don't call yet," Carl pleaded. "Your dispatcher doesn't know there's a principle at stake here. He'll just tell you to back off and take the tires someplace else. Which is OK with me. But backing down is not OK. I don't tell the Burlesons not to raise hogs, and they shouldn't tell me not to plant tires, which smell a lot sweeter than their pigs. It's-a-free-country kind of situation."

The driver nodded. "Hey, I know you've got your rights. I just don't want to get fired because of them. I'm saving up to go back for my MBA."

"Good for you," Lavonne said, giving him a little jab on the arm. "You've got ambitions."

"You think another degree is going to make you successful?" Carl leaned toward the driver. "What a joke. I'm not saying I have the key to getting ahead," he said, sounding as if he did. "But the first requirement to make big money is to stay awake. Most people in this country are asleep at the wheel and don't see the Big Opportunity when it comes out of the confusion and bites them in the ass. Look at me. I've always done well. I sold 1,200,000 matchbooks in '84, '85, and '87. Now I'm making more than then, doing nothing. I'm no genius, but I do have the ability to be in the right place at the right time. You don't learn that in school. An MBA might help you get a job with someone who does have the talent to smell the sweet scent of opportunity; you'll still be driving someone else's truck."

"I'd better call in."

"Sure, kid. The phone is right by the counter," Carl said with an air of resignation. "But if you wait a while, I will give you free of charge one of the greatest business lessons of all time, a real classic. Something you could take and run with."

The driver hesitated. "I don't have a farm I can fill with tires."

"If you did, you'd spend all your energy trying to beat a few cents out of the government with a drought-stricken wheat crop and a mortgage for three times the value of your land. You'd be just as happy as Burleson over there in the middle of the road."

"You don't know that."

"When you run into a challenge, you try the same tired

solutions everyone else uses. You want to be a success in life, so you go to business school. If you can't deliver your load, you go crying to your dispatcher."

"Your neighbor is not my problem." The driver grinned.

"He is in the way of your truck. I'd say he is a challenge we share. Not a problem, a challenge. Notice I don't even think the word *problem*. Problems merely come with solutions. But where there is a challenge, there is an opportunity." Carl always pronounced the word *opportunity* as if it were a religious term.

"So what do you want me to do about your tires?"

"Wait a couple of hours before you turn back and admit we've been beaten by some goofy farmer camped in the middle of the street. Let's try to noodle this through. If we don't come up with something, then it's business as usual for you. And I'm stuck with a bully for a neighbor who knows he can stand in the way of my livelihood any old time he feels like it."

"I like it." The driver grinned. "It's like a war."

"It's the American way." Carl and the driver shook hands vigorously. "Hey, Lavonne, what are you doing out there?"

"Keeping an eye on the Burlesons."

"Come back in here. They've made their big move. Sitting in the middle of the road is as creative as they'll get."

The three of them gathered around the kitchen table. Fresh cups of coffee steamed before them. Lavonne brought out a pad of paper and a marker. On top she wrote *Beat the Burlesons*.

"Yeah, it's like war," the driver repeated.

"We'll let any idea come out and write it out on this sheet of paper," Carl explained. "It's not a matter of arguing if it's good or not. We can do that later. We are setting the proper conditions for a higher wisdom to speak through us, like a gift from the forces of nature."

He took a deep breath and said, "All right, we are ready for inspiration. Remember, the challenge is not just to deliver this load of tires but to make sure the Burlesons don't think they can sit in the way of progress again."

Lavonne raised her hand. "I propose we try to talk with them. We could invite them in for lunch, and then just reason with them. We're all reasonable people."

"Fine. We'll call that approach *Be Nice and Reason with the Enemy.*" Carl printed the words on the yellow pad. "I'll contribute idea number two—*We Go Out and Shoot Their Dog.* Then tell them their firstborn is next if they don't move their butts pronto." Carl and the driver burst out laughing.

Lavonne wrote down idea number two. "It's efficient. Our guy here could deliver the tires and be on his way in a matter of minutes."

"I like dogs and kids. Couldn't we just burn their barn?" the driver put in.

"Now you're thinking," Carl encouraged him. "We'll call that plan *Traditional Rural Intimidation.*"

"I could slip a note to Burley," Lavonne volunteered, "and offer to perform an unatural act with him."

"Are you sure you want me to put that one down?" Carl asked her.

"All ideas count at this stage," she said tersely.

"I'm touched, honey. Indeed I am." Carl wrote *Sex Succeeds* on the pad.

Other ideas followed in quick succession. The driver suggested mediation by a local clergyman. Carl thought that plowing the semi through the Burlesons would do the trick. Lavonne offered to have sex with Mrs. Burleson.

In the end, the simplest idea won the day. Although once things were restored to normal, nobody could remember who had first thought of it. Carl claimed he had.

Ouside, the Burlesons were lined up on their plaid couch, the Mr. and Mrs. at either end, the two kids and the dog in the middle. They were watching Geraldo interview a sex surrogate, a cab driver, a street juggler, and a professor of meta-momentics, all of whom claimed to be angels.

Geraldo was skeptical. He said that being aliens from another planet didn't make them angels. Mrs. Burleson agreed. "They don't look like angels to me," she was saying as the driver emerged from Carl and Lavonne's house and quickly climbed inside the cab.

A moment later the big diesel engine roared back to life amid clouds of blue exhaust. "Could you turn it up a little louder?" Mrs. Burleson asked her husband.

"Sure, honey." He leaned toward the TV set and turned the sound up until Geraldo's sharp excited voice rose above the truck's rumble.

"Well, shoot!" she exclaimed. "We just missed what the professor said about his wings being too heavy to fly. That doesn't make sense. If you're an angel, you're an angel first and a professor second. That sort of proves it to me."

"Proves what, honey?"

"That they're not angels at all."

A moment later Carl and Lavonne emerged from their house and marched toward the Burleson family in the middle of the road.

"Burley," Carl began. "We've been good neighbors for two years. Lavonne and I would like to talk with you before this difference of opinion causes our friendship serious damage."

"You're going to send that smelly truck back to where the hell it came from?" Burleson asked.

"No, not exactly. But I would like to suggest something," Carl insisted calmly.

"Ask him if it can wait until *Geraldo* is over," Mrs. Burleson said, leaning toward her husband.

"Sure, Marcella, of course we can wait," Lavonne put in. "It's not a good time right now," she whispered, pulling at Carl's sleeve.

"Right," Carl nodded. "We'll be here when it's more convenient to talk."

From up in the cab, the driver signaled his impatience with a staccato burst of the throttle. A puff of blue smoke hung above the group before it dispersed under the sunshine.

A few minutes later, Burleson leaned forward from the couch and turned the TV set off. "I'm listening," he called out to Carl.

"It's a simple proposition, a neighborly kind of deal."

"I bet."

"But first let's talk economics," Carl began. "You've got a hundred acres of soybeans out there. You don't eat soybeans. You don't know anyone who eats soybeans. You don't even know what they taste like. In a good year, once you've paid for seed, taxes, equipment, and compensated yourself and your family's labor at more or less minimum wage, you'll net the magnificent sum of $458."

"We're doing just fine, thank you."

"Sure," Carl laughed. "But you would do better selling your land and putting the money into T-bills."

"I'm not selling, if that's what you're getting at."

"I'm not buying," Carl reassured him. "I am willing to let you in on a good thing. I could even let you have this particular load. Back there behind the barn would be a good place."

"Turning good land into a dump is not a good thing."

"It's all temporary," Carl shrugged. "Someday it will be a rubber log factory. We're going to shred all these tires and turn them into logs for fireplaces in Florence, briquettes for barbecues in Brazil, pellets for Peruvian power plants."

"That's crazy," Burleson said sadly. "You can't just send burning tire smoke into the atmosphere."

"The Third World is not picky." Carl paused for a moment. "Think of it as getting paid twice. First for storing the tires. Then for turning them into fuel."

Burleson sat in silence for a moment. "You're not making that much money," he said.

Carl shrugged. "Enough for a sixty-five inch TV with satellite, a Jacuzzi for two in the bathroom, a hair transplant, liposuction, unlimited phone therapy, Jamaican coffee, a nine-foot white leather couch, a Kawasaki Ninja with a hundred-watt, four-speaker sound system, Macadamia nuts by the handful, Jack Daniels by the case, every Nintendo ever made, a '56 Buick and a new Corvette, Buddy Holly's first guitar, Omaha Steaks, filipino mangoes, a Harvard education."

"How about a Whirlpool six-function Tech Way dishwasher?" asked Marcella.

"Yes."

"A twelve-speed Huffy?" asked little Spencer Burleson.

"Yes."

"The five hundred-watt Music Detonator by Sanyo?" asked young Harold.

"Yes. Yes."

"I'm not moving," Burley mumbled after a while. "I said, wasn't moving," he repeated, clearing his throat.

For a long time nobody said a word. The driver sat up in his cab and gunned the engine. Carl and Lavonne looked down at the ground and waited. It was all matter of time, they knew.

Marcella took a deep breath as if steeling herself for one more small battle. "It'll be OK, I'll talk to him," she said, glancing first at Carl, then at her husband. "Honey, we could put some tires behind the barn, like Carl says. We wouldn't even know they were there."

"No," he said. "I'm a farmer."

"Farming's different these days. There's Jerusalem arti-chokes. Ostriches. Ginseng."

"No," he said.

"Well, just consider it," she said.

And the two went on like that for about half an hour. Burley was starting to cave. They could all see it.

The sOund of oNe sHoe

Jason Harter opens the kitchen door and breathes in the air of the first warm morning in May. The smell of new grass and the image of infant crocus bulbs stirring in dark loamy soil rush into his head, nudging his brain cells with the promise of summer. He is ready for work, all tucked and pressed and starched in white and blue; his silk tie pulsates with ripe, quasi-biological nubbles and nodules against a field of electric lazuli. A prudent distance away, he holds a slice of toast dripping honey. An olive-green trenchcoat is slung over his right shoulder. He doesn't think the good weather will last.

"Take an umbrella if you're going out," he says to his wife Stephanie, who stands before a high chair and makes spoon airplanes that carry dollops of mashed banana to little Amanda's eager mouth.

"No way," she says. "An umbrella is precisely the wrong thing to carry on a day like this." It's a moment frozen out of the easy morning routine, with Stephanie's eyes focused on him, a frown on her brow, the spoon poised midflight, the child's eyes clouding with confusion, her head tilted expectantly toward her mother. "You've got to show faith that it's going to be a perfect day."

Stephanie turns toward the child a second before Amanda breaks into cries of frustration at the withheld spoonful. Jason crunches a bite of toast. He cannot shake the look in Stephanie's eyes. The pupils have narrowed to a black pinpoint at the bright light streaming in through the open door. It's a look, he thinks, reserved for the annoying stranger, the casual inopportunist, the guy beside you at the intersection who lights up a cigarette while you are trapped waiting for WALK.

Jason looks back toward Stephanie, but she has resumed feeding the baby. He is suspended in a kitchen-garage limbo. Yes, he was leaving, late for work already. Yes, he was eating breakfast, not ready yet to separate himself from the serenity of his more or less elegant four-bedroom neocolonial in the quiet of Canaan Hills. Left like that to his own devices, he doesn't know whether to go, half-eaten toast in hand, for the drive downtown, or return to the breakfast table for just a few minutes more with his wife and daughter. If he leaves at this moment, he will feel like a stranger the rest of the day, somehow cut off from the affections of his wife, almost as if she did not know him, as if his moods and smells and noises were not part of her loving embrace.

"Stephanie, I hope you two have a wonderful day." He says this not as some casual thought meant to last only until he sees his family again, but as a heartfelt wish, perhaps even a blessing, from someone who believes the world is essentially a dangerous place, in which it pays to be prepared.

"Don't worry about us," Stephanie says.

"I can't help it."

"You're making me nervous. Just go, OK?" Amanda looks up to her mother with an alarmed look. "We'll be fine," Stephanie adds with a soft smile, looking down at the baby, then up at Jason. "I'll lock the doors in the car. Amanda won't take candy from anybody. There's an umbrella in the trunk."

Jason backs his new Saab down the driveway and onto Hyacinth Lane. He feels a vague sadness as he leaves his house behind; though familiar, the needlelike stab at the center of his chest chills him in a fresh, surprising way every morning. There's a shadow of foreboding as he turns right at the intersection with Springer Drive. Then a cold, metallic taste in back of his mouth as he merges into the peristaltic flow of 394's traffic, headed toward downtown with its shimmering glass and steel towers poised to rise and fall like engine pistons.

Jason takes a wary look at the heavy trenchcoat on the passenger seat beside him and looks up at the pristine blue sky for signs of clouds. Ordinarily, he can hardly tell which way the wind blows, much less guess the odds for afternoon showers.

But Jason Harter does have a nose for trouble. There are mornings when he unplugs every appliance in the house, tops off his gas tank, takes a raincoat to work. It may not rain, but other things happen: the client he thought he would never lose is lost; the market research that was going to prove him right proves him wrong; the bird on the branch that was poised to fly shits on the Saab's finish. It doesn't help much on such days whether or not he takes a raincoat to work or checks the pressure on his tires. Readiness is all.

On the freeway, he feels constricted by a lumbering semi on one side and a stuffed garbage truck on the other. In a Cadillac practically tailgating him, a woman applies her makeup and glares at the reflection of his eyes in his rearview mirror. All he can see of the driver of the semi towering beside him is a suntanned arm hanging out the window, silky blonde hairs shimmering in the sun, and, below the shoulder, a tattooed yin-yang symbol. To his left, at times close enough to touch, the garbage truck lists and oozes a green jelly that reminds him of the squashed bugs of his childhood. The four of them roll bonded together all the way downtown.

The view from Jason's office window, twenty-three stories up, still shows clear skies. He hangs the raincoat on a hook behind the door, stands in front of the window, and waits for the phone to ring, for someone to rush into his office, for a meeting to start.

Jason Harter's working life is made up of meetings. The table in his office is round to soften hierarchical divisions and to encourage candor. The people who sit around Jason's round table sell him ideas; he gives them opinions in return.

There are other ways Jason has meetings. Sometimes he has a meeting for a couple of minutes with one or two people in a hallway. Sometimes he has a meeting with someone in the men's room while they are standing at contiguous urinals.

Jason is good at meetings because he comes prepared for trouble. The intuition of trouble might come to him as he stands at the mirror under the clean fluorescent glow of the rest room, searching for something as obvious as nose hair, the pink flush of fever, or the early puffing of a cold sore about to erupt like a volcano on his lip.

Toward the end of the day, Jason leans back in his chair and calls his wife. "Caught in the rain?" she asks.

"Just looking out for the two of you," Jason says, not letting on that her sarcasm stings.

"Hey, guy, I was just joking," she is quick to reassure him. "Sometimes it does rain on us. I know that."

"I'll be home soon," he says, hanging up.

The thought occurs to Jason that signals may have flashed but that he has been too busy looking for them to realize that trouble has already begun. People in the office call this "Waiting for the shoe to drop." The first shoe to drop is a warning. By the time the other shoe drops, you are deep in it. He wonders if listening for the shoe to drop may be the way not to hear it. As an experiment, he pulls off one of his wing tips. He stands up, stretches his arm out, and holds the shoe above the floor.

He is aware of the silence in the deserted office. At this time of the evening, the phones no longer beep, voices are stilled, the Muzak pauses between the end of "Yesterday" and the begining of "I Left My Heart in San Francisco." His heart beats once. He does not breathe.

When he opens his hand, the shoe falls to the floor with a thump so loud he expects security guards to rush in. Even in the midst of the ordinary hum of an office at the height of its activity, the sound of the shoe dropping would be unmistak-able. Once heard, there is nothing to be done except to steel oneself for the other shoe to drop. Just like that, the one-two punch of ordinary physics.

The drive back is uneventful once the evening rush has waned. As Jason turns off the freeway and onto Springer Way, following the narrow road up the hills above Lake Minton, the sun, already behind the top branches of the oaks and maples, casts dappled patterns on the pavement, up onto the hood of the car and through the windshield, warming his hands and face and chest with mottles of sunlight. This is Canaan Hills, last of all the metro-area suburbs in homicide, arson, rape, kid-napping, domestic violence, sexual dysfunction, and divorce rates. Canaan Hills, its mosaic of tender green lawns, the sen-sible two-story-plus-basement houses with attached garages, perhaps a toppled tricycle in front of a neighbor's front door, a single wheel still spinning from the kinesis of a nearby child, spreads its arms to welcome Jason. He is almost home.

It's not until he slows down to turn onto Hyacinth Lane, the street where Stephanie and Amanda await, that he notices on the corner a boxlike structure built of clear plastic panels, steel support columns, and beams. Its purpose eludes him. He slows to a crawl, taking note of several details at once: three sides enclosed in plastic, one open to the street; a simple, slat-ted bench inside; and on a post outside the structure, the logo of the Metropolitan Transit System. That's it, he thinks to himself: a bus shelter. It's unlikely that this plastic box could have been here for the past four years without his noticing it. Now, the thing sits there in stillness, silent, translucent, new.

"Do you know what time buses run down Springer Way, Stephanie?" he asks later during dinner, while between them Amanda observes from her high chair.

"What buses?"

He nods his head. "That's my point."

"Is your car acting up?" she asks. "I could take you to work tomorrow."

"No, I just wanted to know if there was a bus that came by regularly."

"What for? I said I'd drive you."

"I don't need a ride. I don't want to take the bus. I just want to know when it comes by."

"In case you ever want to take the bus, right?"

"Yes, Stephanie."

"Good luck. I've never seen a bus in Canaan Hills."

After dinner Jason insists that the three of them go see this new thing on the corner. He carries Amanda in the crook of his right arm; Stephanie walks beside him, her fingers laced with his. If it weren't after dark, they would seem an ordinary family out for a stroll.

"There it is," Stephanie says as they round the bend on Hyacinth toward the corner with Springer.

The light from fluorescent bulbs on its green aluminum ceiling casts a cool glow inside the big transparent box. Pressed between two layers of plastic on one of the panels is the huge face of a woman smiling through large white teeth, one hand tilting a pair of sunglasses down her nose so we can see right into her blue eyes; the other fingers hold a cigarette with a glowing tip capped by a perfect cylinder of ash. There are no words except on the Virginia Slims package and the cold warning to women about the inadvisability of simultaneously smoking and gestating.

Stephanie and Jason circle the bus shelter. They run their hands along the clear plastic sides, sit on the bench inside, and try to imagine what it might be like to wait for a bus in Canaan Hills. Jason asks Stephanie who she thinks might be taking the bus in their neighborhood, and where they would go by bus, and what times they would expect the bus to come, and where else it would stop.

"I can imagine a woman with long blonde hair in a green silk blouse and big sunglasses with a cigarette in her hand waiting for the bus," he says. "In fact, that is her picture right there."

"She doesn't look like any of our neighbors," Stephanie says. "Not the type to live in Canaan Hills."

"Or to take the bus, either," he points out. "Yet there is her picture. I know about advertising, my dear."

"People who take buses think she does, too?"

"It's scary, isn't it." He reaches for Stephanie's hand as they leave the bus stop and start up Hyacinth toward their house, which is also lit up inside and glowing in the night.

The next morning Jason calls the bus company. "What time does the bus come by the corner of Hyacinth Lane and Springer Way?"

"What are those streets again?" the voice asks.

"Hyacinth and Springer, in Canaan Hills."

"What's Canaan Hills?"

"It's the place where I live," he says. "I want to know if you're going to have buses coming up here."

"I'll pass on your request to have your neighborhood considered for the bus line, sir."

"I'm not requesting anything. I just want to know if you plan to send buses up here."

"Do you personally want to take the bus, sir?"

"Well, not necessarily."

"Then why on earth do you want to know about bus service in Canaan Hills?"

"Just curious, I guess," he says weakly.

"You know, I do have better things to do." The woman hangs up on him.

Driving home that night, Jason slows down at the corner and sees that the bus stop is still there. After his conversation with the transit office, he had expected them to realize that planting their bus shelter in the middle of Canaan Hills was a mistake and that the same people who had stuck it there in the first place would be sent to remove it to its proper place. But even as he is driving away, he catches a glimpse of a figure inside the shelter. He stomps on the brake and looks back at the bus shelter, but the sun setting behind him makes it hard to see through the plastic panels.

"Someone was actually waiting for the bus tonight," Jason announces to his family as the three of them sit around the kitchen table to a dinner of Chicken Florentine by Lean Cuisine and Carrots and Peas by Gerber. "A man or a woman, I couldn't see."

"I haven't heard any buses go by," Stephanie says. "We would certainly hear a bus roaring down Springer."

"The bus company says there is no bus service to Canaan Hills."

"Well, I can sympathize with someone waiting at night for a bus that won't come," Stephanie says, spooning up the remainder of the yellow purée from Amanda's chin.

"How long do you figure someone would wait for a bus before giving up?"

"An hour," Stephanie says. "That's the limit. I once waited for a plane for an hour before I walked up to the counter and learned that the flight had been cancelled."

After dinner Jason waits another twenty minutes until an hour has passed since he drove by the bus shelter. It's still light outside, and the evening has a delicate summer feel to it. Two kids from around the corner are riding their bikes up and down Hyacinth. Lawn sprinklers whirl like dancers. From a backyard nearby comes the scent of grilling meat. This is what one can love about Canaan Hills: its predictability, its sense of ordinary ritual, the cohesiveness of its fabric, a place where you can step out into the spring evening and know yourself to be in familiar territory, a place where your presence is taken utterly for granted.

Jason pushes Amanda in her yellow stroller to the bus shelter. He squints against the glare of the setting sun, trying to make out a figure through the plastic panels. By the time they reach the corner, he thinks he may have imagined someone sitting on the small bench inside. He goes inside the shelter and immediately senses a presence, the certainty that someone has been here until right before this moment. The giant eyes of the smoking woman in the poster seem to point a straight line to the floor just to the right of the bench. There on the concrete floor are five cigarette butts, not crushed but simply dropped to burn themselves out.

He quickly wheels Amanda back home, as if the lingering presence in the bus shelter could be a threat to her. It's not until she has been put to bed, looking up at her parents expectantly while they tuck the pink teddy bear blanket securely around her, that he's able to relax and let the peace of Canaan Hills settle over him. Through the backyard, beyond the tender young birches, he can see lights glowing in warm kitchens, the auras of flickering TV sets, the glimmer of distant traffic.

Later, as he holds Stephanie through the night, Jason becomes aware of still-unfocused dark changes looming ahead, beyond the front door, just down the road.

For the next few days he can't get his mind off the bus shelter. Even when he's thinking of something else, there is the sound of a bus outside his office window or the glint of sunshine reflecting on steel, a stranger's face, deranged eyes, the foolish grin that takes him back to the corner of Hyacinth and Springer. He has visions of buses roaring in from downtown loaded with every panhandler, every menacing youth, every jabbering old woman he has ever met, all of them riding the bus, singing camp songs, telling jokes, plotting mayhem all the way to Canaan Hills. Armies of them get off the bus and start roaming the quiet streets of his neighborhood, tossing sticks at dogs, chucking babies under the chin, ringing bells and asking for stuff, anything, money, cigarettes, directions.

He knows it's happening, never mind that he hasn't seen anyone yet, that days have gone by since the shelter was erected less than a mile from his house, that he hasn't even heard a bus. He knows they are there, that the first interlopers are already edging into the neighborhood. At first they are like some alien strain that starts out being invisible; one day you look around and realize that everything you considered safe has been transformed.

The evidence of their presence grows more tangible. In the evenings after dinner, Jason has gotten into the habit of visiting the bus shelter. He sees things, signs of people having been there that were not there the day before. A copy of the *Enquirer* has been left on the bench. Nobody in Canaan Hills reads that. *People Magazine,* yes. But not the hardcore tabloids, not in public. Every night something new is added. The pile of cigarette butts is growing (Marlboros, Camels,

Kools, Virginia Slims, even roll-your-owns); flattened-out lumps of pink bubble gum stick to the metal support columns; crumpled up Powerball tickets roll with the wind.

Yet when Jason mentions this to Stephanie, she says she has never seen anyone in the bus shelter. Somehow, people are arriving and leaving by bus and hanging out in the bus shelter between the times the people of Canaan Hills leave for work and when they return home. On weekends, there is never anyone there; Jason knows this for sure because last Saturday he walked to the bus stop at least every other hour and never saw a soul.

"Maybe the bus doesn't run on weekends," Stephanie suggests.

"According to the bus company," he reminds her, "the bus doesn't run here at all. And therefore the bus stop doesn't exist."

"Easy, honey," Stephanie says, patting him on the back as if she were pacifying a child.

"Am I the only person in Canaan Hills upset about this?" he asks. "What do the neighbors say?"

"The ones I've talked to say they don't care whether the bus comes or not because they have cars."

"They think that if they don't need the bus they are not affected by it?" Jason hears himself crying out.

"That's the gist of it," Stephanie says cheerfully.

The next morning on his way to the office, Jason stops at the corner as he has for the past several days. This time he grabs his briefcase and raincoat, locks the car, and goes inside the shelter. It is littered with several new signs of its unseen occupants, including a couple of pages torn from the want ads, several scattered tabs from aluminum cans, a limp banana peel, and one unrolled condom. In the warm morning, there's the rising smell of urine. Someone has drawn a black eye patch on the cigarette lady. Behind him, on the main panel, a message has been spray painted with pulsating red strokes, a faint halo glowing around the fat letters: *Hello. Head for the Hills!*

It's at that point that Jason Harter realizes the other shoe is finally about to drop. He sits on the bench, takes out the *Tribune,* crosses his legs, one polished wing tip bouncing above the other, and waits for the bus. It can't take forever, he tells himself. He checks his watch and decides he'll give it an hour.

The gArbAge hOuse

I. THE SIX O' CLOCK NEWS

Like everyone else in the Twin Cities, the Halvorsons saw the whole thing on the TV news—their street, their house, their stuff, themselves.

Sirens howled, tires screamed, and in quick succession the police car, the Channel 8 van, and the social worker's beige Toyota wagon turned the corner from Haskins Avenue and came to a series of lurching, crunching halts in front of the house at 467 Farrell Street. The amber lights on top of the squad car turned and flashed. A spidery antenna rose out of a turret on the van's roof, poised to broadcast news of great significance.

The first ones on the scene, standing on the walkway before the front door to the homey bungalow, were the evening news's Sally Bartlett and her camera operator Skip. As the two police officers, Carla Janson and Fred Grimes, bellied up to the entrance, not actually holding their revolvers but resting their hands on the grip of their holstered .38s, Skip was rolling the tape and Sally was speaking into the microphone in the rapid, breathless delivery that was her trademark.

"Imagine living next door to a garbage house," her voice quavered with anticipation. "Not an incinerator, or a landfill, or some institutional depository of toxic waste, this dysfunctional house on 467 Farrell Street is actually someone's home. It has been reported to contain over three tons of ordinary, all-American household trash. This is Sally Bartlett. Film at six."

The house belonged to Louise and Arne Halvorson. They would have been at work along with the rest of the neighbors, she in the Target shipping department and he at the power company, except that they were called the night before for an appointment with the inspection team. There had been complaints; the whole thing had sounded like some official bureaucratic scolding. The Halvorsons had not expected assorted police officers, a social worker, and the TV celebrity.

On television, Louise and Arne looked like an average couple, even with the tough-looking officer Carla Janson steering them out the front door by the elbows. Clearly these were not crack dealers or porn pushers. They had such a sweet look to them, both bewildered and embarrassed, and they appeared so mortified on either side of the cop that it made people want to call out to them and wish them well.

Arne was around thirty-five, with a round face, doughy like an unbaked cookie, and a beer belly that protruded through his unbuttoned plaid shirt. Not all of Arne's flannel shirts were tight. He wore the small ones in summer, unbuttoned, tails flapping behind him, and saved the newer ones, more suitable to his girth, for the cold months.

His wife Louise was the same age, her body just now starting to puff out at her hips, giving her a rounded, gentle look. Her streaked hair blew across her face, which had flushed to a warm splotchy red. She wore flannel shirts too, but not in the summer. Today she had on a sleeveless sundress with a print of daisies that she liked to alternate with the one with goldfish, each a week at a time.

The Halvorsons had a ten-year-old son. When Wyatt arrived from school shortly after his parents had been taken away, he was kept from going inside by yellow plastic streamers stretched across the doors and windows and by a brittle woman in a stiff blue suit and a red bow around her neck. She introduced herself as Miss Friese, the social worker assigned to help him. They shook hands. His house had been declared a health hazard, she explained, and it would be best to stay away until it was cleaned up. The boy complained that valuable stuff was inside—vintage *Spider Man* comics, an ant farm, a pair of Converse sneakers—as well as Barking Bob and the No-Name cat.

Miss Friese explained that the pets had been taken to something like a hotel for cats and dogs. "The boy appeared distraught and exhibited subtle clues of abuse," the social worker noted in her report; she coaxed him into her Toyota and rushed him downtown for a psychological evaluation. After a two-hour chat with a friendlier woman who watched him play with wooden geometric shapes and gave him Oreos and milk, he was pronounced mildly distressed and confused. She told him he was a nice boy, wished him good luck, and shook his hand.

Most of the Halvorsons' neighbors were away at work and didn't realize what had happened until they saw the news. To Cora and Merle Sollen, who were retired and out on their front porch anyway, it was unsettling to have a full-blown SWAT mission going on in the neighborhood where they had raised their kids and lived for twenty-five years. They couldn't tell from the activity outside the house how bad the situation really was; the Sollens, like everyone else, had to wait for the newscast to see inside 467.

That evening, the Halvorsons were reunited at the Super Eight Motel on I-35. The three stretched out on the king-size bed to share a large pepperoni pizza with extra cheese and to watch their story on the news.

Sally Bartlett's tone was at once brisk and confidential, as if she were taking the audience into a segment of *Lifestyles of the Rich and Famous*. "Imagine living next door to a Garbage House," she began in her clipped, no-nonsense style. "Not an incinerator, or a landfill, or a toxic waste dump, this ordinary bungalow on 467 Farrell Street is actually the home of an average Minnesota family, with a mom, a pop, and a ten-year-old boy. For months, neighbors have complained about the peculiar smell emanating from their home. We have now learned that the house may not have been cleaned in ten years and contains over three tons of all-American household trash. The city estimates it will take a four-man crew three days and two thousand dollars to clean up the mess. This is Sally Bartlett. And this is a Channel 8 exclusive."

"What neighbors?" Arne asked of no one in particular.

"Mr. Sollen," Wyatt said. "I saw him looking through the kitchen windows once." He was proud to be able to contribute this key information.

"I'll kill that old snitch," his dad repeated.

"This is the living room," Sally announced. Not too bad, she pointed out, if you didn't mind the piles of newspapers rising as high as the ceiling, about a hundred empty pop and beer cans, mostly Diet Pepsi and Budweiser, stacked on top of furniture, towers of them leaning against corners or teetering in the middle of the floor.

"I hope they think to recycle that stuff," Wyatt's mother said. "It's not all garbage."

Then came the dining room, which had a table and six chairs that you couldn't see for all the pizza cartons piled on them. Dozens of them, from Domino's to Pizza Hut to Edwardo's, rising halfway to the ceiling, crusted with congealed sauce, macaroons of rubbery mozzarella, and chips of fossilized pepperoni.

"We could own a Domino's franchise by now," Arne chuckled.

It seemed that every room had a theme, Sally Bartlett pointed out. There was order within chaos. The kitchen was mostly stacks of dirty dishes and glasses piled on the sink, skillets with crusted eggs, pots of filmed-over soup remnants. Two overflowing garbage cans and at least four bloated giant-size trash bags stood by the back door.

Then Sally made her way up the stairs, followed by Skip, who kept the camera on her butt for a moment but then shifted to show dog turds and gigantic dust bunnies tumbling along the floor, against corners, and under furniture. Sally Bartlett turned toward the camera and opened her big brown eyes in amazement. "I realize it's beyond what our camera can transmit. The smells of all these things have combined into one unique odor. It's impossible to tell what it is. It's not anything I have ever smelled before. Trust me on this one, folks, you wouldn't want my job right now." She smiled bravely.

"Well, screw you, Miss Smug," Louise muttered. "I'd like to see her house. Bathtub ring. Mirror scum. Toilet rust. Out! Out!"

Arnie laughed. "Call the feds on her. Something smells weird and they should look into it." Then he turned seriously toward the boy. "Things are wrong with this country, Wyatt, when anybody can call the cops on anyone for any reason at any time."

As the camera moved down the hallway, Wyatt sighed with relief; it panned past his bedroom and went right into his parents'. Their huge bed, dressed in tangled sheets and twisted blankets, rose like an island from the middle of the room. Sally stepped inside, lifting her knees high above the swamp of soiled linens, more pizza cartons, more cans, more turds, a few greasy Paul Newman popcorn bags, stacks of old *TV Guides,* and the scattering of unsorted, uncertain baskets of laundry that had long forgotten whether they were advancing toward the washer-dryer or retreating into the closet.

As he watched, Wyatt imagined himself slipping out of the camera's view. He loved his house. He knew places where he could be invisible for days. He recalled burrowing deep inside a closet under a mountain of clothes, or lying flat on his back along the foot of the huge bed, the covers tumbling over him like molten lava, dusty sunlight streaming through the window, filling the small space around his head with a soft glow. Gradually, sounds were muffled, the arguments of his parents downstairs mixed with gales of sitcom laughter as regular as ocean waves. His dad's voice was sharp, nervous, on the edge of anger, always pushing, taunting, his curses breaking up like static. His mother's response was soft and torpid, as if she didn't have the energy to get excited about anything. Even when she was upset, her voice never screamed. On other occasions, when his parents sounded happy and relaxed, Wyatt would come out of hiding.

"This room contains the entire history of the family for the years they have lived on Farrell Street." The camera pulled back to show Sally amid the rubble, like the lone survivor of some natural disaster. "Like anthropologists, the cleanup crew has started digging in and can track, through all these layers, the evolution of a family, from diapers and baby food jars to birthday cakes, booties and bibs to bunny-tailed pajamas."

Sally looked at the camera with such a penetrating gaze that all three Halvorsons felt she was singling them out of her thousands of viewers. "Channel 8 and Sally Bartlett will keep you posted as this story develops."

2. ARNE

Now the whole house smells like a public toilet. Fake pine and chlorine and vanilla and ammonia whizzed together and sprayed all over the place. The smell of ceramic and mirrors and stainless steel urinal fixtures is in our pillows, our glasses and dishes, our toothbrushes even. We can hardly stand to be inside the house. I swear my kid is allergic to it; he's broken out in rashes and sniffles.

Plus, stuff's missing. These Nazis came in here and decided good clothes were garbage. Either that or absconded with some of our things. Sure, why not, just grab it if it looks good. *Abscond* is the word. I'm out two shirts, plaid like this one, only one has more red and the other more green. Louise is out two bras, a sweater, and a real silk blouse. I say they owe me plenty for the lost clothes, the set of very serviceable tires I kept in the basement, and Louise's collection of perfume bottles are not where she left them on her vanity. I've sent a bill to the city.

And they sent me a bill. They say I owe them two thousand dollars for the cleanup and "related expenses." Hell, I've got them by the short and curlies. They want to get paid? First I'll deduct what they owe me. Then I'll sue them for loss of reputation. I'm a professional over at NSP; I have four people reporting to me who no longer respect me like they used to because they think I'm a certified slob.

The truth is we are not the only people who have ever lived in this house. There have been visitors and renters and house sitters. Half the stuff they hauled out wasn't even ours. Then here comes Bitchy Bartlett and points a camera at us, and half the world says, "Oh, yeah, that's What's-his-name. He lives in that dirty house." The *dirtiest* house in the city, no less.

I'm not saying I don't live there. But I didn't live there the whole of my life. Who's to say it wasn't dirty when I moved in? Who's to say we didn't go away for the weekend and that vandals didn't come in and trash the place?

The important thing is, I'm just like everybody else on this street. Before all the TV coverage, I got along with my neighbors. You can ask them. We helped each other out with snow shoveling. I've been to Twins games with a couple of the guys. My wife buys Mary Kay from one of the wives.

Right at 7:20, four of us pull out of our garages at the same exact time. Before this, we'd wave to each other. And then after work sometimes, when we're not doing overtime, we'd pull in, one after the other, like clockwork, at 5:30. We were in sync. We were a team. We'd call out to each other: *How goes the battle. Back to the salt mines. Another day, another yen.* Now they're polite to me. They say, *Good morning, have a nice day.* Not, *Hey Arne, kick some butt at NSP for me.*

It's like I've become a different person. But for years, none of those people gave a damn if my house was messy or not. Take a look at any house on this street; pick one out at random, and tell me they don't have a few old pizza cartons and some dog poop lying around. If there's no dog, you can bet it's cat piss, or bird shit, or hair balls, or mouse crap. Life's a messy thing.

But now that I'm unique, I'm being explained by every so-called expert in town. Like the psychologist who said I was toilet trained too young and then put the whole blame on my mother. Mom watches the program from the Spinway Home where she lives and calls to ask why I am the way I am. It's not her fault, she says to anyone who will listen. I was always a clean baby. She insists the whole fault is Louise's, that if she hadn't been such a slob, I wouldn't be a celebrity. But don't worry, she comforts me, it'll only last fifteen minutes. The woman is old, but her tongue still has bite.

Not that I blame her for feeling betrayed; she had told her fellow inmates that I'm vice president of maintenance and that I live on Lake Minnetonka. Well, guess what, the truth is out. Even as Mother is blaming Louise on this interview with What's-her-face Bartlett, Louise is watching and giving me evil looks.

Now my marriage is getting trashed. I'm the bad guy here and Louise is not talking to me. Last weekend, she packed up the kid and went to visit her parents up north. I mean really far up north, beyond Channel 8 and the *Tribune*. It was a vacation, she said, for her and the kid to be normal. Hell, having to go three hundred miles from home to be normal is not normal.

3. THE FIRST WARM DAY

There are certain things guaranteed to make Merle Sollen crazy. Which is not to say that he is not halfway there to begin with and that these ordinary occurrences just bring the symptom to the fore, so to speak. A lot of people in the neighborhood think that's the case. Still, it gives most everyone comfort that, being retired and home all day, he keeps an eye out for anything that strikes a sour note on Farrell Street. A silver Camaro with tinted windows. Rap blasting away up the street. Tall grass, dead grass, crab grass. These things are more than they seem. To Merle Sollen, they augur larceny, addiction, dissolution.

People think he cultivates these obsessions because he has had too much time on his hands since he retired in '89. Cora, his wife, says he's always been that way. Like years ago when

Lorelei Goodwin started the hair salon on Haskins Avenue two blocks away. She had this great idea to stay open till midnight because she said many people don't have time to get their hair cut during the day.

"What kind of people?" Merle asked her at a neighbors' meeting called to discuss her intentions.

"Just people, is all," Lorelei said. "People who work all day."

"Those people are in bed by ten, not out getting their hair done at all hours."

"Different folks, different clocks."

"You're going to get the different ones, all right." He shook his head sadly. "We're all going to get them. People by themselves in bars with a sudden urge to get a haircut. Loners. Cab drivers. Stewardesses. Strange types." He added this last category in a tone of voice that was at once prudish and conspiratorial.

In the end, the shop was allowed to stay open as late as Lorelei wanted. Merle and Cora and a couple of other neighbors said everyone would be sorry. Sure enough, they had to learn to live with strange cars blocking driveways, sharpies coming on to the flight attendants and waitresses, and even a couple of crack heads who robbed the till, the beauticians, and the customers at gun point. After that, Lorelei got an off-duty policeman to act as a security guard. But the sight of the guy in his blue uniform, the .38, and the big flashlight and the handcuffs and the rest of his hardware dangling from his belt gave the neighborhood an uneasy feeling.

Cora remembers the day that Merle thought something was not quite right with the Halvorsons' house. He had been suspicious of them for years. He was always about to call Arne to complain about his lawn turning into a jungle or the sidewalk disappearing under a thick crust of ice and packed snow. It seemed that just as Merle was about to make the call, Arne would get the message, like telepathy, and the grass would be quickly mowed or the walk shoveled.

On this particular May morning, the sun was shining out of a cloudless sky with the first breath of summer, and Merle wasn't thinking about the Halvorsons. It was the first time in months Cora and Merle had ventured out in their polo shirts and khaki shorts. The sun felt good against the pale winter skin of their bare legs. Cora was proud that Merle was in fine shape, putting out his strong arm for her as they strolled down the street, which they had all to themselves on this wonderful day. As younger people moved into the neighborhood and older ones moved on, no one stayed home anymore unless they were sick or laid off.

The Halvorsons' house was on the opposite side of the street and three homes down from their own. Merle remembers two other families who had lived in the same scruffy house. The first family, the Ansons, put in the covered porch. They were nice people. Then came the Stewarts, who were not as nice because the couple drank and the children screamed; they planted a poplar and put in some hedges. For privacy, they said.

The house had always been beige with brown trim; in the last few years, the paint had started to fall off in flakes as big as hands. It was amazing how one sad-sack house made every other one look shabby, as if the cracking and peeling and scaling were mirrored on the weathered patina of the whole street.

Merle and Cora paused in front of the Halvorsons'. He remembers thinking that they ought to paint now that it was summer and the days were warm and dry, perfect painting weather. Merle said maybe he should give Arne a call.

"Now, don't get into a state, honey," Cora reminded her husband.

"If I'm in a state, then it's a normal state. You'd think a person could show concern and not be accused of being in a state."

"Merle, we were having a nice walk, weren't we?"

"The whole thing looks like it has leprosy. If the paint keeps flaking, the wood is going to rot." He took a few cautious steps across the front lawn and ran his fingers along the windowsill, brushing off the combination of dust and paint. "See? It's rotting already."

"Let's go home. You're meddling."

And then it hit him as he stood in front of the closed window—a foreign, sweetish smell that clung like lint to the tip of his nose. Instinctively, he raised the back of his hand as if the smell were something he could brush off. A flower, mown grass, burgers on the barbecue—these things give their smells a name, an image, an identity. While this, too, was a smell with substance and character, somehow in the warm May morning it seemed to have a life of its own, a nameless, disembodied existence, like a ghost, though not so subtle in form and not abstract at all. It reminded Merle of the presence of the devil, something he had previously sensed in places like the cramped magazine racks in the bookstores on Hennepin Avenue and in bus station men's rooms; like a smell, evil was a tangible, concrete thing that he recognized even if he couldn't see it.

His nostrils flared as he inhaled resolutely, expecting some brain cell to trigger the proper memory. Ah, he wanted to declare, it's paper-hanging glue or roofing tar or burnt beans.

"It smells rotten." He turned to Cora somewhat triumphantly. "The whole place smells like summer road kill."

"Let's go home, Merle."

"Come here and sniff just once. Tell me I'm not imagining stuff."

"It's just dirty socks," said Cora after a moment. "Really dirty socks curled up inside their shoes."

"I'm calling 911," Merle announced as he headed back to his house. "There could be a body in there."

4. THE DAY ARNE BROUGHT FLOWERS

So there I was with the baby and too tired to spit. Getting up to pee in the middle of the night took a major effort. And Arne was no help at all. He slept through the crying and the kicking and the changing and the wiping, and in the morning he was out of the house like a shot. When he got home, we defrosted a pepperoni Red Baron, drank beer, watched TV, and pissed and moaned about how tired we were. We didn't fight about it; we were getting along.

I could sympathize with the man; if I was tired from just sitting around the house talking baby talk, I could imagine him being totally wiped after ten hours at the power company. The very thought of having to be somewhere for that long made me want to curl up inside my old blanket with the Cheese Curls and just blank out. That was the zombie period. I didn't call it that then, but that's what it was. And it was one evening in zombie time that this whole mess started. People think something like this has no beginning. The truth is that everything starts somewhere, sometime. And if you can trace big happenings to the earliest, tiniest moment, then you understand who you are and your place in the social order and why you're on the news and getting more famous by the minute.

There's no way I could forget the day that started this mess; it was the day Arne brought me flowers, the first time since we'd been together. A woman remembers a day like that. I didn't think he knew where you could buy flowers. I mean, he's a good-hearted guy and all, but bringing his wife flowers was out of character.

We didn't even own a vase, so I put some of them inside the percolator. There were so many of them, I took part of the bunch and cut off the stems and floated them in a salad bowl. And then I used a couple of bottles as bud vases.

I took the flowers into the living room. I dimmed the lights, and we had El Chico enchilada platters with candles and the flowers right there on the coffee table. God, the details one remembers. After there were only a few crusty beans and cheesy sauce left to scoop up with the Doritos and Wyatt was in his bed and we were into our third beer, I asked Arne what was going on.

"It's just an idea I had," he said. "A good idea, it felt like."

"Just like that?" I smiled like it was an innocent question. He shrugged and looked somewhere else, as if he expected an explanation to float down from a corner of the ceiling. "An idea out of the blue?"

"Is there a problem?"

"No, Arne. It's just unlike you." We were slouching down on opposite ends of the couch, our feet propped up on the coffee table in front of two dirty plates, a bunch of paper napkins, the crusted plastic trays, and six empty beer cans. Our noisy kid was asleep, and I remember thinking things could get a little romantic. "You've never brought home flowers," I added when I realized he was still scowling. "It was nice. Just very unexpected."

"It's not like you've known me forever."

"I know you always eat the bigger half of the pizza, and that beer makes you fart in your sleep, and that you really like breasts. Arne, I know your deepest secrets."

"You don't know shit," he said. Then he stood up from the couch. He brushed a few crumbs from his lap onto the carpet and stretched his arms so high that they raised the bottom of his T-shirt over his stomach.

The belly was new. One day Arne had a flat stomach, and the next, *boom,* it was like he had swallowed a melon. In school days I had avoided, fled, escaped fat guys. We all did. Now everybody I knew in high school is married to a guy with a gut. Who's playing these jokes on us, anyway?

"I'm going to bed," Arne announced.

"Me too," I switched off *Letterman* in the middle of one of his toothy grins. "Help me pick up."

"Nope," he said, sticking his chin out defiantly. "I do the eight to five. You do the dishes."

I watched his face to see whether he was teasing me or not. But he just stared back with this placid expression. It was like a declaration of war. He knew he had stumped me because while I stood in a daze in the middle of the dining room, he burped and then walked up the stairs without so much as a look back. The next day, as tired as I was, I got up early, checked the want ads, and dropped Wyatt at day care. By the time I came back home around four, I had a job at Tar-jhay. It was easy.

About that time, I realized the dishes and stuff from the night before had never got picked up. The flowers still looked nice. After Arne came home around five-thirty, we had fish sticks, Tater Tots, and Old Milwaukee. And the next day we had meat loaf, which I cooked from scratch because it was Saturday; I made enough to feed us at least a couple more times that week.

By Tuesday, the flowers floating in the bowl were leaving a little scum and the ones in the coffeepot were drooping. I thought they still looked all right and we didn't really need the pot; we'd started drinking instant.

To make room for that night's dinner dishes, I moved the foil trays and the beer cans to the floor and just stacked the clean dishes on the previous night's dirty ones. But it's not like we were planning to leave the dishes for seven years.

Actually, we did pick up now and then. But, you know, if it started out to be once a week, it later became once a month, and then the only time anything got washed was when one of us wanted to use it right then.

Arne hasn't brought flowers again. I still don't know why he did it in the first place. At first I thought it was the guilt thing, like guys will do when they've been messing around or wanting to. Arnie is not the type. He likes things comfortable. Being unfaithful would be too much work. I'm sure of that; we know each other better now than we did ten years ago.

Now all this talk about three tons of garbage. Well, that's just the media blowing things out of proportion. I mean, what did they do, weigh it one bag at a time? We'll appeal. No way we're paying two thousand dollars for house cleaning.

5. SALLY'S DREAM

Sally Bartlett, all rosy cheeked and smooth skinned and fair haired, wakes up in the middle of the night, her heart beating a staccato tattoo into her chest, her breath coming in quick gasps. The dream is in full, vivid color. The reds from pizza boxes and Campbell's soup cans and catsup bottles are redder than stoplights. The green mold shimmers like velvet. Swollen black plastic bags sink like marshmallows beneath her feet. The dream, she knows, is only a dream. She wishes it wouldn't keep recurring.

She kicks off the top satin sheet and lets the cool night air dry the moisture that beads up on the back of her neck, on the insides of her thighs, on her breasts. She has had the sensation of things crawling on her skin. Not insects, more like wet clammy creatures with tiny openings instead of feet, which make tiny sucking sounds as they travel over her body. That's not the dream. It's a physical sensation that comes to her when she wakes up. It's more real than the dream.

This Sunday she rises early even though it's her one day in the week to sleep in. She has a date with Charles Beaulieu, the man who wants to marry her. She stands up from the bed, runs her hands over her skin, and checks her body in the mirror. Nothing unusual. She hurries to the shower.

Charles is a well-known mover-and-shaker type, which is one reason she had lunch with him the day after he left a long message on her voice mail. He said he had fallen in love with her from the Six O' Clock News. A lot of men say this to her. She listens and then tells them it's the dumbest line in the world; the Sally Bartlett they think they know exists only on TV. The last thing she would want to do is fall in love with some guy who sees her as this head inside a box. But someone as rich as Charles Beaulieu can act foolish and be taken seriously.

Charles Beaulieu of Old Beaulieu, Minnesota, appeared in the newsroom the same evening she did the follow-up on the Garbage House on Farrell Street. She had spent all week inside the house taping the cleanup, following a minitractor as it plowed through the various rooms, pushing into the garbage bags and the towers of pizza cartons and scooping up the piles of refuse and loading them onto a truck parked in the alley behind the kitchen door. It had been a dramatic scene. A crew of four big guys in rubber waders and surgical masks had trudged into the house like an invading army, shoveling toys out of the way, trampling on school books and clothes and shoes, kicking a wide swath through petrified donuts, dog turds, and banana peels. And in the midst of it all Sally Bartlett smiled bravely, cheerfully chronicled the two thousand dollar cleanup.

The gArbAge hOuse

Charles Beaulieu shook her hand and left on her skin the scent of expensive lotion. The next evening, over a drink at the St. Paul Grill, she noted his manicured hands, close shave, white, even teeth. His shoes were buffed to a high gloss, his gray trousers pressed to a sharp edge. He had a courtly manner; he held doors open, adjusted chairs, offered his arm whether she needed it or not. A week later, he proposed marriage.

That Sunday, she was still thinking about it. Her misgivings were few: He came with an ex-wife, two grown kids, one cross-eyed Doberman. Also he had confessed shyly to a history of recurrent depressions, some so dark they colored the whole world in hues of dusty gray and Lenten purple and made him hide inside his room and watch TV until his eyeballs burned and were streaked with red from weeping. His crying jags, which lasted hours, could be set off by something as vacuous as an AT&T commercial or a pathetic moment on *Geraldo.* He had been enduring just such a bout with this deep, engrossing sadness when he saw Sally Bartlett inside the Garbage House.

"Talk about depressing," she said.

"Well, yes," Charles said. "Ordinarily, that would be the case. In fact when I get very depressed, I clean the house. It doesn't matter if I had it cleaned the day before. I'll personally do the whole thing all over again, windows, oven, fridge, whatever. Sometimes, if I scrub the kitchen floor for an hour, I start to cheer up. Other times, no matter how hard I work, everything seems dirty, filthy. I just keep buffing and polishing and dusting. People tell me I'm too rich to do my own housework. But it's like Lady Macbeth; nobody else is going to wash her hands."

"Still, the Garbage House must've been a shock for you."

"No, Sally. It was a revelation." Charles leans over and takes her hand. "There you were in the middle of hell. While decay and filth and stink rose all around, you remained untouched by it all. You didn't recoil and say *ish*. You were serene. You were a vision, a spiritual vision. I thought the Six O' Clock News was being done by an angel. And then I thought to myself, that is how I should be. To have the freedom to walk among the dirt and decay of the world and to be untouched by it. Don't you see? There was an important message for me that day. It was inevitable that I fall in love with you."

Charles Beaulieu falls silent. He lifts the bottle of champagne dripping from the ice bucket and pours some for Sally and himself. He raises his glass. "Will you marry me, Sally? Will you walk with me pure and untainted, even as the world rots?"

6. The Longest Day

After the cleanup of the house was completed, the Halvorsons were allowed into their home by a man from the health department. To Wyatt, the man didn't look healthy at all; his clothes were splotched with perspiration and tight against his butt and up his crotch and around his belly. "All right," he said, full of optimism and pep in spite of a long day dealing with rats, bats, and rabid squirrels all over town. "You won't recognize the place. It'll be easier to keep it up now, with all the heavy mess gone. A piece of cake, if you keep one step ahead of the mess. That's the trick, not letting chaos gain on you."

The three Halvorsons took small hesitant steps inside, as if they were feeling their way across a newly frozen pond. Home had been turned into someone else's house, as bare and impersonal as the room at the Super Eight.

"It smells like those white tablets in public urinals," Arne noted for the first time.

"Everything scientifically sanitized from floor to ceiling." The man shook hands with Arne and Louise and Wyatt, as if to put the final seal on a team venture whose mission had been accomplished.

Wyatt couldn't understand what the man was saying even as his voice echoed through the empty house. His room looked as if its inhabitant had moved out with all his clothes, toys, everything except the comic book collection. The forty or fifty comics that had been scattered about the floor were now stacked at the foot of his bed.

The following Monday, he dressed silently in a new white shirt with all the creases and stiff blue jeans. He was about to face school almost a week after they had all been on TV. It had taken him three days to get his nerve up.

During that time, he stayed away from his parents, his friend Donny Ebersohl, everyone. He wandered around the mall and hid in the cool dark of the Multiscreen Cineplex. He had twelve features to choose from. He would buy one ticket, then go into the different theaters, not waiting until one movie was over, but bouncing around in the middle all day long with one child's matinée admission of $2.75.

Wyatt knew he would be called the Garbage Boy even before he walked into his first-period class. It was inevitable. The Garbage Family from the Garbage House. That was them.

"Hey, Wyatt, your mother wears Hefty bags."

"Listen, everybody. You can hear his shoes squish!"

"Talk louder. He's got wax in his ears."

"Hey, Wyatt, what's for dinner? Toe cheese pizza?"

There was more. He had mossy teeth, hair lard, fingernail gunk, and there was enough belly-button lint among the whole family to knit a pair of mittens. Yucky Wyatt was his name.

It was the longest, slowest day of his life. He walked along the hallways with the feeling of a stone in his stomach growing larger and heavier with each passing hour. Suddenly, he was the most famous boy in school. From the first grade through the sixth, every kid knew his name. He felt as if he were naked, a blush starting at the tips of his toes and rising feverishly all the way up to his face.

At noon, he sat by himself in a quiet corner of the lunch room and tried to eat a peanut butter and jelly sandwich. He kept his eyes down on the table so he wouldn't see how everyone around him was watching him. It took every effort he could muster to lift the sandwich to his mouth, take a bite, and chew for what seemed like hours, then take another bite, and another, all the time trying to swallow the growing gummy mass that swelled against the inside of his cheeks.

By one o'clock, word had gotten around school that the Garbage Boy had gone into the first bathroom he had encountered, which turned out to be the women's faculty lounge, and managed to throw up the whole of his lunch and what was left of breakfast. Some of it landed on the assistant principal's white silk blouse. Mrs. Brewster was a tall broad woman with large meaty hands. She took Wyatt by the back of his collar and whispered hoarsely right into his ear, "Where the fuck did you come from?"

Even as he searched for an answer to her question, he had to turn away from her bright green eyes because he had never been looked at with such intensity. Before he had a chance to clean off the vomit that trickled down his chin, she jerked him by his shirt collar out of the lounge and back into the stream of children racing to class after lunch. Now he was the Barf Boy, Puke 'n' Snot, Wyatt Burp.

At two-thirty, when the bell rang at last, Wyatt waited until the classroom emptied and then gathered up pencils and books and notebooks and stuffed them into his backpack. At the front of the classroom, Mr. Farley, the fifth-grade teacher, busied himself clearing his desktop. He was tall and gangly, with a pointed head and stooped shoulders. As Wyatt passed in front of the desk on his way out the door, Mr. Farley followed him. They walked without a word down the hallway and out to the empty parking lot.

"Looks like you missed your bus," Mr. Farley said.

"I don't always ride it," Wyatt said. "Sometimes I walk."

"Would you like a lift home?" the teacher offered.

Wyatt shook his head.

"You know," Mr. Farley said, squatting in front of him, "this has probably been the worst day in your whole life. But there's something to be glad about, isn't there? It's all behind you."

Wyatt could tell the teacher was trying to be sympathetic, but it had little value from someone all the kids called Fartley. "I'm not coming back to school, ever," Wyatt said.

"Sure you are," the teacher said.

"No, I'm not."

"Well, good-bye then, Wyatt." The teacher offered his hand. "It's been really nice knowing you. And having you as a student."

This had become a routine, shaking hands with people. Wyatt marched away, trying to look cocky in his loopy bouncing walk, when he froze uncertainly in the middle of Snelling Avenue. He thought of the stark white spaces of his new house. The light changed and the traffic surged around him, horns beeping and people shouting. For a moment he felt lost, unable to move in either direction. He wasn't returning to school, and he wasn't going home. Then he started to jog down the avenue, dodging cars, picking up speed, finally dropping his book bag so he could run faster.

BroWn hAt, bLue bOx, 1958

Thirty-five years before his wife finally left him, Marvin Lenk
went for a drive in her white Chevrolet Impala. It was a
Saturday morning, and he had just come back from two
weeks on the road selling the famous Mightyplate Roof
Coating from Fort Worth, Texas. This was unusual, Marietta
knew, because he disliked driving her car. Also, the last thing
he would want to do after two weeks and two thousand miles
of sitting on his hemorrhoids was to go for a ride.
"What's up?" Marietta asked.
"I'm just living a small chapter in my life," he said, which
mystified her enough that she couldn't think of anything else
to ask him.
    Years later, even as they were signing the divorce papers, she
remembered the day because when he came back about an
hour later, he had with him his best brown hat, a nice felt
homburg, only it was crushed and smeared with road tar and
bits of gravel. He also had a shoe box wrapped in blue tissue
that he buried in the backyard when he thought she was in
the front of the house watching TV.
    "What's up?" she had repeated, indicating the crumpled
hat with a nod.

Marvin thought most people ought to be protected from asking certain kinds of general, all-inclusive, open-ended questions. They might get an answer that would let them sleep at night. The odds were against it. One could run away from questions; answers stuck to you like dog poop on a shoe.

"It fell off my head," he said. "While I was driving the car, the wind blew it right off my head and out the window."

"I didn't see you wearing it this morning," Marietta observed.

"It happened last night on the way home."

"Did you have an accident or something?" she asked, alarmed.

"No, Etta. It was just a small, tiny incident. Not worth talking about. The kind of thing that happens dozens of times to people in the course of a day and then starts to fade almost as if it happened to someone else. Then you think back on it, and you see your small role in the scheme of things, and it's like watching a TV series. Week after week, things happen to the characters, and one thing leads to another, and pretty soon you just lose all the connections."

"Marvin," Marietta said, "you're a deep thinker. But one of these days I will have had enough." Marvin was struck by her seriousness.

"What did I say?" He made a big helpless shrug.

"Nothing. You never tell me anything."

Marvin Lenk thinks back to the moment, which is receding even as he sees the beefy red Buick—a '56 Roadmaster built soft and heavy for high-mileage road warriors like him—speed down Styles Street, and before he can even stomp on the brakes, run over a small gray dog.

"I tell you what I know, Etta," he said. "Truly, I do."

So what kind of a dog? The truth is that the driver doesn't see what kind of dog it is. Or rather he sees the dog. But not the schnauzer-terrier-spanielness of it. It is just a little ferret-like thing darting into the street. Its toothy jaws are open in a grin. Its bright eyes focus for an instant on the car's chromed grille before it tries to turn and run for safety, its brown leather leash dragging behind it and getting tangled in its front paws. Standing firm on the sidewalk, a six-year-old girl screams at the sight of her dog being hashed under the Buick's white sidewalls.

The kid's young pretty mom is chasing the car down the middle of the road, yelling at the driver ("You blind son of a bitch") to STOP!

A neighbor down the street, Mrs. Miller, who spends a lot of time looking out her window, remembers two letters and one number from the car's license plate and writes them down.

Following a moment behind the Buick, a man in a Ford stops to offer assistance. He is a tall handsome man dressed in a brown suit. He calls the girl's mother *Ma'am*. "We need to get this little guy to a vet," he says, even though he and the kid and the mother all know the dog is dead.

The guy driving the Buick also knows this; there is something conclusive about the thud of bone and muscle and gristle bouncing up against the car's hot steel underbody. With this in mind, there's no point stopping, because it's clear everyone is very upset. As he guns the engine and speeds away, leaving streaks of rubber on the hot pavement, the driver's head jerks back and a sudden gust from the open window blows his hat onto the street. Even as the hat is rolling on its brim along the edge of the road, witnesses have noted that the car is red, the driver is bald, the license plate is F . . . C . . . something . . . 6 . . . something . . . something.

Marvin Lenk is not sure how much of all this he saw and how much of it he has intuited.

There's more.

The little girl grows up to be a relentless activist for animal rights working for the outlawing of furs, cosmetics testing, guinea pigs, Big Macs. She later marries a good-hearted man who welcomes all the strays she finds.

The man in the Ford, who until then was an innocent bystander-good samaritan, falls in love with the girl's mother and persuades her to leave her husband and run away to Florida. When her husband asks why she would do such a crazy thing, the woman can only say it was the man's look of infinite compassion as he held the dead puppy that won her heart. "You wouldn't even touch it," she accused him while waiting for the Airport Taxi. "You couldn't wait to get rid of it."

And he says, "Of course, you are right. I never liked the thing in the first place." But he cares that his life is being changed by something that he had nothing to do with, that happened while he was across town. After that, as things go badly for him, he blames all his troubles on the bald-headed, brown-hatted driver of the Buick. Armed with those small facts and the partial number of Mrs. Miller's license plate, he embarks on a lifelong search of revenge.

The registry of motor vehicles is no help at all because as long as there is not a warrant for the man's arrest, they are not about to humor amateur detectives with lists and lists of possible automobile owners. Puppy hit-and-run, unfortunate as it is, is not a real crime. So the man goes on his private hunt, searching along the streets and freeways, chasing red cars for years, coming at last to an untimely end under the Hennepin Avenue bridge. One night he goes to sleep drunk and wakes up dead.

Mrs. Miller, the neighbor lady, who for years has been watching the traffic outside her window, learns of the father's death when she is called downtown to identify his body.

Upon facing him laid out on a slab looking as pasty and rigid as a store window dummy, she at last gives up the dream she had long nurtured of finding the driver of the Buick and turning him in to the kid's daddy, for whom she has harbored a strong attraction since the day he was left by his wife. She accepts the end of the dream and moves in with her married daughter, who has fixed up a nice apartment with a large window in Chula Vista, California, where the weather is damned near perfect all the time.

The man who set all these events in motion by running over a dog with his red Buick simply hits and runs. He's in the story for about ten seconds, his back visible inside the car only from his shoulders up, most of the time with a hat on. So where does he go?

Marvin Lenk went home. He was tired. He had been on the road for two weeks, stopping at every half-assed warehouse-factory-workshop-restaurant-apartment complex-funeral home-bowling alley-fitness center-massage parlor-type building between St. Paul and Des Moines and Des Moines and Chicago and Chicago and St. Paul. A whole continent of sticky, tarred roofs. He called his sales route the Black Triangle.

His sales technique was to cruise the fringe industrial neighborhoods. He'd stop at a warehouse or a factory and ask the owner when was the last time he'd been up on the roof. Whatever they said, he went up on the roof with them and showed them cracks and blisters and rips on the tarred surface. "Do you know how much an unchecked leak can cost in water damage?" he'd ask his prospects. "You don't want to know. Best of all, you won't have to know." Then he sold them fifty-gallon drums of Mightyplate Roof Coating from Fort Worth, Texas, a black pudding that dries into a rubbery sheath that stretches and contracts along with the roof in the heat of summer and freeze of winter.

Marvin Lenk was so tired that he could barely keep his eyes open. The whole stretch from Madison to Eau Claire and finally into St. Paul was a nervous blank. It was after ten when he pulled his car up the drive of his neat green house at 472 Brimmer. He reached up to take off his brown hat, then realized it was gone, but he still mopped the sweat off his head with a handkerchief. After two weeks on the road, he felt sticky all over.

Much later that night, he lay in bed with Etta, the two of them on their backs, side by side, their plump bodies naked to the soft summer breeze. "Etta," he said. "What are we doing?"

"Why do you ask?"

"I asked first."

"We're lying on the bed in our happy home, while our beautiful child sleeps peacefully in the next room, and we are thinking that the way the breeze makes our new pink curtains billow is wonderful, and that the new white-on-white pattern of the hallway wallpaper, which we can see from here, glistening in the moonlight, is just lovely. Just lovely."

"Right," he said. "Why do I feel so tired?"

"What's going on with you, anyway?" She rose on her elbow and looked down at him.

"Nothing," he said. "Good night, Etta."

"Good night, Marvin."

The next morning, he sat between his wife and his daughter Franny at the breakfast table in their new avocado kitchen, sipping the last of his coffee and reading the paper, when his attention was drawn to a headline on the editorial page that all but named Marvin Lenk as the cold-blooded killer of a German shepherd puppy called Scamp.

STOP THE PUPPY MASSACRE NOW!

It was time, the article said, to rein in the vicious killers behind the wheels of their Detroit murder machines who cruise quiet residential neighborhoods in search of innocent cats and dogs to slaughter. It called for criminal penalties for the wanton murder of children's pets. Marvin closed the newspaper and leaned back in the chair with a quiet gasp.

It wasn't his own life that was particularly demanding. It was the bit parts he was called on to play in the lives of other people. He was the shadow you see in the movie, the extra in the crowd, the split infinitive in the novel, the man in the brown hat. He felt as if he had no control over his own life. Across the table from him, Marietta helped their Franny with the buttons in back of her green plaid sundress. "Hold still," she said. When she was done buttoning, she tied the belt at the waist, making a bow in back. Marvin figured Franny was the same age as the little girl with the dead puppy.

"I had a ten thousand dollar road trip," he announced to his family. He tried to sound casual about it. "And now it feels great to be home."

"So can we buy a puppy?" Franny asked.

"You've already got two goldfish," Marvin reminded her.

"Fish don't do anything," the child protested. "Dogs play fetch and cuddle up."

"Fish swim," he said. "They don't get run over."

Later that day, Marvin Lenk got behind the wheel of his wife's white Chevy. She asked him where he was going and he said just for a drive. Then she offered to go with him but he said he needed to be alone to sort out his thoughts. Instead of his usual brown hat, he put on a straw Panama hat. He wore a short-sleeve Madras plaid shirt with big orange, blue, and green squares. It was his favorite shirt. He wore it because it didn't look like anything a puppy killer would wear. Marvin also took his sample case of Mightyplate Roof Coating along because he never knew when he could be standing in front of a building with a roof that was cracked and parched and thirsty for the black miracle gumbo from Texas.

He retraced his route and soon found himself heading back to Styles Street. He got to the end, just where it runs into the highway, then made a U-turn. From the night before, he remembered only a street lamp and the way the light cast shadows through the tree branches. The street had been a speckled pattern of leaves flickering with the wind. For a second, as the dog darted across the street, the pattern of the leaves had danced on the silvery sheen of its fur.

He was disoriented. The houses on either side, which had been all lit up the previous night, their kitchens aglow, their living rooms sending out bluish TV reflections, their front porches illumined by single yellow bulbs, were now lined up in a repeating series of pastel pink, blue, and yellow façades.

He slowed down when he saw his brown hat lying mashed up against the edge of the sidewalk. A few feet away was a mailbox with the name *Beale.* The house behind it was yellow, and in a corner of the backyard, he saw the girl with her mother. The girl had on a starched white dress, the mother was dressed in a black suit. The girl carried in both hands a parcel the shape of a shoe box wrapped in blue crepe paper and tied with string. The mother carried a shovel.

Marvin parked the car beyond their house and watched them in his rearview mirror. They paced around the yard, going from one end to the other, until they settled on a small rise under the wide branches of a large elm in the corner of the yard. A few minutes later, the girl's father, in faded khakis and an undershirt, came out of the kitchen and let the screen door swing back with a slam. The girl and her mother must have heard the sound but did not turn around. The man walked over to them and, after a brief argument that Marvin couldn't hear, snatched the box away from the girl. The little girl ran after him and tried to pull the box away from him. He bent down, took the girl's hand tightly inside his own massive fist, and pulled her crying back into the house.

Taking a deep breath to steady his nerves, Marvin Lenk got out of the car with his sample case. From outside the front door, he could hear the sobbing of the little girl and the mother's rhythmic rising and falling voice as she appealed for reason and the shouting of the father saying he was damned if they were going to dig up the yard to plant the carcass right there in full view of their bedroom window.

Marvin Lenk tightened his hand around the handle of the sample case as if in the truth of the mysterious waterproofing process from Fort Worth, he could find the courage to pick up where he had left off the previous night. There were faint chimes from inside the house and suddenly the voices were hushed. The man jerked the door open.

"Marvin Lenk is the name." He stuck out his hand at the other man's midriff. "And keeping the rain out is my game."

The man stared at him from deep within his bloodshot eyes. He still carried the box protectively. "We've already got an umbrella."

"Ha, that one's funny." Marvin nodded. "But your house is vulnerable. After all, your roof is out of sight, and therefore dangerously cracking and peeling and blistering while you think everything underneath it is nice and secure."

"This is not a good time."

"If I may differ." Marvin opened up the giant brochure that showed the cross section of a roof with its layers of tar and shingles and woodframe and plaster.

Beale breathed a sigh of resignation. "How long will it take you to give your pitch?"

"Minutes," said Marvin. "May I invite you to climb on the roof? Don't believe what I say but what you see."

Marvin followed the man inside the house. He tipped the brim of his Panama at the mother and the girl standing to one side of the staircase. The two men clambered up a stepladder that led through an attic skylight. Marvin was experienced at climbing roofs with one hand free, the other clutching his sales kit. He wore spongy crepe-soled shoes. Mr. Beale, on the other hand, kept losing his footing and slipping down the steep incline. Still, he kept the blue box lodged under his left arm.

Whenever he climbed a roof in the course of his work, Marvin would often pause and take a moment to enjoy the view; he'd remove his hat to let the sun bounce off his pate and the breeze cool his scalp. "It gives you perspective, doesn't it?" he said to Mr. Beale. "You get to see a bigger world once you climb above your fellow mortals."

"I guess I don't understand what we are doing up here," Mr. Beale said.

"We're looking at cracks and blisters and tears." Marvin gingerly took a few steps toward the edge. "See how the old tar bubbles up?"

"I don't see anything."

"Sure you do, come a little closer to where I'm standing. There are two fat blisters right here. Squeeze them and feel the moisture inside. A roof is a living thing. It's like the skin on your head, the first barrier of protection between the elements and your brain."

The man took a couple of hesitant steps toward Marvin. Still clinging to the blue package under his arm, he sat down just where a vent provided a small ledge on the roof's smooth surface. "So what do you think, Mr. Beale?"

"About fixing the roof?" the man asked.

"Yes. And about life too, what the hey!" Marvin chuckled.

"Persistent, aren't you," the man said.

Marvin shrugged. "Something special happens when people sit together on a rooftop. The isolation and all that. Feel like talking? We could talk about what's inside that blue package you're hanging on to."

"It's a dog." Beale shrugged.

"Shouldn't you let it out for air?" Marvin asked.

"No," Beale said. "It's too late for that."

"Really?"

"Really," Beale insisted. "Want to see it?"

"Later, maybe," Marvin said. "When did it happen?"

"Yesterday. Hit and run. This asshole in a red Buick. A bald guy in a brown hat."

"You saw him that clearly?"

"My wife and kid did. Good thing for him I wasn't there."

"Amazing how attached we can get to a dog."

"I hated the damn thing. And I believe it hated me. That's why I don't want it buried right there in the backyard where I can see its little grave first thing in the morning. That dog barked at me all the time." The man held the blue package next to his ear. "Yap, yap, yap."

"So what were you going to do with it?"

"I don't know," Beale shook his head. "If I knew where the guy in the Buick lived, I would drop Scamp on his porch." He laughed out loud. "That and his hat, which is still there on the ground. See it?" He pointed at a brown spot by the side of the road. "What a stupid hat."

Marvin shook his head philosophically. "About your roof," he started.

"My daughter is upset because she wants to bury her doggie in my yard. And my wife won't talk to me because she thinks I'm heartless. And you want to talk about the roof?"

"It will leak," Marvin said. "By next spring."

"What's with you?" the man said, more agitated now. "Do you know everything?"

"About roofs."

"I bet you know who killed Scamp," the man said quietly.

"Now you're the one who sounds like you know everything. Why should I know who killed your dog?"

"Well, you're bald. Even if you are not the one, bald guys stick together. I have an uncle who is bald and he hangs out with three other bald fellows. They sit around each other's houses and play poker and keep their hats on all the time."

"I'll make you a special deal on a fifty-gallon drum of Mightyplate Roof Coating," Marvin said.

"You're changing the subject."

"You'll see that I'm not," he said. "You buy the roof coating. Pay for it COD. $63.50. I take Scamp." Marvin reached out his hand for the blue box.

Beale thought about this for a moment. He stared, suspiciously at first, into Marvin's eyes. Then his whole expression brightened and he breathed a sigh of relief. "Sure. Fine. OK." He pointed down at the street and added, "You'll take the hat with you, too, right?"

BeYonD tHe nORm

Norman Tresh found something at a garage sale that greatly improved his life. As he rummaged among the polished wooden cases of old surgical instruments and gleaming examining-room fixtures from Dr. Harry Caslon's estate, Norm hoped to find a microscope; he had lately grown bored with books and movies and CDs and expected to gain some elusive new insight from among the germs in swamp water and the bacteria in yogurt, to name just two possibilities.

There was interesting stuff at the sale. The dead doctor's personality hovered like a ghost over his boxes of LP collections, from American musicals to Scandinavian folk songs, obscure medical tools with pincers and hammers and clamps, musty books from the complete Zane Grey to four different editions of *Gray's Anatomy*. But no microscope. Norman was about to leave empty-handed when he saw, curled up like a cat on the bottom shelf of a bookcase, a large naked brain.

The brain floated in a yellowish broth inside a cylindrical jar with a sealed glass top. It seemed in as good a condition as could be expected for an organ so vulnerable outside its skull. It was the color of ivory. Symmetrical. Weighty. Solemn. And terribly silent.

Norm gazed through the murky formaldehyde and decided that the intricate network of folds and fissures on the spongy surface, the sculptural contours of lobes front to back, the dangling medula that hung down like a length of electrical cabling might reveal as many mysteries on close examination as he might find in a glob of spit magnified under a microscope. Here, visible to the naked eye, might be important clues to explain the vagaries of human behavior, the nature of love, the root causes of evil.

"That's an authentic human brain," explained Dr. Caslon's granddaughter Sally, who was running the cash box. "I could let you have it for fifty bucks." At twenty, she already had a brisk, businesslike manner in sharp contrast to her apparent bright-eyed, curly-haired innocence. She wore a huge University of Minnesota sweatshirt and a pair of her grandfather's mostly green plaid shorts. They reached below her knees and were precariously held up by a leather belt she had cinched around her waist.

She looked from the jar to the cash box and back to the jar; she did not look at Norman. Or rather she looked at him only enough to sense that the lanky guy in a Polo shirt and pressed khakis would pay top dollar for such a find.

"I can manage forty."

She shrugged as if to say take it or leave it. "There's sentimental value here. She's been in the family for over fifty years."

"Who?"

Sally finally looked up at Norman. "Mrs. Arveda Gutterman." She indicated the jar with a nod of her head. "She was my grandfather's first official patient. She was brought to him from prison. She was doing life for the murder of her husband and three kids. She was an old, old lady when she was taken to the hospital where he was interning.

They brought her into the emergency room in the middle of the night. She was in the last stages of cirrhosis. He sucked out the fluids and gave her morphine. That's all anyone wanted him to do. She went into a coma and died three days later. She donated her body to science. The med school got her liver. Grandpa kept her brain. He had this saying about patients, 'Easy come, easy go.'" She looked up and held his gaze. She had cool blue eyes. "Am I grossing you out?"

"No. It's interesting." He realized he wanted to continue talking to her. "I mean a brain is not a person, is it?"

"Well, it's not just a thing, either."

"Somewhere in between," he agreed.

"Worth at least fifty dollars," she repeated. "It'll make a great conversation piece. It will help you get women."

That was the clincher. Since moving out of his parents' home and into his own apartment about three years ago, Norman had hardly been able to entice any women into his bachelor pad. He sensed that the neighbors looked at him funny; solitary people were suspect. Norman knew that if he ever committed a crime—and there were several he had considered, from pissing on the fur display at Neiman Marcus to passing himself off as Mother Theresa and soliciting donations on the Internet—the first things they would say about him in the press would be "He was a loner. Stuck pretty much to himself. Sure, he seemed to be a nice guy. But ya never know. Do ya."

When he got to his apartment, Norman placed the jar in the middle of his coffee table. He looked for clues that would provide some insight into Mrs. G's proclivity for intrafamiliar mayhem, some hint of the criminal or the outcast that might be latent in his own brain. But while it communicated nothing, the silent organ affected the way he ordinarily looked at the world.

As he sat on the couch and watched *The Simpsons* on TV, Norman could see part of the screen washed out and made wavy through the formaldehyde soup that held Mrs. Gutterman's brain. Homer Simpson's bright yellow pate and Marge's big blue hair and Bart's eat-my-shorts shorts cast ghostly reflections onto the gray matter itself. Sometimes, depending on which color dominated the screen, the brain would appear to think different kinds of thoughts. Red meant anger. Blue turned it peaceful and serene. Green was cheerful. At night, when there were only the city lights outside the window, the brain became smooth with the sheen of antique ivory. It looked downright meditative.

In time, the brain in the jar, like his poster of Jim Dine's *Red Bathrobe* or the big brown recliner chair in front of the TV, found itself blending into the general ambience of Norman's apartment, its initial dissonance gradually fitting in with the new surroundings.

The way the brain made itself at home reminded him of living with his mother's big figure sketches in dusty charcoals for her art class, which were tacked to the walls in the living room, bedroom, basement, attic, wherever there was space. His two main friends through high school, Tryon Twells, the dentist's son, and Marcus Segura, whose dad was reputed to be with the IRS, were always eager to hang out at the house and were invariably polite to his mother. When his buddies went into Norman's house, the first things they saw were these hefty naked women with doe-eyed expressions and the obligatory thick pubic bushes and tendrils of black hair sprouting from under their arms. The medium lent itself to hair, Norm figured. In time, nobody noticed the nudes; like the petrified wood doorstop and the ficus in the entrance hallway, they were not something you stopped to look at.

It became clear that women would not be lining up to view

Mrs. Gutterman's brain because whenever Norman mentioned owning a fascinating medical specimen in a jar, he was greeted by suspicious looks. That had not been the case with Sally Caslon. She had seemed fond of the brain. It had been obvious, by the way she had taken the jar carefully in both her hands, placed it gently on the table by the cash box, wiped the dust off the glass, and finally handed it to him in exchange for his check, that it made her sad to let Arveda Gutterman go.

He often tried to remember Sally's face, but all he could see was a tumble of blonde curls and her cool blue eyes looking at him with some amusement. He had more success picturing her body underneath the baggy shirt and the flapping green shorts; he decided she had small firm breasts like apples, a little round butt, and a tight belly with a navel shaped like a comma. He thought about her so much, especially in the evenings after work, when he would sit on his couch and watch TV, his glance falling now and then on the brain, that when she called one night about two weeks later, he wasn't surprised.

"This is Sally Caslon," she said. "Do you remember me?"

"Sure," he said, as casually as he could.

"You bought an item at my grandfather's sale."

"Yes, the brain," he said uncertainly.

"Is this a bad time? I can call later."

"No, really. I'm glad to hear from you."

"I imagine you've been wishing you could return the damn thing and get your money back." Her tone was sympathetic. "I'm that way when I buy something on impulse."

"I don't know. It has found its place around here."

"Fifty dollars is a lot for something that doesn't work anymore." After a moment she added brightly, "I haven't deposited your check."

"You can go ahead and cash it. I'm happy with my purchase."

Norman heard disappointment in her voice. "Most people would think having a pickled brain around was disgusting."

"I like it."

"Where do you keep it?"

"Right here in the living room, by the TV. Sometimes I find the brain more engaging than the shows."

"That's quite a life you're leading."

"Thank you, I guess."

"I'll come out with it." He heard her take a deep breath. "I don't think Grandpa would approve of Mrs. G.'s brain going to a stranger."

"I get it now."

"You sound disappointed. If the brain means so much to you . . ."

"I meant that I thought this was a friendly call."

"Well, it can be," she said. "If you want to discuss selling Mrs. G. back to me."

"I was thinking a movie or a beer or something."

"Sure. That, too."

Sally and Norman made a date for Saturday night. They met in front of the Uptown Theater. Norman was afraid they wouldn't have anything to talk about besides her getting back the brain; he arrived early and bought tickets. He had expected her in the old man's shorts again, but this time she was wearing a dress. It was a blue cotton thing with sunflowers. It gathered around her small waist, showed off her cute knees, and rose snugly against her breasts. He decided she had the body he had visualized under the baggy shorts and T-shirt. Norman could tell those things even if he imagined far more bodies than he actually saw. He stared at her for a long time before even saying, "Hi."

"So what's wrong?" she asked. "Green stuff between my teeth, right?"

"No, you look nice," he said. "Just different from the last time."

"I suppose you always wear those shirts and khakis," she said.

"No, I've got different ones."

"I meant that kind of shirt." She looked at him quizzically. "The Polo shirt. You hardly see anyone wearing them anymore. Just older guys who've had them forever."

After the movie, Sally and Norman walked to the coffee place down the street from the theater. "You know why cappuccinos stay hot?" Sally blew on the thick head of frothed milk. "The foam makes a cozy little blanket over the coffee and milk."

"I do have other kinds of shirts, you know." Norman felt he could still improve on the impression he had initially made on her. "It's coincidence that the two times you've seen me I had on the same thing."

"There's nothing intrinsically awful about Polo shirts," Sally said. "They just make you look like you're not much fun."

Norman was silent. He realized there was no way he could persuade someone he could be a fun type of person. That was about showing, not telling. Perhaps, he thought, he should wear his own grandfather's Bermuda shorts. In any case, that was the last time Norman and Sally talked about his Polo shirts because he gave all four of them away to the Salvation Army.

After coffee, they went by his apartment so Sally could pick up Mrs. G. But first, Norman suggested they have a beer and sit on his couch because it was a new couch, he explained, and he had never sat with anyone on it. "I don't think women are attracted to guys named Norman," he said.

The only light in the room came from the small lamp on top of the TV; it cast a glow through the jar's murky suspension. "I like the name Norman all right," Sally murmured.

"It's not me. Norm is marginally better. But it makes me sound really ordinary. Here comes The Norm. Stick to The Norm. Do not depart from The Norm."

"The first time I heard your name, I thought right away of the killer in the movie *Psycho,*" she said.

"Norman Bates doesn't count. He wasn't real. He was a character in a movie."

"Sure, but there was a guy just like him in real life. He ran a motel and wore his mom's clothes."

"I don't suppose *his* name was Norman."

"Listen," she was quick to reassure him. "I didn't mean you were like Norman Bates. Not that at all. The coincidence is interesting, you have to admit."

At about this point in the conversation, Norm reached out his arm and rested it on the back of the couch behind Sally. The tips of his fingers tingled to the warm touch of the skin on her shoulder. He felt her stiffen, but a moment later she relaxed into the soft cushions of the couch and rested her head back. Sally's hair felt fine and silky on his bare arm. For Norman Tresh, this is what being a single guy was all about.

By the end of the evening, Sally and Norman had kissed extensively; he could still taste the strong espresso in her mouth. Once, as if obeying some curious impulse, she rested her hand briefly between his legs; he lacked the courage to ask her to do it again, but the lingering sensation fueled his desire for hours. They continued to explore each other through their clothes and got as close to having actual sex as they dared, given their recent acquaintance. But even as Sally was adjusting her dress and fixing her hair with a brush she borrowed from Norman's bathroom, they still hadn't agreed on where Mrs. G. should end up.

"What do you see in her brain, anyway?" she said.

"The more you examine it, the more you can sense a real personality there. I mean, Mrs. Gutterman was not just a mass murderer. I look at all those little bumps and wrinkles, and I sense she baked great pies, and sang in the choir, and loved growing flowers. It's given me some insights into human nature."

"I think that's cool. Certainly beyond the norm."

Her approval emboldened him. After all, she wouldn't be here if instead of the brain he had bought a set of gardening tools or her grandfather's stationary bike. "I would like to see you again," he said with unaccustomed confidence.

"Fine," she said, like it was no big deal.

"Mrs. G. will be here anytime you want to visit her."

"Fine," she repeated after a moment's thought. "But I'm not cashing your check yet."

That was the most perfect response he'd hoped for, even taking into account her lack of enthusiasm. Norman was happy. He and Sally now shared an unexpected bond. As long as he kept the brain, she would be back. After she'd gone, he gazed deep into the jar's cloudy fluid. He discovered that the hundreds of wrinkles and fissures all over the brain were shaped like little smiles. Now that was an unexpected insight.

EVeTs

It never fails. My hand shakes and my heart thumps and my
stomach knots up every time I buy Powerball lottery tickets.
This happens because I actually expect to win; the thought of
$84 million in the bank, once you accept it as a real likeli-
hood, is enough to make a stone hyperventilate. Today I
spend $280 on Lotto tickets at Doña Chole's liquor store on
Concord Street. My system is to plunk down the money, pick
the numbers, pack up the tickets. Sometimes, I also get a fifth
of Bacardi for rum and Cokes. First there is the investment in
the whims of fate, and then there is the trickle of rum, the fizz
of Coke, the pucker of lime. It's no system at all.

    I blow all this money on lottery tickets because I need to
move away from a certain person. I'm convinced I will win
the jackpot one day; I am one of those people whose whole
existence goes against the accepted odds. For example, when
I was seventeen I went on a personal, one-year crime wave
and held up ten convenience stores throughout the Twin
Cities. I was never caught and straightened out on my own
when I started to feel guilty about scaring people.

    There's more. I have a rare birthmark, a grouping of small

moles located on my left buttock in the exact configuration of the Orion constellation. The odds against such a thing are about 1,250,000 to one! (My two daughters are named Betelgeuse and Rigel, in honor of the two major stars in the group.) There are other interesting, rare things about me: I'm equally dexterous with my right and my left hands. The odds against this are 100,000 to one. My ears can pick up frequencies above 42,000 hertz. I have an IQ of 127. I've been married to Laura for eighteen years, the only woman I have loved since age four. I can touch the tip of my nose with my tongue, my forearm with my thumb, and my erect penis with my chin. Calculate the probability of all these things occurring in one person, and you're into astronomical numbers. Thirty million to one Powerball odds seem downright reasonable.

Once I win the jackpot, we will move far away from here. Not that the West Side is a bad place; we are far enough from St. Paul and North Minneapolis not to be caught in the crossfire yet close enough to cultural amenities. And even though Laura gets nervous about money, she knows there are weeks when I make a lot of it as one of the acknowledged star telemarketers at Sweet Talk, Inc. Ordinarily I net about $12 an hour, not enough to support my big lottery habit. But when I get assignments that operate on pure commission—rare coins, Twins season tickets, senior singles cruises, pre-need funeral services—I make out, well, like a bandit. I'm on the phone at all hours of the day and night, chatting up the East Coast in the morning, the West Coast in the afternoon, Europe in the middle of the night. I can talk to people in English or Spanish, which makes me a very global guy.

I have what is known in the trade as a Sincere Phone Voice (call me Mr. SPV). You can feel my voice worm itself right into your ear canal, squeezing through your eustachian tube, reverberating around your cochlea, to tell your brain we are old friends, that I care, that I understand. It's a voice that opens checkbooks on behalf of anything from the famous Paradise Bay Timeshares of Rosarito, Baja California, to the Saint Theresa Hospice for AIDS terminals (no connection with *the* Mother Theresa, but I don't have to say so unless someone flat out asks).

The one person who knows why I want to move away from here is Doña Chole, the seventy-nine-year-old woman who runs the liquor store. She looks at me through her thick green glasses and calls me *hijito.* It means little son. The store is one of a dozen scattered around the Cities owned by her nephew, whom she calls *hijo de la chingada,* which means son of a bitch, approximately. She doesn't care for him because he pays relatives low wages off the books. I tell Doña Chole that if she gives me a winner, I will write her a big retirement check just before I leave town. She sighs and shakes her head and brushes a strand of white hair away from her face. She says she will miss me. And my brother.

I don't have a brother. But she sometimes asks how my brother is doing anyway, that he hasn't been in the store in a while. I tell her he's fine just to humor her. She wants to know if I will share my prize with him, and I say, "No way." She says you can't escape the influence of a twin, that we are joined together by heavenly forces. I say, "Make me rich and watch me fly." I've spent years hoping to get the money together to quit my job and move far, far away from him.

For years people have told me there's this guy who looks exactly like me. Not that anyone has actually met him, but people have seen him at the grocery store or at clubs or at the mall. Sometimes people have gone up to him and said, "Hello, Steve," thinking it's me; I'm told he gives them a very cool response. Other times, people catch my eye and say something, but I don't much like talking to strangers, at least when they think I'm someone else. A person says, "Hi, thought you were working today." I say, "I don't work on Saturdays," and they say, "I thought you did," and then we both say, "Ha ha, there's been some mix-up. You are not who I think you are. I'm not who you think I am." Like that. It's become clear in all these years that this guy who looks like me does not know rocket scientists or zen masters or beautiful women.

I have often felt I should find this person and have a serious talk with him because the last thing I need is to be blamed for someone else's dirty deeds. I mean, I go to my job, I'm true to my wife, I drive sober. How do I know he isn't stealing, cheating, DWI-ing, drug dealing, gang banging, and otherwise disturbing the peace? Right, I don't.

That's why, for the last ten years, ever since my look-alike started cropping up with increasing frequency, I've always made sure I'm able to account for my whereabouts. And that people remember me: I chat with the couple sitting behind me at the movies; I have memorable exchanges of opinions with McDonald's order takers, bus drivers, hair cutters. Years ago, when Walter Mondale campaigned through here, I even picked a conversation with a guy who I deduced was Secret Service because of the black shades, tiny earphone, and shiny suit with lumps. I said to him I didn't think anyone would try to shoot Mondale because he was too nice a man. Everyone knew that. Except maybe for some fan of the Ayatollah's. Quick wit, no?

I wear conspicuous items of attire. I have a belt buckle with the likeness of Richard Nixon, a Brooklyn Dodgers cap, a hand painted Vargas Girl tie, a Grateful Dead 1972 World Tour T-shirt. These are not only eye-catching, memorable things, they are collector's pieces, not easily duplicated. For a while I also grew a variety of mustaches, fifties sideburns, Lenin goatees. Lately I've tried the opposite tack. I've decided

I want my face to be as ordinary and as forgettable as the next person's because it's too easy for the other guy to grow stuff and look even more like me. I have trimmed my hair to an overall one to one-and-a-half inches, shaved my face clean, and have adopted a bland expression—wide eyes, small smile, questioning eyebrows. It's a popular, perplexed kind of look; the more I look like everybody, the less I look like somebody.

Laura and I talk a lot about Evets. That's the name we've given him because it's easier to refer to him by some name than as The-Guy-Who-Stole-My-Face. At first she said I was making him up. But one time she thought she saw me driving along the freeway while I'd been home. It was a Saturday, and she should have known right away it wasn't me because he was in a red Mustang while I have a blue 1983 TransAm. He was going very fast (I'm usually right within the speed limit) and a cigarette dangled from his lip (I quit ages ago) and his left arm hung out the window with a big plastic watch on his wrist (I never wear a watch). We decided she had seen Evets.

"You believe me. It wasn't me," I rejoiced.

"No, he only *looked* like you."

"Did you find him attractive?"

"What's that got to do with it?" Laura has fair skin that blotches up around her neck when she gets horny or angry. I can usually tell which one it is.

"It has everything to do with it," I insisted. "The guy keeps trying to take over my life. Just tell me yes or no."

"Of course he was attractive. He resembled you."

"Did you find him good looking enough to have sex with him?"

"No. He wasn't you. Why would I want to?"

"But he looked like me, didn't he?" The idea of anyone else touching Laura makes my stomach churn. "Suppose I was dead and you met him at a party. Would you go out with him?"

"Sure, Steve," she said. "If you were dead, he would be the next best thing to the real live you, wouldn't he?" Then she stood up from the couch, her way of signaling that the conversation was over. "On the other hand, I might just head out the door and run."

Whole weeks go by when I don't give Evets a thought. Nobody tells me they have seen him. Nobody sees *me* and thinks it's him. I find myself imagining that he has realized this neighborhood is just too small for the two of us. But then, *wham!* One night around five A.M. after I've been waking up people in Barcelona with my pitch on $799 vacations to Mexico, I leave work and I'm walking down the street to my car, just enjoying the quiet of the dawn, the cool breeze that blows from the west, the sky for once so clear that I can see Orion. I feel good; I've just worked fourteen hours nonstop, and I'm still high from the phone, my voice just now warmed up to a golden sheen. I'm thinking there is nothing I can't achieve by talking—run for office, save souls, tell jokes, whisper secrets, seduce the deaf.

But today I couldn't talk myself out of getting punched in the face by a man I'd never seen before. He must have been waiting for me, leaning against a black Cadillac, totally absorbed with his nails. He was big and squat-bodied and he wore a fedora. Even as he squared off in front of me and was pulling back his arm, like a kid with a slingshot, his hand balled up into a mass of gnarled knuckles flying at my nose, I was speechless. I wanted to tell him I could not be who he thought I was because nobody hates me enough to punch me out like that. He hit and ran before I found out whose nose he thought he had smashed.

The next day I go by Doña Chole's and buy one hundred dollars worth of Powerball. She takes a look at my nose and asks what does it feel like to be hit so hard. I tell her I saw a bright light and that my brain felt exposed to a cold wind and that I have a headache that I expect will last the rest of my life.

"Maybe this time you will win," she says. "To make up for this other piece of bad luck."

I nod in agreement. "I would give you another hundred dollars if I had it."

"You will win a lot of money." Her milky eyes peer at me over the rims of her green glasses. "What will you do with the money?"

"You always ask me that," I smile. "And I always tell you the same thing."

"I ask because it is part of the good luck to have a clear picture of what you will do."

"I will take my family and move to Minnetonka. Everybody lives by a lake except me."

"Will you take your brother?"

"Never in a thousand years."

"In that case," she says. "You will not have good luck."

"Watch it, *vieja.*" I point a finger at her for emphasis. "I buy a lot of lottery tickets from you. I need your good wishes, not your curses."

"Save your money, *tontito.*"

This afternoon at work, I feel I'm a magnet for money, that all I need to do is be in its way when it comes blowing in my direction. That it doesn't depend on Doña Chole or Evets or luck. Money is all around me, ready to be harvested. I put on my headset, bend the microphone so it almost touches my lips, and talk to women across America. I ask them what kind of a day they are having and how they'd like for me to send them three dozen pairs of pantyhose for $17.99 plus $4.00 P&H. I have on my best voice; the breath, the dulcet tones, the incipient boyish chuckle. When I describe the colors of the hose *(cocoa, nutmeg, cinnamon, pecan, flesh),* they can feel my eyes on their legs. When I extol the stockings' texture *(smooth, silky, electric),* they can feel my fingers glide along the inside of their thighs. When I talk about the strength of these pantyhose (thanks to special triple knitting in problem areas like heel and crotch), they can sense me begging at the door of their sacred temple. The orders come in by the bagful. I am the silver-tongued devil. The lips of Midas. A very deep throat. After about two hours of this unbroken litany to the gods of long-distance commerce, my supervisor, a former star of the phone bank who was promoted after he developed a sudden case of stuttering and now signs his memos *T-T-T-Tom,* tells me t-t-t-to g-g-g-go ho-ho-home and not come back for a while. "You need a f-f-f-furlough," he says.

"What did I do?" I want to know. "I was going great."

"You sound like some ha-ha-ha-harasser."

"You were listening in on me again," I complain. "I can't do a good job if I know management is monitoring."

"Steve," Laura exclaims as soon as I get home. "You got yourself fired?"

"Unpaid leave. It is not the same thing. This is temporary. Business conditions and all."

"You were fucking fired," she shakes her head sadly.

I stay cool. "You know we shouldn't use obscene language in front of the girls." Nearby, our two daughters do their homework on the dining table. They are sweet, serious children.

"Betty, Rigel," Laura turns to them. "Go to your room, sweethearts, your daddy and I have money things to discuss."

They sigh in unison, gather their notebooks and pens, and with the air of battle weary troopers, march up the stairs. Laura and I are left alone to hash out our differences. I go first.

"You've made two mistakes, Laura. Before we even start this disagreeable conversation, you've already blown two big ones."

"I'm listening," she says. This is her usual tactic, to let me carry on until I'm all talked out and then wham, she hits me with some last minute, left brained, quasi-logical accusation.

"One, we don't ever tell the children we have money matters to discuss. Children should go to bed at night with full bellies and happy thoughts."

"And two?"

"Betty's name is not Betty. It's Betelgeuse. She was named after a major star. It's a beautiful name, and that's what she should be called. You don't think it matters. But consider what a Betty is apt to grow up to be. A beach bunny, that's what. Betelgeuse will grow up to be a poet or a cellist or a theologian."

"She wants to be Betty."

"She's eleven. She doesn't know what's good for her yet. Call her Betelgeuse. She'll thank you later."

There is not much else to talk about except for the fact that until I'm making money again, we'll need to make sacrifices. Rum and Cokes are out; the Grateful Dead are out; Powerball is out. Then we hug and tell each other things will turn out fine, that they always do, and that the feeling I had earlier in the day about money coming to me with all the certainty of raindrops landing on my head is still there. We make big, sweaty, intricate love. By the time we uncouple at last, rolling onto our backs, wet skin bare to the cool evening air, we've been going at it for hours, performing all kinds of slow, subtle, maddening tricks of finger and tongue. I don't exaggerate. Two examples: Laura wraps my erect manhood in her long, thick brown hair; I flick the tip of my tongue across her eyelids. Enough said.

Much later that night, sometime after two A.M., I slip into

the girls' bedroom to make sure that the harmony that Laura and I have reached after our battle has extended to them. It has been this way ever since they were babies. When Laura and I were happy, small rays of contentment seemed to travel up and down the house, coiling themselves around the two sleeping bodies, cradling them in waves of bliss that you could see in their contented smiles, in their happy gurgling sounds, in their satisfied burps.

Rigel, the younger at five, is curled up in a tangle of sheets, hands balled up into fists on the pillow by her cheek, as if she had dropped asleep while in the middle of some silent boxing match. I turn to the other twin bed and see that Betelgeuse is wide awake, her dark, burning eyes rolled up in her head so that I see mostly the whites, arms stiffly at her sides, lips pursed. When she gets angry, she likes to make believe she's dead, her spirit hovering above the frantic rush and tangle of the wake, the funeral, the burial. She takes after me.

Still, I think I may be able to summon her back to the land of the living for a father-daughter talk on the matter of her identity, the meaning of her name, her aspirations in life. Eleven is not too young to deal with stuff like that. I start by asking her what she wants to be when she grows up.

"A beach bunny," she says.

In the first week since being laid off, I'm suprised at how clearly I sense the presence of Evets hovering around me. Four sightings in one week is not trivial. It's not just the frequency of Evets's presence that concerns me but his proximity.

On Tuesday, he was spotted in a phone booth just two blocks from here at two-thirty in the morning. He was singing "Tommy, Can You Hear Me?" into the phone. When he did not receive a reply to his question, he clutched the receiver like a hammer and banged it on the coin return slot in an apparent effort to retrieve his quarter.

The next night, just around the corner, a man who could only be Evets woke up the neighbors by engaging in a barking match with Sultan, the black Lab that lives at 358 Hilldale. Well, thanks a lot, genius. Sultan got excited, and one woof-woof led to another woof-woof, and pretty soon dogs were barking up and down the street, and Sultan's owners were on the phone to the police. Evets was gone by the time the cops came; it took all night to get Sultan and his pals to quiet down.

Thursday, nothing. Friday, quiet. On Saturday, his behavior got erratic. Evets lost one of his loafers while getting off the bus. There are a dozen ways you can lose a shoe besides jumping on and off buses, which accounts for all that widowed footwear strewn on the roads of America. Most people who drop a shoe pick it up and put it back on. But not Evets. He thought the shoe had stayed on the bus rather than fallen on the street. He chased the bus as it pulled away, half hobbling, half running, one foot bare, the other shod, yelling to the driver, "Stop, stop, you've got my goddamn shoe." He ran for two blocks until he caught up with the bus at the next stop. But when he started to get on to look for his loafer, the driver insisted that he pay the fare. No dollar, no admission to the bus. In the end, Evets gave up, got off the bus, and was last seen wandering up and down the street in search of his lost shoe. The story was told to me by Laura, who heard it from our neighbor Flora Gómez, who was on the bus at the time.

A pattern is taking shape. Evets is closer and therefore more threatening. Has he moved into the block now? Will my children start seeing me being other than me, actually him looking like me? And what will that do to them?

It's like him to take advantage of my defeated, idled status. Some days, when it's too hot to be in the house, I sit in the library and check out books to improve my career prospects: *Chaos, Seven Habits of Highly Effective People.* I also hang around the house; I take naps and watch *Geraldo* and stuff while the girls are at school and Laura steps up her sales of Mary Kay. I don't mind the sitting around part so much; the bad thing is that whole blocks of three and four hours go by in which I have no way to account for my actions, no alibi, no witnesses. I'm at the mercy of Evets, who could do something terrible, and I wouldn't be able to prove that it hadn't been me.

During all these years, I have learned to anticipate people's questions; I can handle Doña Chole's attempts to reconcile us; I've learned to ignore stangers' stares.

By the same token, I figure if I know about him, he must also know about me. Just as I would like to be able to move away, he may also feel his life would be easier with one of us out of the picture. The pattern of the past few days shows him as increasingly aggressive, possibly even going out of his way to embarrass me into leaving. Two can play that game, Mr. Evets.

A plan is born. The first thing is to build Evets from the skin out. While I can't fully picture who I'm supposed to create, I need to uncreate, disassemble, unravel the actual me so that I can replace myself with the other who looks like me but is not me. For this purpose, I'm grateful for the long mornings when Laura is off on her calls and the girls are in school. After nine, the house falls silent. There is just the sighing of the walls, the creaking of the roof under the warming sun, the whirring and humming and ticking of all our electric stuff, somehow alive and alert even when the switches are on OFF.

As *Quality: Japanese Style* puts it, "Trifles make perfection. And perfection is no trifle." I'm naked from the calloses on my heels to the static electricity on top of my head. It takes an effort of will to stand in front of the mirror with no corrective flexing of my pectorals, no tucking in of the buttocks, no withdrawing of the stomach. To stand there, feet apart, arms akimbo, is an education. This is the raw material out of which Evets will be created.

Toenails, which I've always pared to follow the curve of the flesh, are now to be clipped blunt across the top. Hair, which has been parted on the left for forty years, gets slicked back. Part of this exercise demands a painful confrontation with reality. Now, looking at myself as I am, I see that if I can withdraw my belly, not just when I'm under the focus of self-scrutiny but all the time, I will gain a markedly different body stance.

By the following week, I've solved the sagging midriff problem with a corrective girdle made of high tensile nylon mesh, $48.95 from Dr. Kilgore's Cosmoform Technologies of Indianapolis. I stand in front of the mirror, I turn left, then right, check myself from the back. Am I starting to look more like Evets? Other changes I can only wonder about. A reversal of circumcision? Thicker body hair? Idle speculation at this point.

One day I wander the men's section at Marshall's, running my fingers through the fabrics of the 40R sport coats and suits lined up on a rack. I think back to the different sightings of Evets that have been reported, and I realize there hasn't been any mention of what he wore. I try to visualize Evets dressed for work or for Saturday afternoon chores or for a big night on the town. He keeps slipping away. The first decision I make is for a short-sleeved shirt with blue vertical stripes on a pale yellow background, button-down collar, one pocket on the left side.

The shirt sets the pattern for everything else that I get for Evets's wardrobe. The pants are brown houndstooth check. They are a little short, so the socks are important. I'm torn between blue-and-gold paisley and plain green. I go with the paisley. The shoes are penny loafers, one size too big. (That's how he ended up losing one while getting off the bus.) There are other details: a black plastic digital watch, three uni-ball MICRO pens for the shirt pocket, the top caps in blue, black, and red, a pack of Merit cigarettes, and a book of matches advertising the International Correspondence Schools. I steal everything; it's the way to make sure stuff is not traced back to me.

Evets's clothes and accessories go into a round hat case I've hidden in the basement on a high shelf behind Betelgeuse and Rigel's old toys. The shirt, pants, and socks I have washed a number of times; they look as if somebody has had them for years. So far, I haven't had the courage to wear them. I have, however, put on Evets's shoes and gone for walks in our back-yard in order to get them scuffed. After the latest washing and high-heat drying, I am tempted to try on the whole outfit; I decide to hold off until I'm ready to make the move. What am I waiting for? Payday.

A few minutes past eight P.M. on an end-of-the-month Friday, I kiss the girls goodnight and tell Laura I need to return books to the library before it closes. She makes a remark about not knowing I could read, and I say something about improving my mind so it can keep up with hers. We've taken to trading good-natured barbs since I was laid off; it keeps serious conflict at bay. I throw the hat box on the back-seat of the car and then drive two blocks to the Amoco sta-tion on Robert Street.

In the men's room out back behind the alley, it takes me about ten minutes to pull off my tie-dyed T-shirt and the jeans with the rips and to put on the Evets things. I could do it in five except that my hands shake so much that I snag the edge of my briefs in the zipper and have to yank it up and down to get it loose. Then the buttons on the shirt pose a problem because I don't get them lined up and I have to start over again.

I'm ready. I stick the pens in the pocket and open up the pack of Merits, flushing about half down the toilet. Finally, I run gel through my hair and comb it back.

For a moment, as I look at my reflection under the washroom's fluorescent lights, I marvel at my odd new appearance. Ordinary details seem magnified; my teeth are more crooked, the bags under my eyes more pronounced. My breath comes in sharp pants and my heart thumps erratically; I have the queasy sensation of not knowing at this particular moment who I am or where I am or why I am who I am now. The small voice inside that knows me well, even when I'm feeling old or sick or drunk, is silent.

On the way to Doña Chole's liquor store, I practice in my mind this strange and risky act I'm about to perform. There will be first one small step, then another small step. If at any time Doña Chole appears to know who I am, that I'm not Evets, I can change my mind. The plug is pulled. The mission aborted. Ooooops. *Adiós.*

I head out on Concord and slow down past Doña Chole's. I circle the block twice to make sure that the last of her customers has left the place and that she is alone, waiting for her nephew to come for the day's take. The trick is to get in and out before he shows and while the store is empty of customers. But even if someone does show up, the critical part of the evening will only take thirty seconds, and there will be no way to know what is happening until, *Bam!* It happens.

I don't think she hears me come in because I stand at the counter in front of the cash register for several moments before she realizes I am here. Then she comes over to me squinting a little, and I wait for the first test to happen: if she asks me how many lottery tickets I want, then she knows I'm not Evets.

Doña Chole shuffles over and stares at me through her thick glasses.

"Can I help you?" There's no clue whether she knows me or not.

"Yes, I can't find what I came for."

"So tell me what you want. Is it a secret?" Again, she does not offer me any tickets.

"A fifth of Cuervo tequila," I say, instead of my usual Bacardi. Test number two.

She doesn't even blink those big cloudy eyes of hers, just reaches to the left of the counter and puts a bottle of Cuervo inside a paper sack. "That will be twelve dollars," she says.

"There is something else I want," I say. Test number three.

She looks at me for several moments. "Am I supposed to guess?" she asks.

I look behind me for a moment, notice that the store is still empty. Then I stand a little to one side so there's a display of Tecate beer cans between me and the glass front. I say, "I want all the money in your cash register, señora. Put it in the bag with the bottle."

"Would you hurt an old woman?"

"No, señora. I'm just going to jump behind the counter and take your payday money," I say. "Unless you put it in the bag for me."

"Do you have a gun?"

"Unfortunately, yes, señora," I lie. "It's in my pocket."

She sighs. She presses down the NO SALE button on the old register, and the cash drawer slides out with a metallic clatter. I lean across the counter, grab handfuls of bills, mostly fives and ones, and stuff them into the paper sack. I leave a twenty on the counter in payment for the tequila.

I say *gracias* to Doña Chole and back out the door, clutching the bag with the tequila and the money close to my chest, making sure she doesn't reach for the phone yet.

"I know who you are," she calls out to me from behind the counter. "I will tell your brother about this. You are polite like he is. But he will not be happy to hear you are a thief."

It's a few minutes after ten when I get home. Even with a stop at the Amoco station to change back into my own clothes, then a swing to return books to the library, where I push the books in through the night slot and shout behind them that the *Habits of Effective People* are a load of b.s., the whole thing has taken an hour. I put the Cuervo and the $876 from the cash register inside the the hat box. Laura is watching *Cheers* reruns and doesn't pay attention to me while I take the stuff down to the basement. Later tonight, even as I'm drifting off to sleep, Doña Chole will be talking to the police. She will tell them that a robber came to her store, threatened her with a gun, bought a bottle of Tequila, and stole her nephew's money.

The word will be out: Find Evets.

BUddiEs

Until this week, Ed Beechum hadn't personally known anyone who'd had a quadruple bypass. Vasectomies, procto-
scopies, and hemorrhoid laser zaps, yes. Also, some C-sec-
tions among the wives in their circle, plus rumors of an occasional rhynoplasty, a liposuction, or the rare, unhappy mas-
tectomy. "But it's different with women," he commiserated
with his friend Neil Haskell. "Women have a greater toler-
ance for pain."

Neil nodded, as if giving the matter lengthy consideration.
He was sitting against a pile of pillows bunched up strategi-
cally to keep his torso more or less vertical. His face, through
the prickly black stubble of three days' growth, appeared gray
and dry as paper. His eyes were dull, the whites around the
opaque brown irises were the pale yellow of soft butter. He
had tried to comb his hair without a mirror but had succeed-
ed only in rearranging the thin strands on top of his head to
reveal a latticework of pink scalp.

"How do you feel, anyway?" Ed asked, shifting his gaze
away from his friend's head.

"Okay, I guess." Neil tried to describe his condition for the first time since emerging from intensive care four days earlier. "Aside from the pain."

"You look hung over."

"Right," he smiled weakly. "Too much to drink and then run over by a truck." Wincing at the pain, he started to undo the buttons of his blue-and-gray striped pajama top. "Want to see the tread marks?"

"No, thanks, buddy. I believe you." Beechum stood up from the chair and paced about the room.

"It's impressive," his friend insisted. "They saw through your breastbone and pull the ribs apart with steel clamps. They disconnect the valves while they keep the blood flowing through plastic tubes. They grab some natural piping from a tough old vein down in the leg, then they reattach every-thing, push the ribs back together, and sew you up. Bingo."

Ed wondered if his friend had owned those pajamas before the operation or if they were something his wife had bought for him to convalesce in. There was something depressing about the blue-and-gray stripes, a design common in mat-tress ticking; they belonged on asylum inmates or, buttoned all the way up to the chin, on old men with thin blood. He ventured a glance toward the bed and saw that Neil had opened the front of his shirt to reveal a thick gauze pad the size of a small pillow attached to his skin with satiny adhesive tape. "Fooled you. *I* don't even know what it looks like down there. I do know that my chest and legs looked like a boy's once they shaved all the hair off." Neil tried to grin even as he was convulsed by a weak, hacking cough. "It only hurts when I laugh," he said.

Then, after a moment, he added seriously, "It's great of you to hang out with me while Mary Ann is out. I told her I could stay by myself, but they're all worried that I'm so weak I'll fall from the bed and not be able to get up."

"Hey, buddy," Ed raised his hand in protest. "Don't even mention it."

Neil closed his eyes. After a few seconds, his breathing became deep and rhythmical, almost as if he'd fallen asleep in midthought. Ed remembered what Mary Ann had said about her husband's energy being low, about needing these quick small naps as his body began to recover from the exhausting experience of having its heart handled like plumbing. "It's natural. Let him sleep. If he's hungry, there's soup on the stove. If he's thirsty, he can sip grapefruit juice through the built-in straw." She'd held up a plastic Mickey Mouse cup with a tube sticking up between its ears. "As long as you keep Mickey's head screwed on, it's spillproof. See?" She turned the cup upside down.

Ed looked at his watch. The sudden intimacy of sitting in his friend's bedroom, which was dark and gloomy and smelled vaguely of medicine and wilted bed linens, made him feel as if he were being pushed against some stranger inside a packed elevator: someone else's aftershave, the press of another's body under unfamiliar clothes, and the moist breath redolent of garlic or tobacco or antacid mints. There was no relaxing in a situation like this. While he had known Neil Haskell for over twenty years, ever since they had been classmates at William Mitchell Law School and then, for a brief time, associates at the same firm in St. Paul, this was the first occasion in years they had spent even an hour alone together without wives or colleagues or children around. He wished Neil would continue to sleep.

"How about a drink?" his friend spoke suddenly, his eyes popping open as if he were surprised to be awake. "I haven't been a very good host."

"Sure, I could have some juice with you," Ed indicated the cup on the night table.

"The carton's in the fridge," Neil said helpfully. "I'd get it, but it would take an hour for both of us to trudge down the stairs and then back up again."

When Ed returned a couple of minutes later, his friend was clicking the remote through all forty-five channels of cable. "There's got to be a game on. Want to watch a game?"

"It's Wednesday morning," Ed shrugged. "Nobody plays anything on Wednesday mornings."

"Except bowling on ESPN," Neil offered, pausing on the channel. "It's women's bowling," he smiled apologetically. "Makes it more interesting, though. Women bowlers are known for their great bodies, you know."

"Yes, almost like gymnasts," Ed ventured.

"We can have it on without the sound," he said, pressing the mute button. "Do you bowl?"

"Do I bowl?" Ed repeated.

"It's not a dumb question, is it?"

He shrugged. "No, I don't bowl. Do you?"

"No." Neil tilted his head forward from the massed pillows behind him and asked seriously, "Why is this conversation weird?"

"I didn't say it was weird."

"I'm the one says it's weird."

"Maybe because we've known each other for over twenty years and if one of us bowled, the other would know about it."

"That's it." Then, holding out his glass, he signaled a toast. "Salud, old buddy."

"Cheers." Ed leaned across the bed to click glasses.

"There's some Stoli in the den, buddy."

"Should you be drinking?"

"I'm not driving anywhere." And then he added in a mock whisper, "Synergy. Vodka punches up the Vicoden." When Ed came back with the bottle, he saw that Neil had fallen asleep again. The only sound in the room was the quiet hum of the TV, its bright image sending flickering reflections over the walls and dresser mirror to one side of the room. He poured some vodka into his juice glass and sat back on the chair to watch the women's bowling tournament. The Milwaukee Beer Maidens and the Duluth Ice Queens were fighting it out for first place. How'd you like to run into one of those Maidens in a dark alley, he wanted to say to Neil. But his friend was sound asleep.

There was a shot of the four women from Milwaukee, a strong-looking group with sturdy thighs, large square butts inside their jeans, and plump breasts under the crisp lime-green bowling shirts. The captain's name was R. Mostov; it was embroidered above her heart. She held the ball in front of her eyes, squinting as she tried to get a bead on the key front pin, her brown hair feathered and blow-dried, right out of the seventies. As the camera held on a close-up, he saw her pucker her lips and kiss the shiny black surface.

She swung it back and, as if she were unleashing a wrecking ball, sent it skating over the gleaming hardwood into the apex of the triangle. The ball disappeared in a tumult of exploding white pins that tumbled up in the air, flying and ricocheting in different directions, and ended up scattered about like dead soldiers.

"Did you see her kiss the ball? What a moment," Neil sighed as the camera cut to Mostov the Beer Maiden still holding her final position, one leg outstretched, the other bent at the knee, her fingers extended and, surely, tingling still from the ball's release.

"I didn't realize you'd woken up."

"I wasn't asleep. I had my eyes closed because I was praying for her to get a strike." He took a sip from his cup. "I thought you put vodka in this."

"Not yet. I was waiting for you to wake up." Ed twisted off the cap and poured some into the top of Mickey Mouse's head. "Say when."

"Don't worry about me, buddy. I didn't know it, but during the last couple of years I was this close to keeling over from a heart attack. I'm a survivor. We should drink to that." Neil took a long pull from the plastic straw. "I used to think I didn't want to die drunk."

"What are you talking about? You should be thinking healthy thoughts."

"Hey, I'm the patient here. I'll talk about whatever I want to, OK?"

"No problem with me." Ed was quick to mollify him.

He took a deep breath and closed his eyes as if to collect his thoughts. "Whenever I'd go on a business trip, I never drank during the flight, even when I flew First Class and the booze was free. I didn't drink because if the plane crashed, I wanted to go thinking clearly. Don't ask me why. I just felt that dying was such a big step that to take it drunk would start me off on the wrong foot. Do you know what I mean?"

"I can tell this conversation is getting deep," Beechum laughed.

"Who do you go to when you want to get things off your chest?" Neil asked tentatively.

"Not your cardiologist."

"You're not listening." Neil sighed and let his head fall back against the pillows. "I mean, I think I've got something important to say. Can we try again?"

"Sorry, buddy," Ed shrugged. "Mary Ann said I should keep you from getting too glum."

"I wasn't talking about death. I was talking about getting drunk. That's the issue. I believe you shouldn't drive drunk. That you shouldn't pick fights drunk. That you shouldn't dance with other guys' wives drunk. But after being under all the sedation and anesthesia, I realized it doesn't matter if you die drunk."

"I can't say much for dying sober, either."

"Know what? My wife doesn't know shit about glum or happy," Neil explained. "Right now, what would make me happy is for you to pour us each another drink. Go ahead, kick back. We can talk."

Ed nodded. He poured a shot into his glass and into Neil's cup and topped both up with juice. "Cheers. I'm putting my money on the Beer Maidens."

"You would." Neil took a sip from his cup and made an elaborate wink in Ed's direction.

"They're the better team."

"Well, sure. Now it turns out you're an expert on bowling."

"I sure as hell could be, couldn't I?" Ed laughed, concentrating on the next bowler up. "For all you know, I was a champion bowler in another life."

"Or you banged one in this life," Neil chuckled. "Look, here she is now."

"What are you talking about?"

"Miss Mostov from Milwaukee," Neil nodded toward the TV as the grim-faced team captain selected her ball from the carousel. "Who does she remind you of?"

Ed thought for a moment. "Nobody."

"Just look at her." The two men were quiet as Mostov went through her paces and gracefully bowled another strike. "Jesus, it's amazing, isn't it?"

"I can't believe we're sitting around here talking about bowling."

"I'm not talking about bowling," Neil said. "I'm just pointing out that the captain of the Milwaukee Beer Maidens bears a strong resemblence to a woman in your—in our—past."

"Really? Somebody we knew?"

"You knew her better than I did."

"Somebody from law school?"

"No," Neil answered coyly.

"Somebody's wife?"

"Not anybody's that we knew."

"Newburn, Stollard, and Green?"

"Bingo." Neil smiled broadly for the first time that day. "Actually, she only worked there one day."

"Mostov the Bowler?"

"Yes, Roberta Clements was her name then." Neil pronounced the name with relish. "She was a temp," he added after a moment. "Honestly, doesn't the bowler remind you of her? Same hair, same tough look, initial *R.*"

Ed looked at his friend curiously as Neil gestured toward the TV. Ed turned away in time to see the captain of the Beer Maidens accept a trophy on behalf of her team. She still had that serious, almost scowling look. Then, as the camera pulled back to show her lifting the trophy above her head while her three teammates cheered, she allowed herself a brief, radiant smile. A moment later, when she shook the judge's hand, her face had regained the tough, streetwise look.

"Hey, she's going to say something," Neil exclaimed, straightening himself up on the bed. "Victory speech."

"We'd like to thank the H.G. Heileman Brewing Company of Milwaukeee, Wisconsin, and Local 31 for the time off and the money to make this tour. It shows what happens when everybody pulls together. Also thanks to our parents, three boyfriends, and one husband, and the Starlight Bowling Palace of Kenosha for the free practice time. All right, Beer Maidens!" She ended on a big note, raising the trophy above her head to applause and scattered cheers while the theme from *Chariots of Fire* played in the background and the credits for the Regional Bowling Championships telecast scrolled down the screen.

"All right, Beer Maidens," Neil echoed, making his voice deep. "Don't you just love that voice? It's so throaty, like it could growl, given the right circumstances. That's how Roberta Clements talked."

"You sound a lot better."

"I feel somewhat better," Neil gestured to Ed with his Mickey Mouse cup. "Just a little juice with my vodka," he said. "Or I'll be pissing all afternoon."

"To bowling," Ed said, raising his glass.

"This is not about bowling. Bowling is not about bowling," he tried to clarify.

"Well, here's to R. Mostov."

"No, asshole. Here's to Roberta Clements."

Ed shrugged in mock surrender. "Oκ, who the hell's Roberta?"

"You really don't remember?"

"Well, if she worked at Newburn, Stollard, and Green, it's been twenty-something years."

"We were getting a brief together. About three hundred pages for Intelco's board meeting the next morning. It was going to take all night. We got this temp to help with corrections and copies and collating. No big deal. She was just some kid taking on part-time work to help out with school. I think it was her first job in a big office."

"That was Roberta?"

"Right. By eight or so, it was just the three of us left in the office. We all knew it was going to be a long night. I'd only been married about six months. It was a big deal calling Mary Ann and telling her I wouldn't be home."

"So what happened?"

"It was a mess, at first. We had to show her how to run every-

thing, the copier, the collator, even the fucking coffeemaker."
Neil laughed. "First the green button, then the number buttons, then the red button. Lift, pull, snap. Over and over."

"I remember now. I think."

"Finally!" Neil let his head fall back against the pillow. "It
all comes back to him."

Ed recalled that by midnight the building's air-conditioning had shut itself off, and a dense stillness had fallen over the
empty law office. Other sounds were magnified, their voices,
the whirr and click of the copying machines, the tinny disco
music coming from Roberta's small transistor radio.

"I can't work without music," she had said. "I hope it does-
n't bother you guys."

She couldn't work with music, either. Typing was for her a
process of constant exploration, every strike of a key a small
discovery, every paragraph without error a triumph. The
completion of a page was cause for celebration.

As the night progressed, Ed knew their careers at Newburn,
Stollard, and Green were in someone else's hands. If in two
years they were passed over for partnership, if they were ever
sued for legal malpractice, if their Supreme Court justice
nominations were not confirmed, they knew they would
have Roberta Clements to thank for their ill fortune.

Meanwhile, Roberta seemed unaware of the disasters she was
courting. She actually appeared confident that she was improving her typing by the hour and mastering the process of copying, binding, and collating; she was starting to enjoy herself.

By eleven, she was moving around the office with assur-
ance, aware that the two guys had little else to do but watch
her as she went about her work, confidently now, swinging
her hips from side to side as if she were on a dance floor. She
would lean over to place a document on a desk and offer a
glimpse of her breasts rising out of the knit halter top. Hands

would brush when they exchanged papers. She pressed a breast against Neil's arm when he explained how to unjam the copier. She pushed her chair close to Ed so their knees touched as he pointed out yet another typo.

"She was driving us nuts, wasn't she?" Neil asked. "Did you bang her?"

"I don't remember," Ed replied.

"We finished the briefs around two A.M. I wanted to take her home. She wanted me to take her home." Neil sighed, as if the effort of recalling the episode was too much for him. "*You* ended up taking her home. How did you manage to butt in?"

"I thought you should go home to your wife."

"So you banged her for me?"

"I don't think so."

"You banged her." Neil took the Mickey Mouse cup and raised it in a small toast before taking a long sip. "You knew she was coming on to us. Jesus Christ, to you and me both."

Ed shrugged. "She just wanted to make up for messing up the project."

Neil shook his head. "There was a real tension in the room with just the three of us there. I've never had anything like that happen to me again."

"What a waste, right?" Ed forced out a small laugh. "After she finished, the three of us sat around for a while, just staring at the mountain of briefs in their green Newburn, Stollard, and Green, binders. And then I drove her home."

"You don't remember if you slept with her? It's not like you've had hundreds of women. I know you that well."

"I think I wanted to, but really, I just dropped her off," Ed said.

"We could've had an orgy, for Christ's sake."

"That would've been different. You don't forget your first orgy." Ed turned to the TV. Bowling had given way to golf.

"Is this conversation weird?" Neil asked. "I don't know," he answered himself. "Ever since I came to from the surgery, I've been getting these questions. As if I had to sort out the loose ends of my life. Could I have banged Roberta? Did you bang Roberta? Would Roberta have banged the two of us? I mean, nobody else cares."

"You're the guy who almost died. You're entitled to talk about anything you want."

"If you remembered banging her, you'd tell me, right?"

"I think so," Ed said. "Why wouldn't I."

Neil turned away and stared at the golf tournament. He was silent for several moments. He seemed to have put the matter to rest. He had been dozing off and on when he woke up suddenly. "Jesus, that was a fine putt," he said. "Did you see that? Twenty feet."

The tHinGs he rememBers

In the dark, the giant TV screen, all sixty-five inches of almost
high definition, crystal sharpness, vibrating phosphores-
cence, exudes a luminous presence that bathes the whole
room in a palette of screaming primary tones; it washes over
the seated figure of Jeff Garza, making the golden skin on his
face and hands glow like fever. Jeff surfs along the universe,
ah how he flies, hand firmly on the remote, eighty channels
of digital satellite stuff booming in Surround Sound. Jeff
hungers for close-ups. *Lawrence of Arabia* does not belong on
TV; all those acres of undulating dunes seem crammed into a
sandbox populated by plastic cereal box tokens. Television is
about intimacy.

Jeff Garza clicks to a huge head, all pink skin and white teeth
in crisp detail, down to the nose hair. *Click.* A single gleaming
spoonful of Cocoa Puffs swimming in milk. *Click.* A butt in a
bikini, lime green on coffee brown. *Hold that thought.* Lust
bigger than life. The adrenaline rush of the nightly news, big
laughs for small jokes, sublime hair, teeth, hands.

Jeff Garza remembers the very last thing he saw on TV. Not
too many people can make that claim. It's usually in one eye

and out the other. Perhaps someone is lying in bed, propped up on a couple of pillows, a wife breathing heavily beside him, and one moment he's watching, and the next he's asleep, the screen left on its own to flicker and hum through the night. Imagine those being the very last images someone sees on TV. Imagine not remembering.

Jeff remembers a woman in a white coat—your basic, straight-ahead pitch in a flat medium shot but wide enough to include the pen in the breast pocket, glasses hanging from a gold chain, pink silk ruffles under the medical smock. She held her hand palm up toward the camera as if she were begging. That's what got Jeff's attention in the first place, the apparently empty hand. When the camera zoomed in, Jeff could see that in the middle of her palm rested a tiny curled piece of plastic shaped like an embryo. It was a Magic Ear. She picked it up, using the thumb and index fingers of her other hand as delicately as tweezers. Jeff noted her finely manicured nails, the delicate blue veins on the inside of her wrist, and the deep lines on her palm that augured wealth, a faithful husband, and a long life. The woman looked right past the camera directly at him, her energy bursting out of the screen and filling the small cluttered room; Jeff wondered what was the point of talking to the deaf.

He leans back on the couch, tilts his head back, and falls asleep with his mouth open, as if in the middle of being surprised. He is startled awake by the buzz of the off-the-air station and the brilliant white light of the empty screen shining on him. When he closes his eyes again, the bright light remains trapped on the inside of his eyelids. He stretches out along the whole length of the couch and stays there, dozing on and off through the night. He keeps waking up and for a moment panics, but then he sees the light from the screen and goes back to sleep. In the dark he can't see much else, not the TV cabinet or the cluster of shiny black knobs below the screen or the table on which the TV rests. The light fills the whole of his vision. In the morning, the glow is there wherever he looks. Jeff feels around for the phone, gets Dr. Lucians's long-forgotten number from 411, and makes an appointment for the earliest open slot.

The slow grinding transition from the bright night into the metallic gray dawn of the city is a melancholy time. In the morning the apartment feels cold and much too quiet, and in spite of its compact size, empty with a kind of windblown desolation, as if the drafty downtown canyons all managed to converge in the third floor of The Holland House building. He feels better after his second cup of coffee.

The Holland House, with its pots of plastic tulips on the windowsills and posters of Amsterdam in the lobby, is a squat, red brick four story between downtown Minneapolis and the warehouse district. It houses a lawyer looking for his first big score in product liability, a couple of graphic designers, a silkscreen T-shirt printer, and taking over the whole of the fourth floor, the Elysian Health Club, which features scented oil massages by a team of plump Vietnamese women who, for a modest gratuity, will apply a dollop of Jergen's Lotion to the customers' genitals and coax from them a hasty climax.

There are two restaurants across the street, one Mexican and the other Italian, separated by an alley just wide enough to let a sanitation truck through to unload the rusting, battle-scarred dumpster they share. On some days, the dumpster is closer to the Italian place and on others, to the Mexican. Jeff wonders how the spattered steel box travels from one side of the alley to the other, driven perhaps by its mood swings and cravings, but probably content with the resulting meld of brown guacamole and browning pesto, arroz, and risotto, burnt beans and charred bruschetta, as if one distinct taste experience could be conjured up from the world's two most satisfying cuisines. Pancho and Francesca's Mexicalian Café.

At nine, all the bells and buzzers and beepers in Jeff's apartment, from his clock radio to the oven timer, go off in close succession. Cleverly-named OmniLingua, Inc., is open for business, a translation bureau of which Jeff Garza is It, Mr. Ichi-ban, El Manda Más, Le Chef, Il Capo, titles that are the result of being laid off from his job in the international marketing department of General Grains.

He turns off the TV set and waits for the phone to ring with a hot assignment. Last week it was the translation into Arabic of the surgeon's installation procedures for a cardiac pacemaker. There was also the owner's manual for the Cadillac Seville into Urdu. The lyrics of all the Beatle's songs into Catalan.

If the assignment is in any romance language except Rumanian, Jeff will handle it himself. Otherwise, he will look into the directory of foreign students at the University and seek out cheap help. His requirements are definitely Equal Opportunity. If applicants speak English with a quaint accent and wear at least one item from their country of origin, be it an African dashiki or Bulgarian shoes that creak with every step, they get a trial assignment. That's about it for quality control. It's the real-world feedback that counts—if anyone had died because of an installation error of the pacemaker during surgery in Riyadh, Jeff would never hire Rashid Il Abnat from the med school again, even though several months ago, over Bohemias at the Mexican restaurant, Rashid had declared himself to be Jeff's soul brother.

On this particular Monday, Jeff Garza has little more to do than stare at the phone and picture it in his mind, Norman Vincent Peale-style, ringing itself merrily off the hook, a stream of silver coins pouring like a slot machine's jackpot out of the earpiece. Outside, the roar of a semi rattles the window. An early bird customer for the massage parlor scurries down the sidewalk, glancing at both ends of the street before he ducks into the building. Jeff watches a couple of kitchen workers from the restaurants meet in the alley to smoke cigarettes, and perhaps, thinks Jeff, also to trade recipes, Board of Health tips, tortilla chips for crostini. And then he sees the girl, tapping her way along the sidewalk with her white stick.

She tilts her head up to the sun, as if to feel the warmth on her eyelids, on her lips. She appears to be about seventeen. She's wearing a brown leather bomber jacket, unzipped halfway down, a black T-shirt, blue jeans, clunky lace-up boots, a green paisley bandanna rolled up and tied loosely around her neck. From her left ear hangs a silver earring that ends on a single turquoise teardrop. Her black hair is cropped short: hair she can wash and air-dry without having to look in a mirror. She has a serious expression, lips pressed together, chin lifted, as if to make the whole of her face more alert to the sounds around her. From the middle of the sidewalk, her thin white stick poised before her, she must sense how people make a wide circle around her so she can walk in sacred, inviolate space, safe from jostling, accidental bumping, the occasional, insinuating whisper.

She appears disoriented, as if she had been driven here and then dropped off to fend for herself. She breathes deeply to calm the beating of her heart and to arm herself with resolve before walking. She takes three or four steps and starts swinging the white stick from side to side, its tip grating against the sidewalk. The stick bangs against the support pole of a parking meter. She pauses, lifts her left hand, and caresses the curved top, feeling its rounded sides, her fingers pausing on the coin groove, the glass window over the time gauge. Then she steps toward the right and swings her stick until it hits the side of the building. She's more confident closer to the walls.

She wanders into the alley and is suddenly batting the stick around in empty space. She takes a step or two, more cautiously now, and the tip finally hits the side of the garbage dumpster. She reaches out, her fingers wiggling in the air, then pressing against the pitted sides of the garbage box. Jeff watches her pause again, almost able to follow the course of her thoughts as she smells the ripe garbage, almost sweet on this warm spring morning.

He can see from the way she flails away, reaching out for some anchor that will help her find her way back, that she's bewildered. She turns first to the right, then to the left, then full circle, always reaching out the whole length of her arm and swinging the white stick. She narrowly misses the back of the dumpster, the side of a delivery van loaded with produce, the door to the Mexican restaurant. She's floating alone in some vast empty space, every move a random, undirected stroke that takes her no closer to safety than the previous one. She turns again full circle until she's facing him, her head lifted to catch the sounds of traffic, the smells of exhaust and garbage.

Behind him, the phone rings. "Have you forgotten me, you sinister third world exploiter? It's me, Gurcharan Das, your Hindi connection."

"There just haven't been any assignments." Then, before Gurcharan can say anything, Jeff adds, "I need to go, I'm busy."

"And I'm desperate," Gurcharan says.

"How much money do you need?"

"Enough to get me through the next three or four days. There has been a mail strike in Delhi. Those rabble-rousing postmen are squeezing me into poverty."

"Sell something, Gur."

"What have I got to sell?" he squawks in Jeff's ear. "Tell me you are making fun of me so I can have a good laugh."

"Sell plasma," Jeff suggests. "Twenty dollars and free orange pop." Jeff holds the receiver at arm's length. "I've got to go now," he says. "There's someone outside my apartment."

By the time he gets back to the window, the girl is gone. The spot where she had been standing frozen in confusion is now empty, leaving in Jeff's imagination only a small circle of energy that continues to pulse with her presence.

During the next week, he can't stay at his desk for more than a few minutes before he finds himself at the window, searching the street. He remembers the brittle sound of her walking stick against the concrete sidewalk and the fronts of buildings, on the dumpster's sheet metal, on the steel poles of the parking meters. There are other sensations—the sound of her breath, a bitter taste in his mouth, a shiver down his back.

In the middle of the day, Jeff Garza breaks off from work to take long walks along the back streets of downtown. He starts seeing blind people everywhere. He sees them at the public library hunched over the cassette player tables, their faces tilted as if to catch a faint, inner glimpse of light or an elusive sound, rapt in concentration, broadly expressive, frowning quizzically, at times breaking into large unguarded smiles. He sees them where he least expects to, in bowling alleys and skating rinks and tennis courts. He even sits next to a blind woman in the movie theater. It's a double feature of *Manhattan* and *Annie Hall*. The woman laughs even before the lines are out of the actor's mouth. ("Tell him it's an emergency, I've forgotten my mantra.") Later, as they file out of the theater, Jeff asks her if she doesn't miss *seeing* movies.

"I know many of the scenes down to the details," she says. "I remember Woody's hair, and Diane Keaton's hats, and

Mariel Hemingway's eyebrows. I haven't been blind forever."

"Do you ever go to new movies?"

"I did at first." She turns approximately in his direction. "But they don't make them like they used to. Not even Woody Allen."

Some afternoons Jeff doesn't go back to work but instead finds himself riding the buses all over town, sitting behind blind people, stopping finally in front of apartment buildings and houses in the suburbs. He waits for them to lead him to the girl. He eats in cafeterias and lunch counters, watching how they move their spoons from bowl to mouth without spilling.

He watches a stocky man in a music store search through the racks of CDs, flipping his fingers over the tops until he pulls out *The Golden Years of Motown, Vol. 3*, easily, as if he had known it was there all the time.

"How did you do that?" Jeff asks.

"I was here yesterday," he explains. "The clerk showed me, but I didn't have any money. It was twelve CDs back, fourth bin from the right."

"You remembered that?"

"Pain in the ass, isn't it," he laughs.

"Why didn't you just ask the clerk for the record?"

The man turns so that Jeff's vaguely apologetic expression is reflected in a pair of large black lenses; he is shocked to see himself as if from the other's point of view. "Because he had already shown me once, obviously." He holds the record close to Jeff's face. "The Supremes, The Shirelles, The Coasters. Fabulous music. Right?"

"Yes. But what if you had picked up Manilow instead of Motown? Would you want me to tell you?"

"Use your effing head, man," the man says with a groan. "I don't like to feel helpless. But I like Manilow even less."

"You got Motown. But you couldn't be certain."

"That's what makes being blind so interesting," he says, standing closer to Jeff. "You learn to live with uncertainty."

"I'm pissing you off, right?"

The man touches his fingers to his wristwatch. "Nice talking to you. Really." He guides himself by running his fingertips along the tops of the CD bins straight to the sales counter. He pays for the disc, then turns to face a point some two feet to the right of where Jeff stands. He speaks in a loud voice, as if he's already lost his sense of the distance separating them. "I'm going down the street for coffee."

"What's with you?" he asks Jeff, once they're sitting at a booth close to the entrance of the cafeteria. "Most sighted people are afraid of talking to me."

"There's a blind girl that I'd like to find."

"People fall in love with blind girls. It's like a good deed."

"I don't know her. I only saw her once. She didn't see me."

"No shit."

"I meant that she didn't know I was watching her."

"What was she doing?"

"Practicing traveling. Learning to make her way downtown."

"She knew you were there. Not you, exactly. Just someone watching her."

"How do I find her?"

"Look for her in the dark."

In the evening, Jeff covers his eyes for the first time. First with a bandage that wraps around his head four or five times and is gathered in back with a metallic fastener. Then a sleeping mask made of black velvet, held snug by two elastic bands. He sits at the kitchen table for several minutes, waiting for the black fog in front of him to lift. At first there is the continuous dance of dark shadows, the hovering blobs of blue and purple and dark red, the echoes of the shapes around him—simple, ordinary things like a chromed toaster, a glass coffee carafe, the white enameled sink—swimming like amoebae in a black, inky soup. Gradually thoughts slow down. The day's memories fade into small, round impulses, translucent, like raindrops on a distant screen.

The murk begins to lift. The black void and the hovering shapes are replaced by a pristine, flat wall like brushed steel. When he stands up, the floor seems as insubstantial as quicksand. He stands back from the table and turns forty-five degrees to the right. He tries to remember. Three even, measured steps take him to the counter. On the right is the stove. To the left, more counter space, then the dish rack and the sink. He turns toward the cabinets, raises his hand, and finds that it meets the exact spot where the door handle is. The hands know. He lets them take down a large mug. From its texture and light weight, he recognizes the Mexican earthenware cup with the brown glaze and the blue-and-yellow flowers hand painted and then overglazed. He reaches for the row of knobs on the side of the stove and turns the farthest one, corresponding to the front right burner, up to the first click. His fingers dance over the top of the teakettle, make sure it's in place, square on the burner. Then, while the water boils, he reaches further to the right to open another cupboard and feels his way through several jars and cartons until he takes out a box of tea, brings it close to smell, and identifies it as Earl Grey. The kettle's whistle signals that the water is boiling. It gets tricky from here. With his left hand, he takes the position of the cup, his fingers resting lightly on the rim, and with his right he lifts the kettle, the water still bubbling, carefully tilts it so that a trickle of hot water pours into the center of the mug.

Happy sounds. The water strikes the hard ceramic walls of the mug with a thin, metallic note. Then, as it starts to fill, there's a light gurgle, and rising to the rim, it becomes a light, musical splash. Jeff turns off the burner and places the kettle back on the stove. He touches the sides of the mug—dry; the surface of the counter—not a drop. He picks up the cup and gradually feels his way out of the kitchen, the fingers of his left hand brushing the walls, his feet stepping haltingly, one before the other, toes reaching forward, feeling for obstacles. He bumps into the back of a chair, a couple of steps later his shin hits the edge of the glass-topped coffee table. He steps around it, feels his way to sit on the edge of the couch, and takes a long sip of the hot tea.

The first time Jeff Garza was in this room, he was twelve years old. He had sat on a leather couch between his parents and listened as they talked about him with Dr. Lucians. He wasn't called upon to say anything. He found himself agreeing to everything his parents said about him. Yes, he was doing his exercises. No, he did not have headaches. Yes, he was keeping up in school. He's only been back occasionally in the years since then; the conversation runs much the same.

He doesn't remember the room being so dim. This afternoon, the only light comes from a slender, burnished pole culminating in an inverted parasol that throws a yellow glow onto the ceiling. He wonders if mood lighting is becoming fashionable in the offices of accountants and lawyers as well. Jeff feels himself sinking into the soft middle of the familiar leather couch and thinks that the intervening years have served mainly to make him heavier and the springs weaker.

Jeff jokes with Dr. Lucians that his office, with all those browns and ochres and dark reds, looks more like a psychiatrist's office. The thought of him moonlighting as a shrink makes him smile. On the other side of the desk, Dr. Lucians, now close to seventy years old, heavyset and preoccupied of expression, looks at him intently. Jeff can't read his face, but he knows he's being serious, brow probably furrowed, lips unsmiling, his splayed fingers touching as if in prayer. "On occasion, I am called to practice a little psychology to help people along with their situations."

"You can use all the psychology you want on me." He pauses for a moment. "There's this glow inside my head wherever I go. But the rooms keep getting darker anyway. I don't know if it's something I'm seeing or imagining. That's where a shrink would help. Right?"

Dr. Lucians is silent for several moments, as if he were considering his next words. "Do you remember what we talked about when you were a boy?" he asks finally.

"I haven't forgotten," Jeff replies. "Not for a day."

"You've made preparations?"

"I live and work in the same place. I have two restaurants across the street, friendly women upstairs," he says.

"It is taking place, you know, the last stages of a type of RP," Dr. Lucians begins. "What we knew would happen eventually, the final degradation of the eyes' rods and cones, is happening now."

"When now?" Jeff can hardly hear the sound of his own voice.

"Anytime. Tonight. Next week." Then he adds, "You need to discuss this with your wife, other family members."

"No wife yet, not much family," Jeff says. "I'll talk it over with someone. Right now, I think I'll go home and watch TV. After all, it's one of the few things still bright enough to see more or less vividly."

"You must get out and about. Get training. Learn the streets."

"Of course. Maybe I'll bump into someone I'd like to meet." He senses Lucians's bewilderment and adds, "A girl was walking along my street one morning a few weeks ago. She was very pretty. But she hasn't been back." Jeff laughs self-consciously and stands up to shake the doctor's hand. "What if I'm in love?" he says. "What if I never see her again? Imagine that."

WaYs of bEinG

Under the evening's hazy, reddish light, the village of San Miguel seems to burrow deeper into the natural pocket created by the surrounding mountains. The sudden cooling elicits an agitated cackle from the hundreds of starlings perched deep within the overreaching foliage of the elms around the plaza. At its center is a kiosk topped by an ornate copper foolscap resting on six fluted columns.

Pablo Hobart, feeling too old and weathered at forty to be a schoolboy, the teacher's pet no less, sits on a wrought iron bench by the kiosk and ponders the mysteries of *ser* and *estar* in his textbook, *Hablemos, Amigos*. The idea of returning to Minneapolis empty-handed, without having mastered the two ways of being, depresses him.

The square, the town's living room, also functions as Hobart's living classroom. In the morning, old men melt away the kinks of the night under the sun, idly stringing out a conversation with the ritual phrases that may orbit the same thought for an hour before any conclusions are reached. Pablo Hobart listens. He picks up new words. Learns about weather. Is it cold or warm or wet or dry? Compared to last year. Compared to the last ten years. Are the rains early or late? Will they be good for those who rushed to plant or for those who wait? One has a cousin who waits and waits to put in his seed. Because he thinks the rains will be late? No, because he's lazy. And poor. *Con razón* he writes on the margin. With reason? Rationally? He will ask Mireya, his teacher. In return, he teaches her authentic American idioms, street slang, popular obscenities.

In the early afternoon, children swarm out of the school at the bell's ring, screaming out in different directions, and converge on the square. They dance and swirl around Hobart's bench. They ask him questions in Spanish, then stamp their feet and laugh uproariously at his answers.

Cómo te llamas? they ask. He thinks about this. His real name is not Pablo; that's the name he uses in his Spanish class because Mireya gives her students Spanish names. His permanent, lifelong name is Paul. So he says, eager to be as precise as the beautifully unambiguous Spanish language will let him, *Estoy Pablo.* That is, he is only Pablo for the time being, for now, while he is in San Miguel for the role he plays as student of Spanish under Mireya's exacting tutelage. He wishes he could explain all this to the kids to keep them from laughing.

At dusk, the square turns into a courting parlor. Young women in groups of three or four circle the perimeter while men with hangdog expressions follow several steps behind. They joke among themselves and push one another forward, encouraging, taunting, daring each other to speak to the women. But this is a system where courtship is a hesitant, timid ritual. The simple act of speaking to a woman, drawing her away from the safety of her friends, is a public commitment. Once made, it's awkward to turn back. The next step is to walk with only each other for company. Then to pick out a bench and sit together. Sometimes the woman, at her parents' insistence, will be accompanied by a younger brother. Often the man will give the kid a coin in order to send him away. The children feel this extraction of money is fair compensation for chaperoning someone as dull as their sister and her misguided admirer.

At seven, Hobart closes his book and waits for Mireya. He prepares a sentence in his mind to show her he has worked diligently on Lesson Three. He opens the book and pretends to study at first, too absorbed in the new lesson to be aware of her presence when she stops in front of him. Then, he does see her small feet with the lovely curve of their high arches and the perfectly shaped brown toes inside the open-weave sandals beyond the edge of his book.

He looks up in mock surprise, takes her hand, and pulls her down to sit on the bench beside him. *"Soy enamorado de tu."* I'm in love with you, Mireya, glowing ember of my cold gringo heart, song of my deaf gringo ears, light of my myopic gringo eyes. Run away to Minnesota with me.

"Tontito," she corrects him. *"Estoy. Estoy enamorado."*

"No, no, no," he insists. "My being in love with you is an eternal condition, I'm permanently afflicted by the symptoms of my racing heart and my short breath and my stirring you-know-what. I will always be in love with you, Mireya. *Soy enamorado de tu."*

Mireya winces. "Two mistakes out of four words. I think it's better we speak in English. I need a break, my dear." She puts a small hand over the back of his, her fingers barely reaching his middle knuckles.

"Are you happy, Pablito?" Mireya has been asking him this lately.

To be happy, he thinks, is a daunting enough premise without having to deal with two ways of being happy, one temporal, the other, if not eternal, certainly ongoing for the foreseeable future, a stable condition, like being North American or bald or stupid.

"How do you mean, happy?" he teases her. "Happy right this minute? Or happy all the time, happy when I'm hung over, when I'm broke, when I'm cold because you've curled up and stolen my half of the bedcovers? Do you want to know if I *soy feliz* or if I *estoy feliz?*"

"I want to know if you're fucking happy." He likes that about Mireya. She is as blunt as rain. "Or happy fucking. It's confusing, no?"

NEtWorKing

Martin Knight had stories to tell. In the first forty years of his life, he had counted the legs of a centipede, driven thirty miles on a flat tire, and made soup from bones and cheese rinds and potato eyes. In younger days he had been a jerk, a jock, a snake, a rake, and a frat boy. He had picked at scabs, shat worms, passed stones, pinched pustules, and coughed blood. He had also heard butterflies' wings fluttering, had seen the northern lights twice, had felt deep at the center of his solar plexus the world's hunger. He had pushed the boundaries of science in the search for the Perfect Tomato. He had climbed the ladder, high up where the air is thin and friends are few, and then fallen off. And he had loved Della Starr, though she had not loved him.

We are the sum total of our past, he liked to say. The distillation of our pain, our shame, our pride, our fame. The result of our atrophied brain cells, squandered sperm count, fractured chromosomes. What I am now is the inevitable sum of my many parts, the reaping of my sowing, the walking miscarriage of all my fine intentions.

Martin Knight wanted to tell all to one person at a time. He felt the age of mass media was over and that the millennium would welcome its survivors to a new intimacy. Television bellowed, e-mail was a faceless ether, phones had been taken over by a single voice. People yearned for closeness, for the smell, the feel, the sound of another. In the coming age, anyone with something important to say would have to repeat it one day at a time, to one person at a time, a million times.

Martin would seek out adolescents and tell them how, once, he had also raved. Women with babies would know he remembered the taste of mother's milk. To the sour bellied corporate hack, he would say, "In a former life, I headed a company with five hundred million dollars in revenues and three hundred employees. Then I was betrayed. It could happen to you."

Martin started close to home. In those days, a former life indeed, the Knight family had lived in a comfortable four-bedroom neocolonial in Canaan Hills. There were no weeds on the lawn, no flakes in the paint, no cracks in the drive, no loose shingles on the roof.

It was a crisp autumn night; the evening frost had given the brilliant maple in front of the house a fine dusting, causing its red and orange leaves to glow in the moonlight. Inside the warm house, in the oak paneled den, Martin paced as if he were looking for a way out of a locked room. Janet Knight sat on the couch in her cozy blue chenille robe, hands folded in her lap, her eyes following his erratic movements. It was around ten-thirty. The children had been sent to bed, the TV was switched off, the stereo softly played Janet's favorite piano pieces by Satie.

A passerby driving down Hyacinth Street might have slowed down in front of the large picture window above the garage and seen Martin Knight pacing back and forth, hands gesturing in an agitated manner, while Janet sat quite still, her head tilted to one side. It would not have been clear to the observer whether she was straining to catch the point of his words or shrinking from it.

Martin talked faster than he could think. He heard his own words roll out unguarded; even as his own mind tried to grasp what he had just said, he was moving on to the next subject in a random threading of insights, threats, accusations, confessions. He spoke to Janet of his career at Zycledia Genetics. Of the three years it took to develop the Perfect "Better-than-Homegrown" Tomato™. (A rare achievement, if you take into account that it took a hundred thousand years for nature to come up with the first version.)

He related every detail of his final confrontation with penis headed, brown nosed, pucker lipped Tucker Blount, his rival for the top post at Zycledia Genetics. The stakes were high; Zycledia was the developer and licensor of the Perfect Tomato, which boasted a texture like chicken and the size of a melon.

"Can you believe this?" Martin exclaimed. "He was scratching his balls even as he waved the resignation letter in my face. Then, after I'd signed it, he offered to shake my hand." He added, "With the same hand he'd been scratching with."

Sometime around midnight, Martin talked for the first time of his love for Della Starr. He sat stretched-out on the carpet and spoke very slowly, as if every detail had to be right—the coppery luminescence of her hair, the cold light in her blue eyes, the energy that emanated from her flushed skin so that even seeing her in a meeting or standing in line behind her at the company cafeteria, he would experience a tingle in the back of his neck and a shortness of breath.

The extent of his obsession took Janet by surprise. He confessed he thought of Della while shaving, driving, eating, even while he and Janet made love. He would call her home number to hear her answering machine. On weekends, he went to her empty office and stood there surrounded by her Things. These Things—the stapler, the mug, the mouse, the pencils, the phone, the picture of the dog, the picture of the house, the picture of the child—were not ordinary things; they pulsed with her presence. He took some of them—a pencil with her teeth marks, a Post-It note with her writing—and carried them around in his pockets. Sometimes when he changed clothes, he would be surprised to find a button or a paper clip beating like a small heart in his coat pocket. "I was forty years old," he shrugged, as if that explained everything.

Janet grew tired of sitting in front of Martin. She nodded in and out of sleep; a chilly sadness overtook her as the night wore on, driving her deeper into the warmth of her blue robe. Martin reached up and lifted her head by the chin, gently coaxing her awake. "There's more," he whispered.

The next morning, while Martin slept, Janet bundled up Jason and Lisa, packed swimming suits and a change of clothes, and checked in for the ninety-nine dollar Family Getaway Special at the Holiday Inn. Free sundaes for kids, free champagne for adults. She wrote Martin a note that she and the kids were visiting her parents, that they would be back Sunday night.

Martin wiped the steam from the full-length bathroom mirror and dripped in all his nakedness, all 175 pounds of him, jiggle bellied, wispy haired, fuzzy brained, one hand holding the phone against his ear, the other pushing his stomach in.

"Is that you, Martha? I need to speak to Janet. Tell Janet I will not put clothes on until she comes to the phone. I will sit here on the floor curled up like a naked dog." Martin walked up and down the room.

"Are you all right, Martin?"

"I'm naked."

"You've told me that, Martin."

Martin said he was fine but that his skin was white and flaky in spots, and there was a mole the size of a penny on his left buttock. This was something new, he was sure. He wondered if it had grown on him overnight. He wanted to ask Janet about it because if she had noticed it coming on, then he wanted to know why on earth she hadn't warned him. Those things are not always decorative, he insisted. They can be the work of cells gone helter, gone skelter, reproducing like bunnies, chain reacting in exponential progression until in a matter of days, his whole ass cheek would be one big mole. "So you see," he pleaded with Janet's mother, "it's important."

"I'll have her call you," the woman assured him. "But this mole of yours. Well, maybe you should have it looked at."

"Do you want to look at it, Martha?" After a long silence on the other end, he added, "I don't think Janet wants to see it, either."

"I meant by a doctor."

"I know, I know," he said, and hung up.

When Janet finally called, Martin asked to speak to the kids. "I want to tell them how their father once had a chance to eradicate world hunger. That's what the Perfect Tomato was all about. I wanted to be a hero or a saint, but Tucker Blount just wanted to get rich. I'll never have an opportunity like that again."

"I wouldn't go into all that, Martin. I don't think they'll understand."

"Don't try to keep me from talking to them, Janet. They're my kids, too."

"Talk to them all you want. Just don't confuse them."

"What do they want to know?"

"Well, they're worried that with no job, we won't have any

money. Jason asked me where people lived if they were homeless."

"Tell them their dad was a smart guy and that he had a golden parachute—severance pay, stock, continuation of life insurance, major medical, and even a dental plan that straightens out teeth. Not many do."

"That's a good start," Janet said. "You tell them about it, Martin. I'm sure it will set their minds at ease."

"Fine, put the kids on."

"Hello. Hello," the little voices spoke.

"Hi, Lisa! Hi, Jason!" He pictured them with their heads close together, trying to share the phone. "Can you hear me?" he asked. "I was working on the Perfect Cucumber last week before I stopped going to the office. It would look like a regular cucumber, and it would taste just as good and clean and fresh. But it would have no seeds. That's good, kids," he added after a moment's silence. "No seeds, no gas."

And then he told them about jumping off into the bright, blue space with his parachute. He told them the earth was far away and very tiny. That he could see their house right there in the middle of Hyacinth Street, and that he was falling and falling, and it occurred to him that if he didn't open his parachute, he was going to come crashing right through the roof.

"Or through the chimney like Santa Claus," Jason pointed out.

"Very shrewd of you. Well, I was lucky, you see. A lot of guys get thrown out of airplanes without a parachute. But I had a big, silky golden one. So I pulled the cord, and then I floated down to earth, just hanging from those golden ropes like a baby in a cradle, swinging back and forth, so peacefully it nearly put me to sleep. When I landed, I just went *ploof,* right on the soft green grass." He waited for a reaction from the other end. "So, are you guys still there?"

"Yes, Dad," they answered.

"Are you having a good time?"

"We had burgers and fries and Cokes for dinner. And huge sundaes."

"Okay," he said. "Good night. Sleep tight."

On Sunday, Martin woke up to the sounds of a church service on tv. It was a solemn mass, with bells and puffs of incense and a choir, with three priests and a couple of altar boys bumping into each other at St. Patrick's in New York. He gazed at the lead priest, the archbishop, he supposed, all dressed up in his vestments, pointed hat, and a staff at his side.

Martin saw himself reflected on the screen, a whole twenty-four hours later, still naked. He felt innocent and vulnerable, as if being free of clothes made him more worthy to witness the ritual on the screen. He was like a baby put up for baptism or a sacrificial lamb for holy sacrifice. Blessed are the naked? Along with the hungry, the meek, the shy, the stupid, the tone deaf. From way back, from his other lifetime as a boy in St. Paul, Martin Knight remembered the mass. He stood for the Introit, hands clasped in front of his penis. He knelt for the Consecration. Here it was, the presence of God in the food and the drink of the world. From a bag of corn chips in front of the couch he took one and lifted it up to the heavens. *This is my flesh.* He crunched the chip between his teeth.

When the mass was over, he rose and went to the kitchen. Walking around naked when there was no reason to be naked made him feel light and buoyant, as if he were somewhere above his head, watching his own feet move this way and that with a will of their own, so that every step he took was spontaneous and effortless, like dance.

Ordinary sensations became new. The different textures of the house caressed the bottoms of his feet; he felt the grip of the carpet in the family room, the varnished hardwood of the hallway, and the rough concrete of the basement floor. He sat down with the newspaper and marveled at how the edges of the pages tickled the top of his belly and how their weight rested on his soft penis.

From the middle of the room, Martin fired the remote like an automatic weapon, skipping through channels until he stopped at a golf tournament taking place somewhere lush and green and warm. Standing in front of the TV set, he gripped an imaginary putter and dug his heels into the carpet. He looked up for a moment to get a bead on the hole framed by the shoes of the caddy, the slender flagpole, its shadow angling away from the hole. He wiggled his hips and stroked the ball across the velvety green and, imagining an agreeable metallic clunk, into the cup.

There was warm applause. Martin was dancing around the room, waving at the gallery, when the phone rang. "For Christ's sake, mister. If you're going to be naked, at least draw the curtains," complained an angry male voice.

The voice had sounded like Tucker Blount.

It was just like Smelly Fingers to keep on gathering dirt about him even after he had left Zycledia. They already had records of his expense accounts. They knew what he had for breakfast, lunch, and dinner, down to the last four green peas speared on the tines of his fork. There were records of what movies he had rented, when he paid his bills, and what numbers he called at odd hours of the night. On business trips, there was a trail of his taxi rides, his in-flight conversations with fellow passengers, his middle-of-the-night cries in strange hotel rooms. Logs detailed how he had spent every day of his fourteen years at Zycledia, neatly divided into ten minute segments *(10/4/89 2:46-2:56: Meeting with Della Starr!)*. Conversations with a colleague at the urinals were invariably overheard by the anonymous feet in the next stall.

"Quiet, the feet have ears" was a common expression at Zycledia.

In the very depths of the mainframe computer, down in the remotest corner of the last microchip, there was a record of every word he had tapped into his PC. The letters and memos and e-mails he had deleted were still a faint echo that could be revived, the prints of his dirtiest words, thoughts, and deeds faintly surfacing under a light coating of electronic dust.

All the information was in the file Tucker Blount had used in order for Zycledia to ease him out the door. The file showed how much money he made in salary and bonuses, his reviews by the board of directors, the vows of secrecy he had signed so that what he knew about seedless cucumbers, chicken-textured tomatoes, and skinless kiwis had to stay inside his head for the next ten years. That was Blount's greatest fear: Martin would take everything he knew about Zycledia, and, in spite of the signed confidentiality agreements, spill it to the competition.

"This is your noose" is the way Blount had put it during that last meeting. "This is your life."

"But why?" he found himself wondering out loud.

"Because you are conniving. Perverted. Incompetent. Mediocre. Careless. Wasteful. Untruthful. Disloyal. Slothful. Lubricious. Cruel. Weak. NTP."

"Something new, this NTP?"

"Not a Team Player."

"I'll grant you I am all of those things," he said. "They still don't add up to one good reason for firing me."

On his last day, a Saturday, Martin waited until after five and slipped into the building to clean out his desk. He emptied his drawers into trash bags without bothering to check what he was throwing out. He zapped his PC hard drive. He stuffed his briefcase with a picture of Janet and the kids, the paperweight Lisa gave him last Father's Day, Jason's drawings.

On the way out, he stopped at Della Starr's office. He looked around for a minute, breathing in her presence, almost seeing her there, sitting at her desk with her back to him, the tilt of her head, the long, manicured fingers holding the phone. He touched the warm back of her chair.

When Janet and the kids returned from the Holiday Inn sometime after three that Sunday, Martin was still sitting around the family room watching golf with his clothes off. As soon as he heard the car in the driveway, he stood up and walked to the kitchen. The kids were the first in. They started to rush toward him but stopped suddenly. They stood like that for several seconds, their eyes wide open, while Martin swayed from one foot to another, no one knowing what to say. Finally, he shouted "Hello!" and the kids ran off to their rooms.

Then Janet came in, took a look at him, and asked if he was all right.

"What do you mean, am I all right?" Martin asked back. "Do I look sick?"

"What happened to your clothes?"

"Nothing happened to them," he snapped. "They're fine."

"Why aren't they on you?"

"I'm not going anywhere."

"The children think it's weird how you just hang around the house naked."

"I can fix that," he promised her.

The next morning, Martin emerged from the bedroom dressed in a pinstriped suit, white shirt, and a blue tie with tiny red tomatoes. His black shoes were polished, his hair was slicked back. He carried his Hartmann attaché.

"Are you going somewhere, dear?" Janet asked.

"The airport."

"Will you be back in time for dinner? I mean tonight?"

"Oh, sure." He put his briefcase down and and hugged Lisa and Jason.

Once at the airport, he systematically walked up and down the various concourses, briskly, like a man with no time to waste between flights. He sat at the boarding gate lounges and struck up conversations with people with long layovers, delayed flights, missed connections. He told them about Zycledia Genetics and The Perfect Tomato. "The home-grown taste is bred right into it!"©

He told people of his betrayal by Tucker Blount, the cesspool bottom feeder of corporate life. And of his love for Della Starr. He told the story many times. For the most part, people were sympathetic. In return, they told him about lost luggage and the weather in places where they'd been. Occasionally, frequent flyers remembered him. They said, "You were here on Monday. You were here this morning. Don't you ever go anywhere?"

When Martin came home at night, he and Janet would relax with a glass of wine. She would ask him how his day had gone; he would say terrific or OK or so-so, depending on how many times he had been able to tell his story. "I'm actually enjoying the networking," he would say.

The next day he would dress, kiss the children good-bye, and again head for the airport. He paced up and down the red, the yellow, the green, and the blue concourses. He went from Gate 1 to Gate 91. He stopped at the World Club and at the Pizza Hut.

After a few days, when he'd sit down and tell his story to someone, right away there would be the funny looks. Airline employees recognized him. Other guys in suits avoided him, saw him as a harbinger of bad luck. "Hey, it happened to me. It could happen to you." Finally, two airport security men with tiny microphones pinned to their lapels and coiled black

wires emerging from behind their right ears suggested there
was something odd about his behavior.

"Am I being disorderly?" Martin objected mildly.

"Not exactly, sir."

"Soliciting, panhandling, accosting?"

"No, sir."

"Am I threat to the passengers?"

"Not in any visible way," one of them admitted.

"I'm supposed to be in Chicago by noon," Martin said,
glancing at his watch.

"You're actually going somewhere?" the younger one with
the mustache asked.

"I am at the airport, aren't I?" Martin picked up his mostly
empty Hartmann and marched to the Northwest counter,
where he bought a one-way to Chicago.

During the flight, he sat next to a woman who was a sales
rep for a computer software company. He bought her a drink
and told her the story about Zycledia Genetics and The
Perfect Vegetables. "These tomatoes, they're the size of vol-
leyballs. Some of them, anyway." He left out the part about
Della Starr; he didn't think she would be sympathetic. When
they landed at O'Hare, Martin found many people who had
not heard his story.

Around seven he got hungry, so he went up to the
American Airlines counter and asked when the next flight
serving dinner was leaving. He bought a ticket to Bangor,
Maine, and, while he squirted the butter out of his chicken
Kiev, he talked to the guy next to him, who was a professor at
Colby College. He told him mostly about Della Starr. Doctor
Al Jonas, a national authority on equine behavior, red wine,
and midwestern weather patterns, ran his hand across a tan-
gle of red curls and nodded understandingly because he had
also on occasion fallen in love with a student. "We all do it in

academia," the professor said. "It's the unspeakeable yearning for the young and the promising."

"Well, I didn't actually yearn for Della," Martin defended. "It was simpler than that."

When he got to Bangor, it was almost nine P.M. and the small airport was almost deserted. There was nobody there to listen to his story. Air New England's was the only counter open. So Martin flew to Boston on a mostly empty plane. He tried to talk to the flight attendant about the fabulous tomatoes that would be available in years to come, thanks to the work he had done at Zycledia. "Imagine a sensuous new taste in airline food," he boasted.

When Martin got to Boston, he walked the whole length of Logan Airport with no one to talk to except a sleepy clerk at the United counter. "Hold the plane. I'm the tomato king." He got the last seat on the last flight to New York City.

Even at two A.M., La Guardia was crowded with red eyed travelers slumped on benches throughout the terminal. Martin talked until six the next morning. "It's easy. If you understand DNA, you understand the Perfect Tomato."

Then he withdrew money at a cash machine and rode a van into Manhattan. He talked along the way to a couple of muffler salesmen from Rockford, Illinois. They had not heard his story before.

When he arrived at Grand Central Station, Martin found himself being drawn into the center of the human maelstrom. Crowds flowed past him in all directions. Everyone was talking to each other at once. The cacophony of voices rising from the marble floor, pouring out of the ceiling loudspeakers, bouncing from windows and columns ascended toward the vaulted nave like celestial music. People of all ages and sizes and colors, hundreds of them at a time, zoomed past him like a blizzard of electrons swirling around an atom.

He found that here he did not have to look for anyone to hear his story. All he had to do was stand at the center of the cavernous hall and, lifting his eyes toward the ceiling, start talking. The tomato of the future. The love of Della Starr. Tucker Blount's betrayal. People would sometimes pause, nod, shake their heads, occasionally drop a coin at his feet. And always, people kept coming, one after the other. He knew he would be here a long time.

THe aMazing fRog bOy

It runs in the genes. On my father's side, Grandmother
Loomis did birdsong impressions. She actually became something of a celebrity in her youth with her renditions of such
little-known warblers as the Red Breasted Sprinster and the
Dove Winged Parsifano in the early days of coast-to-coast
broadcasting. People swear to this day that her trills and
chirps were sweeter and more melodious than the real thing.
My grandfather, the original Boomer Loomis, managed her
career with rare dedication. For a time, he brought her out of
the carnie circuit into real show business with bookings in
the big Broadway houses, sharing top billing with such great
acts as the Hinky Friedman Roller Follies and Morty
Moriarity's Laughter Machine.

Remember Morty? He used to drag this contraption on
stage that looked like a cross between a cement mixer and a
tank festooned with ribbons and colored lightbulbs. The
machine cranked out jokes printed on rolls of toilet paper,
and Morty would tear out reams of the stuff and read them to
the audience. The jokes were just awful, so the audience
would start to boo and hiss and drive old Moriarity into a

frenzy, first cursing and threatening the machine, then plead-
ing with it for anything that might get him a laugh. Believe it
or not, the damn thing would creep toward Morty, alive with
a real personality; all wheezes and sputters and blinking lights,
it would turn against its master and chase Morty all over the
stage while flinging cream pies at him. That got laughs.

Grandmother always complained about following Morty's
act with her birdsongs. The crowd loved the pie throwing and
would still be hooting and whistling as she daintily made her
way down the stage, one hand lifting the hem of her dress,
taking great care not to slip on one of Morty's pies. At first,
the people wouldn't be aware of her, but as soon as the first
liquid notes poured from her throat and hung suspended in
the air, even the toughest audiences became pudding under
her spell.

My father, Boomer Jr., remembers waiting backstage, nervously at first and then swelling with pride as the air was filled
with thousands of invisible birds chirping away like crazy.
That's how he met my mother, Lila, the very plump child of
a unique husband-and-wife juggling team. They used to
spend all their time perched up in the catwalks watching the
shows for nothing.

My mother grew up to become Two-Ton Lila, and on her
side of the family talent leaned toward fat. Grandfather Two-
Ton weighed in at 480 pounds and could balance six champagne glasses on the outward swell of his belly. Grandmother
played a tiny ukelele while he danced a minuet without
spilling a drop. The tune she played on the uke is still one of
my favorites, an old Bubbles Mahler number called "The
Bumblebee's Lament."

When I was born, it was understood I would grow up to be
fat. Fat freaks were a big draw in those days, what with the
Depression and all. To keep my act interesting, Two-Ton Lila

would round it out with some minor skill like hoop juggling or rhythmic belly jiggling. My livelihood was assured.

The truth is, I didn't get fat. Even as a baby, I was thin and often sickly, even though Lila's breasts held enough milk to feed an orphanage. And it was all for me. I got rashes and pimples and diarrhea. But I did not get fat.

Years after, I had a recurrent dream of my face pressed against Mother's breasts, warm and massive in my memory, and sinking helplessly into their yielding oatmeal softness. There's a brief panic as I punch and stab at them with my tiny fists, struggling to pull my face free for a quick breath. Meanwhile, Lila rocks me, squeezes me tighter to her bosom, coos delicious endearments. Then, just as I'm about to pass out in her arms, a sudden stab of light jolts me like electricity. I give up the struggle and surrender to my mother's embrace; a warm tender current seeps in through my arms and up my legs, and a taste sweeter than honey fills my mouth. I fall into a quiet, peaceful state, without a breath or thought, but wide awake and utterly content. After some time, Lila would disconnect me from her nipple and I would come to with a sonorous, curdled burp.

By the time I was seven, it was clear to everyone I would not make it as a juggling fat man. Boomer started my training in earnest, for no carnie kid could be allowed to grow up without an angle. We tried barking. It was something Boomer knew a thing or two about. Before rising into management, he had been one of the great midway barkers of all time. I have heard his pitches picked up, word for word, by barkers all around the country. Some of his spiels were downright poetic.

She crawls on her belly like a reptile!
She flies through the air like a bird!

She makes grown men faint
and brave hearts stop in their tracks.
She is the one and only
Dagmar from Denmark!
And no one who wears pants
can miss this one and only chance
to see Dagmar perform
her Viking dance!

For the bark to be effective, the rhythm had to be just right, the pitch and roll of the words somewhere between a song and a rant. I grabbed a strawboater and a megaphone just like Boomer showed me and sang out in my thin falsetto:

One minute, folks . . .
One minute to show tiiiime!
Get your tickets here
Get your tickets now
and hold on to your socks and pants
while Dagmar does her Viking dance.

Boomer shook his head unhappily. I squeaked when I yelled, I was too small, I was afraid of crowds. I didn't have the presence to be a barker.

By the time I was ten, Boomer and Lila had pretty much written me out of the business—the first Loomis in history without an angle. That left school. As we traveled across the country doing car dealer promotions, radio station ratings wars, supermarket openings, Lila pushed me in and out of classrooms, hoping I would pick up a useful trade along the way. It was a hectic life. And something akin to agony to be the new kid in school three or four times a year as I enrolled in one place after another, all the way from Florida to Minnesota and back down again.

I had seven different teachers during the fifth grade. In one place, I didn't stay in school long enough to learn where the boys' bathroom was. At another, they suspended me after the first day for peddling the sword swallower's French postcards in the playground.

A serious consequence of all the moving about was that I had to change best friends as often as I changed schools. Often, my one friend would turn out to be the one kid who had been left pretty much alone until my arrival, because he was either too homely or too smart or too stupid or too dirty.

"Just pick a seat there in the back, Jasper," the teacher would say, and give me a gentle, encouraging push into the arena. It was always a seat in the back. I had a back-of-the-class mentality from the start. As I shuffled down the aisle, I'd brace myself for the inevitable wiseass who'd try to get my goat. "Woooow, would you believe his name is Jasper? Jasper!" As I sat down on the one available chair at the back of the room, somebody would lean toward me and whisper sympathetically, "Don't pay any attention to him. He's the class turd." This was always useful information, knowing in advance who the class turd was. The other kid, the one kind voice in the wilderness, would end up my best friend.

In Faribault, Minnesota, it was Xavier Planck, the optometrist's son. We were great buddies during most of the seventh grade. There was more to our relationship than a shared solitude; it turned out we both had unusual, almost magical skills.

Xavier had learned from his father how to roll his eyes so far up into his head that all you could see were the whites. He could stay like that for hours, it seemed, staring blankly at people with his two white eyes big as golf balls. We'd walk into a store and then, while he paid for a comic or a candy bar or something, right in the middle of handing the money to the lady at the cash register, Xavier would roll up his eyes and just stand there with a demented grin. The cashier would get so flustered and shaky at the experience that we'd often come out ahead by a nickel or more.

My particular ability was not as dramatic as walking around with two blank eyeballs staring at the world. But I did impress Xavier Planck by holding my breath for as long as three minutes at a time. I didn't think there was much to it, just something I'd done for years while I sat at the back of the class waiting for the recess bell to ring. I liked the way my whole body would go limp after the first minute, everything coming to a hush inside my head, and I'd end up floating around somewhere up in space, miles from the drone and buzz of the crowded classroom. Xavier was sure we could make some money.

It was to be a scientific demonstration of my curious talent; we would sell tickets for a dime, with the added inducement of a double-your-money-back guarantee in case I failed to hold my breath for a full three minutes. Xavier estimated we'd each clear a dollar and become sought after celebrities at school as well.

On the appointed day, we pushed together four cafeteria tables to make a stage and waited for the crowd to gather. We stalled for about twenty minutes and then began the show in front of an audience of twelve skeptical classmates. Xavier rolled his eyes up a few times as a warm-up for the greater thrills to come. But everyone knew all about his eyeballs. "Get on with the show, Planck," someone whined, and the the rest of the kids joined in with hissing, booing, and vigorous accusations of fakery.

Xavier finally explained to the audience that I would hold

my breath for a minimum of three minutes, which would be a world record, according to the *Guinness Book of World Records*. "Don't believe me? Look it up," he challenged them. At the center of our makeshift stage, I felt rumbles in my stomach and a tightness in my chest as I braced myself for either one more humiliation or the glory of setting a new record. To dismiss any suspicion of trickery, I asked the audience to name two volunteers who would stand beside me on the stage and hold a mirror under my nostrils. They readily nominated the Class Turd and his close friend, a little thug known as Moosehead.

"Preeee-senting!" Xavier announced, taking a cue from Boomer's barking style. "For the first time in Minnesota, and following a string of smashing engagements across the whole USA, none other than Jasper Loomis, The Amazing Frog Boy!" He's the one who gave me my name, just like that, on the spur of the moment during my very first appearance.

I took a deep bow, which elicited some scattered giggles, and began the technique I had learned from an encyclopedia article on frogs. First, I swallowed great gulps of air until my belly swelled as tight as a basketball. Then I took a few deep breaths to fill my lungs, while the air stayed in my stomach as if inside a reservoir. I closed my eyes when Xavier clicked the start button on the track team's stopwatch. "The clock is running," he announced in a hushed voice.

The air around me was filled with distinct, crisp sounds. The ticking of the watch was sharp and metallic. I could hear Class Turd's breath as clearly as my own. There was the rustle of clothes, a restless shifting about as the audience got ready to wait me out. There were even three or four deep inhalations as Xavier started the clock. In the next minute, I heard the same kids, one by one, give up with loud gasps. And then the ticking of the seconds became a loud, staccato drumming, the lazy buzz of a fly surged into a roar, my pulse thumped like a deep bass chord. I get all these sensations today just like I did that first time. The first ninety seconds are the hardest; my diaphragm flaps in and out in sudden spasms, but I manage to keep a lock on my windpipe so that no matter how much my lungs thirst for new, clean air, the path is sealed.

"Two minutes."

The flutters in my chest relaxed. Even as my whole body was stilled, my head remained erect, my posture straight. The ticks and rustles around me sank into a dense silence. The thoughts in my head blurred into formless shadows. I drifted into a peaceful revery filled with smoky visions of Lila's blue-veined breasts, of Boomer's dancing straw boater, of the road whirling past us as we drove with the carnival from Wilmington to St. Paul to Madison to Columbus and down again past Gary past Paducah past Nashville, all the way to St. Pete for the winter, and always the road snapping past, the poles strobing by, and the electric wires and the telephone lines buzzing, humming, whispering by like a song.

"Three minutes!" Xavier's voice quavered.

But I wasn't ready to come out yet; I felt as if I could go on forever without needing another breath, as long as I was left alone with my memories and shadowy dreams. As long as I could go past all sounds and tastes and smells into a world of thick, cottony silence that settled over everything like a blanket of clean, new snow. After all those years on the road, I was coming home.

I stirred under Xavier's hand nudging me awake. "Are you all right, Jasper?" His voice sounded very distant, too far for me to bother to answer. Then, pushing Moosehead and Class Turd out of the way, he told everyone to stand back. "Give him a little space. Can't you see the man would like to breathe?"

I let out a long, long sigh and then started drawing hungry breaths through my mouth. I blinked a few times as my surroundings came into clearer focus, and then I looked into Xavier's grinning face; his eyes rolled up and the whites stared all about in mad triumph. "Three minutes and twenty-four seconds," he informed our stunned audience. "Son of a gun!" Xavier whispered.

Well, we got to keep the money, although the day's take was only $2.80. Still, it was a promising start for me in show business. I didn't know it then, but I was well on my way to becoming a real midway character. It must've been in the genes after all. Years later, the summer I got my high school diploma by way of fourteen different schools, Boomer took me aside for the first real man-to-man talk of our lives. It was around two A.M., and the midway had just shut down the music and turned off the lights and most of the acts had closed for the night. It was the middle of July and felt cooler to sit outside on the steps of Lila's caravan.

He began hesitantly. "I'm not sure I have much to say to the first educated man in the family." He shrugged and held out his hands helplessly. "But have you given any thought to what you'll do with your life?" He sounded as if a high school diploma was a handicap to be overcome only with serious effort.

"I've got an act," I answered, eager to set his mind at ease.

He stared at me skeptically. "Tell me about it," he said, unable to hide his disbelief.

I handed him my watch and breathed frog-style to fill my stomach with air. Then I took a couple of deep breaths and signaled for Boomer to start the clock. He stared at the sweep of the second hand, his amazement growing with each passing minute. That night, I held my breath for five.

"Are you sure you want to do this for a living?" he asked as a look of concern clouded his eyes. "Being a freak is not for everyone." He stumbled over the word *freak,* glancing over his shoulder to see if Lila had overheard. Then he looked at the watch again. "You're in a class all by yourself," he whistled. "A real carnie original."

"Lila," he called out. "Come out here, quick." Then he introduced me proudly: "Meet Jasper, the Amazing Frog Boy."

By the time I opened in Greenville, South Carolina, the Pickens County fair as I recall, Boomer had his bark down pat.

Eeeeeevolution comes full circle!
Man lives again underwater
without any source of oxygen.
JASPER, THE AMAZING FROG BOY
has mastered the ancient oriental art of
SUSPENDED ANIMATION
and will remain submerged inside
a SEALED glass tank
without taking a BREATH longer
than any man before him.
Get yout tickets here
for this SCIENTIFIC demonstration
of the FROG BOY'S amazing powers.
Only two minutes till SHOW TIME!

To tell the truth, I was never a big hit around the midway. For one thing, Boomer's talk of evolution and oriental arts didn't sit well in some circles. Still, he put a lot of thought into the act's show biz appeal. First, there was the glass tank that made me look like some giant aquatic mutant in the costume Lila made for me with an iridescent leotard, a green satin cape, and a jewelled headband to keep my long hair out of the way. There was a huge timer with lights around it and a loud fire bell to ring off each passing minute. Outside the tent was a huge painting of a very realistic frog with my face on it.

As I became well-known, there were always a few people willing to pay a dollar to enter my tent and look at me inside the water tank. They seldom had the patience to stare at me for the full ten or twelve minutes I eventually managed. As Boomer figured out soon enough, "The act just doesn't have any action in it."

Still, people did come to look. Seven times a day they lined up outside the tent, then gathered around the tank and stared at me as if I were some ancient, prehistoric relic come back to remind them of their own origins. The clock above me showed how long I'd been holding my breath. At times, someone would be genuinely interested.

"How in the hell do you do it?" a man grumbled one day as I came out of the tank. "My boy here wants to know what the trick is." He indicated the silent child at his side.

"No trick. I fill my belly with air," I explained directly to the boy. "Just like frogs, you know."

"The boy wants to know what's the longest you've stayed in that thing."

"Twelve minutes and forty-two seconds." The boy stared at me with large, pale eyes.

"But that's impossible," the man laughed.

"What do you think?" I looked into his milky blue irises. The boy shrugged self-consciously. He took a couple of gumdrops from his jeans pocket, inspected them, then popped one of them inside his mouth and offered me the other one. I took it, even though it was full of lint.

"Do you believe I can stay underwater as long as I want to?" I insisted.

He nodded his head seriously.

"Doesn't he ever say anything?" I asked his father.

"When he feels like it."

I turned to the boy again. "If you come back tomorrow, maybe I'll go for a new record."

By then I'd been sitting inside the tank for years, had in fact become more of a frog man, thinning hair and sagging belly, than the Amazing Frog Boy and no longer cared much if people didn't think what I did was remarkable. That's what I told myself, that I didn't care, every time I ducked into the water. Still, I was flattered when the next day the same pale kid showed up out of nowhere. Suddenly, there he was, his face almost touching the glass wall of the tank. I gave him a wink to let him know I remembered him, but he simply stared back as silent and unresponsive as he'd been the day before. I looked around the sparse audience for his father, but the boy was alone.

It was a real summer scorcher in Fostoria, Ohio, that day, and as the tent started to fill up, it became stifling inside. It was a cinch no one would stick around long enough to see me pop out of the water after the full twelve minutes. From outside, the familiar words of Boomer's spiel floated inside the tent, disjointed, like leaves caught in the wind. The people gathered closer around me, pressing the boy tighter against the tank.

"Where's your pa?" I asked him.

The boy merely looked at me with his eyes open and unblinking, so compelling in their translucent glaze I had to make a real effort to pull away from them and turn to the audience with my spiel about how I was the world record holder for survival in a zero-oxygen environment and all. Nobody listened, really, but I went through the whole of my act anyway, out of habit. That day there was the usual gathering of farmers checking out the fair's exhibits, their wives with pink plump faces and the smeared, rumpled children at their sides. Today a small group of teenage girls would break into giggles every time the freak looked in their direction. I'm sure none of them understood what I had learned from the world of frogs. As usual, I inquired if there was a doctor in the house in case an emergency should arise. As usual, there wasn't. Not that I ever expected to find a doctor among the audience, but asking for one gave the act some added suspense.

I threw off the cape with a flourish and stood inside the tank with water up to the middle of my chest, while all the time swallowing gulps of air until I could feel the reassuring tightness and swelling of my stomach. I was barely aware of the crowd now. Above their heads, in a far corner of the tent, I had painted a round blue dot the size of a dinner plate. As I took my breaths, I kept my eyes on the blue spot until the color began to grow and fill the whole range of my vision with a deep, cool blueness that spread over everything in sight. Then I took one last gulp of air and switched on the the timer with its lights and bells.

I lowered myself beneath the surface and sat cross-legged on the tank's floor; the murmur of the audience was dulled, muffled in my head by the slow beat of my heart and a low hum droning in my ears. I took one last look into the kid's glassy blue eyes and sank into darkness. The memory of their brilliant sparkle mingled with the afterglow of the blue dot imprinted on my retina, its coolness settling all around me. I thought of the kid and how I'd like to shake him from his strange, mute stare by going for a new record. This time, thirteen minutes. The magic number had a fine carnie ring to it. *See the Frog Boy take a thirteen-minute dive into the dawn of man's evolution.* What do you think of that, kid? The idea of pushing through my own limitations, of breaking past earlier boundaries filled me with purpose. *The Amazing Frog Boy floats again.*

Dimly, through the blue mist, through the hum in my ears and the thumping in my veins, I heard the timer bell mark the first minute. The second and the third. Then, as often happened, I lost count.

A lot of bells must've rung by the time I opened my eyes to check the crowd's reaction, because the only person left in the tent was the kid. His face was right against the glass, a circle of moisture where his breath fell. His eyes locked into mine and I figured as long as he remained with me, I'd keep trying for a new record. I waited for the bell to ring again; its length would give me some idea of how long I'd been inside the tank. When it finally went off, it kept ringing so long I thought the damn thing had gotten stuck. Then it stopped abruptly. I was trying to figure out why it had gone crazy like that when it clanged again, sending deep reverberations through the still water above my head. It stopped, then started again, then stopped, over and over, until I gave up keeping track of it. Instead, I thought of the boy watching me from the other side of the glass.

He would be the witness I needed to make the new record official, to sign the forms, take the oath, record the pertinent facts surrounding the occasion. That was important, the filling out of forms. I tried to remember the date, come up with a sponsoring organization, the purpose and relevance claimed for the feat on record. The kid wasn't much of a talker, but after he gave me one of his gumdrops, I figured I'd gotten through to him somehow. Hey, kid, I'd ask him, how long was I under? What's the date, the day of the week, which city, county, state?

I opened my eyes, expecting to see the boy's blue stare in wide amazement, but he was gone. I tried to find him beyond the murky water, thinking he would still be there, maybe not as close as he'd been, but certainly in some corner of the tent's steamy vacuum. I refused to believe he had simply grown bored and gone off like the others. Not him, not my star witness.

I closed my eyes and waited for the timer to ring. Somehow, even with the kid out of sight, I sensed I was not alone in the tent, that another presence stood nearby. My lids parted and I became aware of a vague shape drifting toward me from the right side of the tank. My heart beat faster. The boy was still here, teasing, maybe playing some game of hide-and-seek. Well, I'd catch him in the act. I opened my eyes as wide as they'd go, ready to give him the old eyeball as he tried to sneak past the tank. I waited.

The form came closer, took shape, finally came into view. Instead of the boy staring at me, I saw the face of a pensive, middle-aged man. He had blonde, thinning hair, and his skin was smooth like a baby's, pale pink and well fed, with a soft double chin and fat, rosy earlobes. His blue eyes were half-hidden by drooping lids. He stood right in front of the tank, his head cocked to one side in a bemused, perplexed way. I tried to see past him to find the kid. After all, as Boomer would put it, it doesn't matter what you do if no one knows about it. And I'd been holding my breath forever, it seemed, but the only person who knew about it had disappeared.

The blonde man stepped closer to the tank. There was in his pale eyes, for a brief moment as they met mine, a piercing look of recognition. He appeared as if he were about to say something but in the end didn't find the right words. He put his hand deep into his coat pocket and took out a gumdrop. He picked some lint off it and put it in his mouth. He sighed and looked at me with a sad bewildered gaze. I wanted to ask him what the matter was, but instead I closed my eyes and went on as before, waiting for the timer bells to ring.

coLopHon

This book was designed by Jinger Peissig, and was set in Adobe Garamond and Courier typefaces. It has been printed on acid-free paper, and smyth sewn for durability and reading comfort.